T0381463

CHRYSALIS
AND HER
MONSTERS

Charlotte "Lottie" Brown

authorHOUSE®

AuthorHouse™
1663 Liberty Drive
Bloomington, IN 47403
www.authorhouse.com
Phone: 833-262-8899

Published by AuthorHouse 11/04/2024

ISBN: 979-8-8230-3724-2 (sc)
ISBN: 979-8-8230-3723-5 (e)

Library of Congress Control Number: 2024923431

Print information available on the last page.

This book is printed on acid-free paper.

Because of the dynamic nature of the Internet, any web addresses or
links contained in this book may have changed since publication and
may no longer be valid. The views expressed in this work are solely those
of the author and do not necessarily reflect the views of the publisher,
and the publisher hereby disclaims any responsibility for them.

"Exciting Chrysalis, your 15th birthday is in three days," said Ocieana.

"Yeah it is." said Chrysalis.

Chrysalis is a very beautiful and very kind girl and a very famous singer. Chrysalis' family are all famous singers too she lives with her 13-year-old nonuplet little sisters Natasha, Patty, Gege, Blinda, Zadie, Ocieana, Whittneya, Amelia, and Tiana, their mom Marleen, their dad Walter, their grandpa Tarson (their mom's dad), their grandma Elsa (their mom's mom), their grandfather Jimonthey (their dad's dad), their grandmother Nessia (their dad's mom), their great-grandfather Ard (their mom's grandfather and also their grandma Elsa's dad), and their great-grandma Sasha (their mom's grandmother and also their grandma Elsa's mom)who isn't just a famous singer she is also the owner of the music studios they work at, and they are also the biggest and most popular studios in the world.

"Hey guys check out this new human to monster formula they made two days ago," said Blinda coming up to Chrysalis and Ocieana with her phone out.

1

"Wow weird and another new human to monster formula they're what people use to become monsters and all the formulas has anyone who uses it become a monster but, they turn back when they become engaged in case it's against Jesus that a person is a monster when they are engaged and the person is also not able to be or become a monster from the formula until after getting married, after having babies, and after before having baby after getting married in case it's against Jesus if you are a monster during those times including if both human/monsters are the same human/monster, and they have the formulas not make a person become a monster during having a baby in case the baby won't have a soul if they are born a monster instead of a human and in case it would be against Jesus having a baby born a monster or the baby being a monster before it is born." said Chrysalis.

"Yep that's spread to everyone to know." said Blinda.

"There's also a turn back to normal formula too." said Chrysalis.

"Hey guys, Blinda showed you guys the new human to monster formula?" said Gege who just appeared to them.

"Yep." said Chrysalis.

"Did you guys think it looked weird too?" said Gege.

"Yeah it kind of does." said Chrysalis.

"I agree too, and no I was not eavesdropping I just heard you guys while I walked over here." said Whittneya who just came into the room.

"Yeah you think they be inspired by better looking ones to do better work." said Ocieana.

"I know right." said Gege.

"But guys remember if someone wants to look like that then we have to respect that." said Chrysalis.

"Yeah you're right Chrysalis." said Blinda.

"Sure, anyway I'm excited about your birthday Chrysalis, what is like Chrysalis planning a birthday for yourself because being a nonuplet you don't do that?" said Whittneya.

"Well it's nice but you guys sharing a birthday means you guys get to do something you all want to do, not one of you nine gets to hear about a party you don't want." said Chrysalis.

"She is right on that Whittneya." said Tiana.

"True." said Whittneya.

"Hey guys." said Patty who came over and looking worried.

"Hi Patty, is everything okay?" said Chrysalis.

"Actually, no I lost my bracelet." said Patty.

"Which one?" said Gege.

"Um the one you guys would be surprised that I lost." said Patty.

"Are you talking about the bright light music love bracelet?" said Chrysalis.

"Yeah, that's it." said Patty.

"Are you serious?" said Blinda.

"Hey did we just hear what we think we just heard about Patty losing her bright light music love bracelet?" said Natasha walking up with Zadie, Tiana, and Amelia.

"Yep." said Ocieana.

3

"I'll help you find it Patty." said Chrysalis.

"Thanks Chrysalis." said Patty.

Chrysalis' sisters all joined in too.

"You know what, I might have left it at the music studio that's closest to here." said Patty.

"Okay, then we'll go there." said Chrysalis.

So they left. Meanwhile, at a house where a family of six human/snake monsters live at who they are pink, they have flat lines pointing out non-sharp spikes at the back of their heads, humans familiar-looking chest and waist and neck and arms, hands with three fingers which their thumbs are higher up than their other end fingers, no fangs, no scales but human skin instead, three feet taller than they would be in their human forms, regular human eyesight, ear holes hidden in their spikes, and human tongues. One of them named Kylestone was sitting at the table looking at a card with his dad on the cover feeling sad.

"What are you looking at baby? Oh, one of your birthday cards with your dadda on the cover. I know that one was from him." said his mother, Zinnia.

Kylestone's father is the same human/ snake monster they are.

"Yes mother." said Kylestone.

"Are you okay?" said Zinnia.

"Just huh, wishing he was here." said Kylestone.

"I know how you feel I wish he was here too." said Zinnia.

"I never thought it would be possible how he died." said Kylestone.

4

"Well look you know he's in a better place now with Jesus." said Zinnia.

"I know I can never forget that." said Kylestone.

"Hi dad are you okay?" said Kylestone's 14-year-old daughter Ariel who is the same human/ snake monster they are placing herself in his arms and while placing herself on his lap.

Kylestone kissed Ariel on top of her head.

"I'm fine, did you make any friends?" said Kylestone.

"Can you please stop asking me about that?" said Ariel.

"Baby, you know one of the reasons why we moved here is so you can try and make friends here since you weren't able to where we used to live at." said Kylestone.

"I'm sorry dad but, it's not easy for me because grandfather died from being murdered." said Ariel.

"Accidently murder, to make it less freaky than someone killed him on purpose." said Zinnia.

"Baby if you don't start making any friends your mother and I are going to get worried about you being alone." said Kylestone.

"I can't promise you that I will." said Ariel.

"Can you at least try?" said Kylestone.

"That I can promise you." said Ariel.

"Good now go do it." said Kylestone pointing his finger out.

"Now?" said Ariel.

"Yes now." said Kylestone.

"Dad." said Ariel.

"Come on baby please." said Kylestone, getting up from his seat with Ariel.

"Okay but don't get mad or upset with me if I still haven't made a friend." said Ariel.

Then Ariel slithered out.

"Don't be pushing her," said Zinnia.

"I'm not going to push her, but I don't want her to be alone. She's an only child and when it was just me and you, after, father died and before I met my wife Regina I still felt like we needed to meet others because we don't have enough company." said Kylestone.

"I'm sure she'll find a friend soon." said Zinnia.

Upstairs, Ariel's mom, Regina, who is the same human/ snake monster as Ariel, Kylestone, and Zinnia are. Regina was looking at photos in picture frames of Ariel when she was a baby.

"Honey." said Kylestone, coming up to Regina, putting his arms around her.

Kylestone and Regina kissed each other on the lips.

"Just look at our little baby when she was a baby." said Regina, holding the picture frame.

"Adorable, by the way, she left." said Kylestone.

"I'm hoping this is finally the day she makes a friend." said Regina.

"At least we know she tries to keep herself safe." said Kylestone.

"True but I'm sure it's a nice neighborhood here." said Regina.

"Wait that got me thinking we don't know much about this neighborhood. We just moved here. We should go find her and stay with her while she's slithering around." said Kylestone.

"Well okay but don't worry," said Regina.

"I know, but you know that the lady who made my father die was never caught, and I don't know what she will do if she finds us and finds out who we are, our little baby is out there by herself I don't want anything bad to happen to her, but we will go catch up to her calmly." said Kylestone.

"Exactly." said Regina.

"What are you two talking about?" said Tarzan (Ariel's grandpa who is her mom's dad) who is the same human/ snake monster Kylestone and Regina are and is coming up with Pocahontas (Ariel's grandma who is her mom's mom).

"Ariel is not in trouble is she?" said Pocahontas who is the same human/ snake monster they are.

"No she's not but Kylestone and I are just going to go see Ariel out of the house." said Regina.

"Oh good you had me worried a bit." said Pocahontas.

"Me too." said Tarzan.

At one of Sasha's studios where Chrysalis and her sisters and her friends are looking for Patty's bracelet.

"Found it," said Gaddy, holding it up.

"Oh good thanks Gaddy." said Patty, while Gaddy handed it to her.

"Still can't believe you lost yours. We all use them a lot." said Jerrica who is a human/ black cat monster who has no whiskers, no claws, five fingers, five toes, no tail, and no

7

sharp teeth and so is her husband Aaron next to her and their less than a year-old daughter Sue who is in Jerrica's arms.

"I know I'm surprised too." said Patty.

"So Chrysalis is everything going good for your 15th birthday?" said Stacya, who is a human/ monster who looks like a human with pink skin and a black cat nose and has four sisters Lotusa, Jannia, Bentha, and Tarika and the five of them are quintuplets and the same human/monster.

"Everything is going good." said Chrysalis.

"Ah man I'm so excited." said Cherryette who is a human/ monster who looks like a human with green skin, snake teeth, parts of her skin is snake scales instead, scales around her eyes, a snake tongue, and a snake nose.

"Is everything going good like how I've been keeping my stuffed cat good for the fashion show at the GLAMOR PAL MALL." said Dakota who is a human/ white weasel monster with no claws, no sharp teeth, longer fur at the sides of her face, pointy ears, no whiskers, and a pink nose and is holding out her stuffed cat.

"You're going to have your stuffed cat be in the fashion show, as in being a model for stuffed animal clothes?" said Darent.

"Yeah I asked Kiri's mom, and she said why not." said Dakota.

"It's true I was there, and I agree with Dakota having her stuffed cat in the fashion show." said Kiri.

"It's also too cute how could you say no?" said Dakota holding it by her head.

"Yeah it is." said Chrysalis.

"You know asking you about what it's like planning a birthday for yourself got me thinking, what's it like being the eldest sister?" said Whittneya to Chrysalis.

"Well you're the first one having to take responsibility." said Chrysalis.

"You know this talking of bright light music lover bracelets got me thinking when I got mine." said Jerrica.

Jerrica got hers out of her pocket.

"I got mine for Aaron here when we were boyfriend and girlfriend and sweet husband he is now," said Jerrica.

"Thanks hun," said Aaron.

"I remember the song I sang when I first sang with it on my wrist. Hey Chrysalis, can you hold my baby girl Sue for a few minutes?" said Jerrica.

"Sure and I believe I know why," said Chrysalis, while Jerrica handed her Sue.

Jerrica put her bright light music lover bracelet on her wrist and set her phone on the app that plays instruments in the rhyme of the song you're singing, and she started to sing the song she sang when she first got her bright light music lover bracelet, and it shined green light with black jaguar patterns and orange and blue diagonal colored stripes and while she was doing that she bought her husband Aaron up to her to dance and they both danced together until Jerrica stopped singing. Then Jerrica put her phone away and bracelet into her pocket and Chrysalis gave Sue back into Jerrica's arms. Everyone loved watching what Jerrica did and with Aaron.

"Wow awesome," said Chrysalis.

9

"That is the song you first sang when you got your bracelet, right?" said Tiana.

"Yes it was." said Jerrica.

"And you still sang it as great as you did the first time." said Aaron.

"Aw thanks hun." said Jerrica.

Then Jerrica and Aaron kissed each other.

"Hey Kert did you finally ask Slecks out on a date?" said Candace.

"Oho is it finally happening?" said Ratia.

"Please tell us it is." said Colleen who is Ratia's twin sister.

"Well actually Candace, Colleen, and Ratia, no I have not." said Kert.

"Aww." said Colleen and Ratia.

"What you haven't." said Kert's second youngest-sister Lalo.

"That's a low down." said Cherryette.

"You tell it Cherryette." said Gaddy.

"I was going to but, she was having a photo shoot and I had to wait and while I was waiting I had second thoughts." said Kert.

"So you didn't like Slecks?" said Zila who is Kert's third-youngest sister.

"No I do." said Kert.

"Then why don't you ask her out, it sounds like you don't." said Javada who is Kert's eldest little sister.

"They got a point there." said Gaddy.

"Huh yeah you guys are right I will next time I see her." said Kert.

Just then, Jistopher and his girlfriend Trudy came to them and also Slecks.

"Hi guys," said Jistopher.

"Hey Jistopher, Trudy, and Slecks." they all said.

"Hey guys I came up with a new song, you guys want to hear it?" said Slecks.

"Sure yeah." they all said.

So Slecks went up the stage in the room and sang, and they all loved it and during her singing Kert, still had the courage to ask her out.

"Hey Kert, now's your chance to ask Slecks out." said Tinka.

"Um." said Kert feeling nervous again.

"Get over there you heard my little sister Tinka." said Dannya.

"Hey Slecks." said Kert.

"Yeah?" said Slecks.

"Ah ah ah hi there Slecks." said Kert.

Slecks felt weird and Kert felt embarrassed, and he turned and looked at Dannya and Tinka, who were behind him looking like they, saw an odd show.

"Hi there Slecks isn't good enough." said Tinka.

"Kert has something he wants to tell you Slecks." said Darma who is Kert's youngest sister.

"Oho is it happening?" whispered Ratia.

"Oh really what's that?" said Slecks.

"I think it is sis." whispered Colleen.

"Uh, are you doing anything tomorrow?" said Kert.

"I don't have any big plans tomorrow why?" said Slecks.

"Well I was wondering if you would want to go on a date with me that day." said Kert.

"Really yeah, I just feel bad that I wasn't brave enough to ask you." said Slecks.

"Yes." said Colleen and Ratia.

"Wait you were feeling the same thing with Kert that he was with you?" said Tiana.

"Kert was like that with me?" said Slecks.

"Honestly yeah." said Kert.

"Then yes." said Slecks.

Then Jistopher and Trudy kissed each other.

"That's sweet." said Tarika.

"Hey Beatrix where are you and your boyfriend Jaser going again on your guys' date?" said Trudy.

"The SWEET NON-SWISH place." said Beatrix.

"We both subjected it at the same time." said Jaser.

"I'm going there too with my girlfriend Navia." said Princeson while holding Navia's hand up.

"Same thing with my boyfriend Darent and I." said Venelope.

"It's true." said Darent.

"Is that where you want to go for our next date?" said Jistopher.

"Uh yeah sure." said Trudy.

"Alright then that's where." said Jistopher.

"Hey guys look who's back." said their friend Raymen with his wife Taffada and their new baby daughter Trixie.

The three of them are also human/ cat monsters that are light bluish green and they have triangle pointed out hands and thumbs and they have triangle pointed out feet and no tails or sharp teeth or whiskers.

"Oh my gosh you guys are back and with you guys' new baby Trixie." said Chrysalis.

"Ah she's so cute." said Bessa.

"Yep she is Bessa." said Taffada.

"Hi Trixie." said Chrysalis.

Trixie smiled and giggled. Raymen notices Kert and Slecks holding hands

"Hey you guys are holding hands are you two going on a date?" said Raymen.

"Yes we are." said Slecks.

"Thanks for helping me Javada, Zila, Lalo, and Darma." said Kert.

"Ah it's sweet that your little sisters helped you." said Slecks.

"You know I'm glad that Trixie was born in time for Chrysalis' birthday and for that outdoor flea market happening soon." said Taffada.

"Oh yeah right I forgot about that." said Justina.

"I can't believe I forgot too." said Agnesa.

"LuLu and LeLe and I will be doing that after our hula music video." said LiLi who is LuLu and LeLe's triplet sister.

"Are you guys ready, you're going on in a few minutes?" said Cherrycake who is a human/ cat monster who is orange with black stripes, has blonde hair on her head, no claws, no whiskers, no sharp teeth, five fingers on both hands, and five toes on both feet.

"Yeah we are Cherrycake, we're always ready for our performances." said LuLu.

"LuLu, LeLe, LiLi are you guys ready?" said Agnesa's dad who is a director.

"We are, and we're coming." said LeLe.

"Oh and Agnesa can you do me a favor when you go to the flea market to look for any jewelry for your mom and I to wear for our next concert we might be very busy?" said Agnesa's dad.

"Sure thing dad." said Agnesa.

"Thanks." said Agnesa's dad.

Where Ariel was slithering her parents came up to her.

"Mom dad, you guys are here too," said Ariel.

"We thought it would be safer if we came along with you until we know this area better. Are you okay with that?" said Kylestone.

"Oh well okay." said Ariel.

"Hey look over there they're having a flea market." said Regina pointing at it.

"You want us to go there?" said Kylestone.

"Sure." said Ariel.

So they slithered over. Chrysalis and her sisters and friends arrived at the flea market too.

"Wow this flea market is pretty." said Nillia.

"Yeah I want to look everywhere here." said Arianie who is Nillia's twin sister.

"Remember you guys said when Jindy, Tira, Irenie, and Candace' parents open their jewelry cart here we'll head on over because I want to see it, but I'm supposed to be watching you guys." said Fawn who is Nillia and Arianie's older cousin.

"We know and we promise." said Arianie.

"Plus we want to see it too." said Nillia.

"Wait until you guys see it." said Candace.

"We're all looking forward to it." said Chrysalis.

"Yeah you guys know making jewelry is one of their talents." said Candace.

"We also helped set it up." said Jindy who is Candace's eldest sister.

"Hey Agnesa, remember what your dad told you to do." said Tira who is Candace's second-eldest sister.

"Yeah and you should get started because this place is filling up." said Irenie who is Candace's youngest eldest sister.

"Oh yeah I don't want to upset my parents." said Agnesa.

"Wow." said Chrysalis, looking around.

Just then, while Chrysalis was looking, three women walked up by her.

"Hey look, where you are heading when you see us move and give us space." said one of them madly to Chrysalis.

"I'm sorry I wasn't meant to hit you guys at least I didn't." said Chrysalis.

"Doesn't matter to us don't you ever let it happen again." said a second one who was mad at Chrysalis.

Then they started walking away.

"You guys are acting mean," said Chrysalis.

Just then another lady came over.

"Is something going on guys?" said the lady to the three girls.

"We're being bothered by this gal." said the first one who spoke to Chrysalis.

The lady who just came over and looked at Chrysalis.

"Hi my name is Carlica," said the lady who just came over to Chrysalis.

"Hi I'm-." said Chrysalis before getting interrupted by Carlica.

"Don't need to know and stay away from my friends Mesha, Manora, and Mingmi." said Carlica.

"Oh so that's their names." said Chrysalis.

"You don't need to speak." said Carlica.

Carlica and her friends Mesha, Manora, and Mingmi left. Where Ariel and her parents were looking at items, the three women went up to them and stopped where Ariel was looking at jewelry.

"Hello and move over, we want to look here." said the first one of the three women with a mad face.

"Just a minute," said Ariel.

"Excuse us but when we say something we mean it now." said the second one of the three women angrily.

"Simmer down." said Ariel.

"Didn't tell us what to do." said the third one of the three girls.

Her parents heard and knew what had happened.

"Hey you ladies!" said Regina.

"We better go," said the first one of the three women.

Then they ran off.

"Are you okay baby?" said Regina while she and Kylestone wrapped their arms around Ariel.

"Can I go home now?" said Ariel.

"Don't you want to look around here more?" said Regina.

"I don't want to." said Ariel.

"I could take her home while you look around more." said Kylestone to Regina.

"Alright thanks Kylestone if you guys want me to come home just tell me." said Regina.

Chrysalis and her friends and sisters were excited to almost begin Jindy, Tira, Irenie, and Candace's parents', jewelry cart.

"Hey Chrysalis, where's your great-grandparents Sasha and Ard and our senior citizen friends Poppy and her little sister Epe?" said Constance (who is a human/ monster that looks like a human with pink skin, blue eyes with no white and only one black dot in the middle of each of them, has twelve fangs six on top and six at the bottom with regular teeth between them separating three).

"Oh they're coming." said Chrysalis.

"Hey guys we're about to get started." said Jindy, Tira, Irenie, and Candace's dad with their mom.

"I hope Sasha, Ard, Poppy, and Epe aren't going to be too late." said Tira.

"Oh coming quickly." said Chrysalis.

Chrysalis and her sisters' parents and grandparents and Chrysalis' friends' parents all showed up too.

"Hey guys, I see that the jewelry cart isn't out yet," said Walter.

"Nope, but it's about too." said Jindy, who is Candace's eldest sister.

"Hey mom dad you guys came." said Agnesa.

"We ended up finishing on time." said Agnesa's mom.

Chrysalis was looking upset.

"Is something wrong, Chrysalis?" said Irenie.

"I ran into some mean ladies who were mean to me." said Chrysalis.

"Oh were their names Mesha, Manora, and Mingmi? We ran into them on the way here." said Fawn's mom.

"You guys have," said Chrysalis.

"Yep they were mean to us too, but you got to not listen to them." said Gaddy's dad.

"I know, I also met another friend of theirs named Carlica who was mean too." said Chrysalis.

"They were all being hard on you Chrysalis." said Marleen.

"Well if they run into me, they will be talked to too." said Walter.

"Thanks, but I'm sure they will try to cause trouble." said Chrysalis.

Just then, Chrysalis' great-grandparents come over with their friends Poppy and Epe, who are sisters on Poppy's motorcycle. They parked by them and took their helmets off.

"Hey everyone," said Ard.

"Hi." Chrysalis and her friends and family said.

Then they walked over.

"Did we make it in time before the cart was revealed?" said Sasha.

"Yeah you guys have." said Gaddy's mom.

"You know Jindy, Tira, Irenie, and Candace. It has been a long time since you girls' parents did a jewelry cart at a flea market." said Stacya, Lotusa, Jannia, Bentha, and Tarika's mom.

"Yeah they last time they did it was when they were kids, I remember that time." said Stacya, Lotusa, Jannia, Bentha, and Tarika's dad.

"Oh yeah we know we like hearing stories we you guys all hung out with each other when you guys were kids." said Candace.

"Did you guys and Sasha and Ard and your other friends who were kids when you guys were kids, were friends during when you guys were kids too?" said Nillia to Poppy and Epe.

"My little sister and I and our friends who were kids when we were kids have been friends since we were kids." said Poppy.

"I believe that." said Cherryette.

"Hey Ocieana you have been staring at Poppy's motorcycle for a while." said Cersanthama.

"It looks so sparkly and shiny." said Ocieana.

"That's because I just cleaned it." said Poppy.

"Oh man big sis everytime Ocieana sees your motorcycle clean she stares at it for a while." said Epe.

"Okay guys here's our cart." said Jindy, Tira, Irenie, and Candace's mom pushing it over after walking to go get it.

All of them love looking at their jewelry designs.

"Wow after all these years you guys still got with setting up an amazing cart of jewelry." said Walter.

"Thanks Walter." said Jindy, Tira, Irenie, and Candace's dad.

"Thanks." said Jindy, Tira, Irenie, and Candace's mom.

"Do you like this necklace Trixie?" said Taffada holding the necklace to Trixie being held in her arm.

Trixie laughed and smiled.

"I'll take that as a yes, I like it too," said Taffada.

"These are lovely," said Cersanthama, looking at the necklaces.

"Hey Ratia do you think my neck looks weird with this necklace?" said Colleen.

"I think you mean our necks we do look alike." said Ratia.

"I think you girls look pretty with it." said Colleen and Ratia's mom.

"Thanks mom." said Colleen and Ratia.

"But these necklaces are nice." said Colleen and Ratia's dad grabbing them.

"Oh yeah, thanks dad." said Colleen and Ratia grabbing them from their dad.

Chrysalis' friend Rowshella was admiring the jewelry. Rowshella held a necklace out and turned around and was surprised because a teenage boy who is the same age as her was behind her, who was surprised that Rowshella turned right at his face.

"Sorry I didn't know you were behind me." said Rowshella.

"It's okay." said the boy.

"You know you do look good in this necklace." said Rowshella holding the necklace up to his neck.

"You know I think I do too." said the boy.

"If you're interested in it I'll let you have it." said Rowshella.

"Oh, thanks, but I think I'll look around for something else." said the boy.

"Okay I think I will too." said Rowshella.

Everyone saw Rowshella with the boy and wanted to meet him.

"Hi," said Chrysalis to the boy with Rowshella.

"Hey," said everyone else to the boy with Rowshella.

"It's nice meeting you Rowshella and the rest of you guys, I'm Calvis." said the boy.

"Well I don't have to tell you my name." said Rowshella.

"I'm a very big music fan and I love to dance I do it a lot." said Calvis.

"Really can you show us?" said Kathleenie who is a human/ monster that looks like a human with blue skin, pink cheeks, and silver glitterly parts of her skin on her arms.

"Sure." said Calvis.

So Calvis did that and they were impressed.

"Wow that was great, are you interested in having a talk with me later after I'm done looking around the flea market?" said Sasha to Calvis.

"Sure yeah." said Calvis excitedly.

"Great." said Sasha.

"You know Rowshella I'm glad to be meeting you I know a lot about you." said Calivs.

"Really well now I get to learn about you. Do you use the music app on your phone that plays the instruments you pick to play in the rhythm of the song you're singing?" said Rowshella.

"Yes I do, you know I think this necklace is good for you." said Calvis holding up the necklace.

"Yeah you're right." said Rowshella.

Then they started staring at each other's eyes. While they were looking a lady who is a human/ monster that looks like a human with blue skin, a purple tongue, six fingers, and is five feet taller than her original height came up to look and went next to Chrysalis.

"You're a thief aren't you?" said the lady to Chrysalis while sitting on her knees.

"I'm not a thief." said Chrysalis.

"You don't have any friends here do you?" said the lady.

"Yeah I do and family." said Chrysalis.

"Are you someone who likes to cause mischief." said the lady.

"No mischief is wrong." said Chrysalis.

"Well I don't know who you are I never heard of you I'm Falyby." said the lady.

"My name's Chrysalis." said Chrysalis.

"Doesn't ring the bell but why would you say your first name only?" said Falyby.

"Oh you want to know my last name it's Loom." said Chrysalis.

"Nope, I still don't know you." said Falyby.

"Okay, do you like the jewelry at this cart?" said Chrysalis.

"Are you upset?" said Falyby.

"Upset about what?" said Chrysalis.

"But if you're a famous singer why would you not say your full name to have people know who you are better to try and get them to know you better to have them know you're famous, you're not upset by that?" said Falyby.

"I don't care about fame and I thought you didn't know who I was and that you never heard of me." said Chrysalis.

"Well I-." said Falyby.

"You know I am upset that you lied to me." said Chrysalis.

Calvis noticed what was going on.

"Uh, I'm guessing she's not a friend of Chrysalis," said Calvis.

"What?" said Rowshella.

Rowshella turned around and saw Chrysalis talking to Falyby.

"I don't think that lady is a friend of any of us," said Cersanthama.

"Oh yeah, I believe you guys are right." said Rowshella.

"Is everything going okay?" said Marge Kathleenie's twin sister who is the same/ human monster she is but with golden glitterly skin parts on her arms.

"Can we make this good?" said Chrysalis to Falyby.

"Hopefully with you and me it will." said Falyby to Chrysalis.

Then Falyby walked away.

23

"Huh man," said Chrysalis.

"Are you okay?" said Dannya.

"I think I need to walk far out." said Chrysalis.

"Are you feeling upset?" said Tinka.

"I'm just feeling kind of bugged, don't worry about it." said Chrysalis.

Then Chrysalis walked away from the cart. Regina was still at the flea market, then she got out her phone to look at the time.

"I should go home now." said Regina.

Chrysalis was walking until she walked by a dark dead end walkway between buildings she got the idea to walk down there, and she started to get out her phone and set it up, and she started to sing while dancing then she got out her bright light music love bracelet, and it made bright golden, yellow, and red lights shine out of it while she sang and dance, but she didn't know that Regina was walking by where she was, but Chrysalis spotted her once she looked at her Chrysalis continued sing and dancing while looking at her until she finished and grabbed her phone and took off her bracelet and put them on her pocket.

"Wow." said Regina.

"Thanks, who are you?" said Chrysalis.

"I'm Regina and that was an amazing performance and wow, you are pretty." said Regina.

"Thanks and nice to meet you I'm Chrysalis I was singing and dancing with my bright light music love bracelet because I was having a bugged out time." said Chrysalis.

"My daughter Ariel did too which was why she left the flea market early after being bothered by three mean ladies." said Regina.

"Did they look alike with black held up hair, moles on their cheeks, and red clothing?" said Chrysalis.

"Yes, do you know them?" said Regina.

"I just met them once, and they were not nice to meet either." said Chrysalis.

"Were they the ones who made you upset to do your wonderful performance?" said Regina.

"It was after meeting another mean lady named Falyby." said Chrysalis.

"Oh well I just moved her with my family." said Regina.

"Oh are you liking it here so far? It can be very nice here," said Chrysalis.

"True it can be." said Regina.

"Your family should have happy times here." said Chrysalis.

"You know you should meet my daughter Ariel. She doesn't have any friends." said Regina.

"Oh really sure when?" said Chrysalis.

"Well you could bring your parents with you to go walk to my house right now. Am I able to meet them?" said Regina.

"Sure they're at the flea market. I can bring you to them," said Chrysalis.

"Okay," said Regina.

So Chrysalis brought Regina to them.

"Did you guys know that lady who Chrysalis was talking to?" said Beatrix's dad to Chrysalis' parents.

"No," said Marleen.

Then they saw Chrysalis come up with Regina.

"Hey mom dad I feel a lot better now after meeting my new friend Regina here." said Chrysalis.

"Hi." said Regina.

"Oh hello." said Marleen.

"Do you guys know her?" said Beatrix's mom to Chrysalis' parents.

"No we haven't either." said Marleen.

"That's because I just moved here with my family, and I was wondering if Chrysalis would like to come to my house with you guys her parents to meet my daughter Ariel so she can make a friend because she doesn't have any, and I thought you wouldn't want her to go to someone she just meet at their house alone you're also able to walk there." said Regina.

"No friends, that's sad." said Butterscotch who is a human/ dog monster who has pink fur and yellow fur on her limbs, yellow hair on top of her head, no neck, no sharp teeth, no tail, and half a foot tall.

"Yeah that is sure." said Marleen.

"We can do that." said Walter.

"Great are you guys okay with going right now?" said Regina.

"Can we?" said Chrysalis.

"You are okay with going right now hun." said Walter to Marleen.

"Sure." said Marleen.

"Okay then." said Walter.

"Yes." said Chrysalis.

"Come on." said Regina.

Chrysalis and her parents went with Regina. At Ariel's house, Kylestone sat with Ariel wrapped around his arms, kissing her and rubbing her to make her feel better.

"I'm sure it will turn up here," said Kylestone.

"Can I never leave the house again?" said Ariel.

"No baby girl that's bad for you." said Kylestone.

"Doubt it matters." said Ariel.

"Don't be like that baby." said Kylestone.

Just then they heard the door open.

"Sounds like your mother is back, if you tell her what you told me she'll agree with me," said Kylestone.

Regina slithered to them, but they didn't see Chrysalis and her parents.

"Hi you two, Ariel, I think I'm going to make your day when you finally make a friend." said Reginsafire.

"Did you bring someone here?" said Ariel.

"Did you bring anyone here?" said Kylestone.

"Yes and her parents, and they are very nice." said Regina.

"Hi." said Chrysalis appearing to Kylestone and Ariel with her parents.

"Whoa wow you are beautiful." said Kylestone to Chrysalis.

"Thanks are you Kylestone?" said Chrysalis.

"Yes and standing over there is Ariel." said Kylestone pointing at her.

"Oh hi I'm Chrysalis I'm glad to be meeting you to get to know you." said Chrysalis.

Ariel stood silent.

"Oh, I'm sorry if I'm scaring you," said Chrysalis.

Still Ariel stood silently.

"Ah man." said Kylestone worried.

"She's being all silent again," said Regina worried too.

"Do you want to show me around your house, or can I look around your house with you following me? Are you okay with that?" said Chrysalis.

Ariel nodded yes.

"Okay, come on," said Chrysalis.

So they looked around Ariel's house.

Meanwhile, at Calvis' house. Calvis' dad was sitting on his chair reading in the living room while Calvis' mom was doing the dishes in the kitchen. Just then Calvis entered inside through the back door and walked to the living room where his dad is reading.

"This has been amazing! Dad, I have a career happening" said Calvis.

"Calvis don't expect you'll get a music and dance career just because you think you will not everyone gets one, but that's okay." said Calvis' dad.

"No dad I'm serious." said Calvis.

"What you ran into Sasha Coldrock, and she thought you were talented enough for one?" said Calvis' dad sarcastically.

"Yeah that's what happened I also met the singer Rowshella that I like-." said Calvis.

"What?" said Calvis' dad getting up from his chair surprised.

"Did I just hear what I think I just heard?" said Calvis' mom entering the living room.

"Yeah I just got back from meeting Sasha Coldrock after I met her at the flea market-." said Calvis.

"Wait you went to the flea market you weren't supposed to go until after you went to the hardware store to get a new broom and finished sweeping the garage." said Calvis' dad.

"Yeah I know, but the flea market was on the way there, and I thought I could look a little before continuing going there, but I did get the broom and I can also make it up to you guys by bring you to see Sasha Coldrocks studios I just got back after already got hired by her at one of them." said Calivs.

"You mean you went to one of her studios without us knowing and you just got back so you weren't sweeping the garage?" said Calvis' dad.

"Uh well yeah." said Calvis.

"Calvis." said Calvis' mom.

"I'm sorry I would have told you guys where I was going, but I got so excited I forgot, but please let me make it up to you guys by bringing you guys there." said Calvis.

"Why not hun we know Calvis doesn't usually make mistakes like that." said Calvis' mom.

"Okay, but after you're done sweeping the garage but remember even though you work for Sasha Coldrock we can still have you quit if we want too." said Calvis dad.

"Yes I know and you guys won't have that happen." said Calvis.

"By the way you said you met the singer Rowshella you have a crush on?" said Calvis' mom.

"Yeah I'm supposed to be meeting her later because I had a job to do at home." said Calvis.

"Well I'm glad you didn't forget that." said Calvis' dad.

At Ariel's house, Chrysalis and Ariel were upstairs.

"You know your mom told me that you were bothered by those three mean girls that made you want to leave the flea market early. Sorry about that," said Chrysalis.

Ariel felt upset thinking about it.

"Hey, these are photos of you and your family, huh," said Chrysalis.

Still Ariel stayed silently.

"Hey this is a photo of Ivern he's known for being a famous singer, but he's dead now, wait, your dad's name is Kylestone, and that's the name of his only child is Ivern, your grandfather?" said Chrysalis.

"Yes." said Ariel quietly.

"Whoa, wait this why you're nervous to meet others because he was accidentally killed 20 years ago because he was taking a slither until he ran into a lady who was jealous of him and when she meet him during his slither she lost it so much she pushed him but accidentally into the street and a car ran over him and the lady was never found." said Chrysalis.

"Yeah." said Ariel.

"It's too bad that happened to him, I love his songs and I also love singing too." said Chrysalis.

"I'm sorry I keep feeling too scared to talk I'm afraid of what someone will do to me like what happened to him." said Ariel.

"It's okay I get it when you're ready to talk then talk." said Chrysalis.

"Thanks." said Ariel.

Where Walter and Kylestone are in the house.

"Ivern is your dad," said Walter holding the picture frame with a photo of Ivern.

"Yeah," said Kylestone.

"Do you sing, I sure do." said Walter.

"Sometimes." said Kylestone.

"I hope it works out with the girls, it should Chrysalis is good with others." said Walter.

"I hope it goes good too." said Kylestone.

Where Chrysalis and Ariel are in the house.

"Do you own one of these? These bracelets are really fun. They make lights come out of them and the more you love the song you're singing and the more the ones hearing your singing loves it, the brighter the lights and more it makes and does while you're singing." said Chrysalis holding out her bright light music love bracelet from her pocket.

"Wow and no." said Ariel.

"Here let me show you." said Chrysalis.

Chrysalis got out her phone, set up the app and started to sing and dance, and the bracelet did what Chrysalis said and Ariel loved it. It really made her happy, like she was not shy.

"Wow," said Ariel.

"Do you sing? Do you want to try using my bracelet?" said Chrysalis after putting her phone away.

"Well, I do, but I prefer to be alone doing it." said Ariel.

"Oh, okay here keep the bracelet so you can enjoy what it does by yourself, I can get a new one." said Chrysalis.

"What really?" said Ariel

"Yeah." said Chrysalis.

"Wow, thank you I'm hoping I will be willing to sing in front of you someday and you liking it." said Ariel.

"I'm sure you'll do good if you show me." said Chrysalis.

Ariel's family and Chrysalis' parents come over to them.

"Did we just hear singing?" said Pochontas.

"And very beautiful singing." said Tarzan.

"That was Chrysalis." said Ariel.

"Oh wow, and she is very beautiful herself." said Zinnia.

"Thank you." said Chrysalis.

"Yep she's a famous singer alright." said Walter.

"Wait she's a famous singer." said Tarzan.

"That's believable." said Ariel.

"Yep Walter and I are famous singers and our friends and family." said Marleen.

"You guys too." said Regina.

"Wow, am I dreaming?" said Zinnia.

"Well even though we're famous singers you don't have to treat us like royalty." said Marleen.

"We're good with being treated like ordinary people." said Walter.

"Ariel, where did you get that bracelet?" said Zinnia.

"From Chrysalis she gave it to me." said Ariel.

"Hey you guys interested in seeing one of my great-grandma Sasha's music studios?" said Chrysalis.

"Wait is your great-grandma Sasha Coldrock?" said Kylestone.

"Yeah and one of her studios is the music studio where Ivern used to work at where you guys used to live." said Chrysalis.

"Really." said Zinnia.

"Yes that's my grandma." said Marleen.

"I don't think I'm ready to meet other people yet." said Ariel.

"They're really nice, but you don't have to come." said Chrysalis.

"But I want to hang out with you more if I go there with you stay with me and make sure I'm okay?" said Ariel.

"Sure of course." said Chrysalis.

"Thanks, friend?" said Ariel.

"Yeah." said Chrysalis.

"Huh." said Regina quietly.

"Finally." said Kylestone quietly.

At one of Sasha's music studios where Chrysalis' friends and the rest of her family are at Calvis brought his parents with him to there.

"Wow," said Calvis' mom.

Chrysalis and her parents and Ariel and her family arrived at the same studio too.

"This is bigger than the one my father worked at." said Kylestone.

"I hope you'll get along with my sisters to make it easier to have you come to my house sometimes." said Chrysalis.

"How many sisters do you have?" said Ariel.

"Nine all younger and nonuplets." said Chrysalis.

"Hold on what?" said Zinnia.

"Did she just say you guys have nine more girls?" said Kylestone to Chrysalis' parents.

"Yes we do." said Marleen.

"My that's a lot." said Regina.

"And you had them naturally?" said Pocahontas to Marleen.

"Yep." said Marleen.

"Hi Chrysalis." said Calvis with his parents.

"Hi Calvis, are those two with you your parents?" said Chrysalis.

"Yep, who are those guys you're with?" said Calvis.

"This is my new friend Ariel and her family." said Chrysalis.

"Oh hey I know you." said Walter to Calvis' dad.

"Hi Walter and Marleen." said Calvis' dad.

"You know them dad?" said Calvis.

"We went to school together, and after we graduated your dad moved because he wanted to go somewhere more formal than here." said Walter.

34

"What, dad, you wanted to go live somewhere less fun." said Calvis.

"Well we're here now and that's better than continuing where we lived right?" said Calvis' dad.

"You're dad's right." said Calvis' mom.

"Yeah okay well I'm going to go look around." said Calvis.

"Come on Ariel let's look around." Chrysalis said.

"Ariel will you be fine if you're just with Chrysalis?" said Kylestone.

"Uh, sure." said Ariel.

"I'm going to come with you guys too." said Calvis to Chrysalis and Ariel.

"Are you okay with that Ariel?" said Chrysalis.

"Are you shy?" said Calvis to Ariel.

"She's nervous around others." said Chrysalis.

"Oh I'll try making it easy for you." said Calvis to Ariel.

"Okay thanks." said Ariel to Calvis.

"Come on." said Chrysalis.

"Don't feel nervous about meeting your former classmates." said Marleen to Calvis' dad.

"They're here too." said Calvis' dad.

"Oh that's nice you get to meet the ones who were your classmates again." said Calvis' mom.

So they walked further into the studio. Where Chrysalis' friends and sisters are in the studio. Just then Chrysalis, Calvis, and Ariel appeared.

"Hey Calvis and the rest of you guys," said Rowshella, going up to Calvis.

Rowshella put her hand on Calvis' shoulder.

"Rowshella and I have really bonded," said Calvis.

"Hey Chrysalis and Calvis, who's that you're with?" said Navia who is Princeson's girlfriend looking at Ariel.

"This is Ariel but be careful with her because she's shy." said Chrysalis.

"Oh you're Regina's daughter we meet her at the flea market earlier, I'm Navia." said Navia.

"And I'm Navia's boyfriend Princeson." said Princeson.

"Uh, hi." said Ariel.

Ariel was surprised when Kert's four little sisters came up to her.

"Don't worry about my little sisters Javada, Zila, Lalo, and Darma, they're nice." said Kert.

"Hi, do you love stuffed animals?" Swifta said to Ariel and Swifta is a human/ monster that looks like a human but has part of her skin snakes scales and a snake tongue.

"Yeah." said Ariel.

"So do I you and me getting along should be easy. My name's Swifta." said Swifta.

"Fun seeing you." said Dava.

"Hi, who are you?" said Ariel.

"I'm Dava." said Dava.

"And I'm her triple sister Bemma." said Bemma.

"And I'm their other triple sister Loua." said Loua.

"The three of us girl sisters are a singing group." said Bemma.

"And we're a fun family group." said Loua.

"Oh okay." said Ariel.

"And I'm-." said Mirabel who is a human/ monster that looks like a human with dark green skin a black bear nose, a zebra tail, and cheetah ears.

"Oh you're Mirabel who sang in that TV show you were the stars in it I've been watching Mirabel in her show since I was five, and she was eleven when she started." said Ariel pointing at Mirabel.

"Yep that's her." said Gaddy.

"I love watching that show I was into." said Mirabel.

"You've been watching Mirabel's show since you were five." said Shenatha.

"Uh, I, well." said Ariel feeling embarrassed.

"Don't feel embarrassed Ariel I still watch their show and I'm twenty and my name is Belyndica." said Belyndica.

"Same thing her with me, I'm also twenty and my name is Cherryette by the way." said Cherryette

"A lot of us do and some of us are adults my name's Dakota by the way." said Dakota.

"Okay I feel better now." said Ariel.

Chrysalis' parents brought Ariel's family and Calvis' parents to Chrysalis' friends' parents. When they entered the room, they saw Belyndica's mom singing on stage in front of Chrysalis' friends' parents. All of them enjoyed it and when she was done they all looked and saw Chrysalis' parents, Ariel's family, and Calvis' parents.

"Hey guys." said Belyndica's mom to them.

"Wow, that was great singing." said Regina.

"Thank you." said Belyndica's mom.

"My wife's a good singer." said Belyndica's dad.

"Oh you're a cop." said Kylestone to Belyndica's dad.

"Yep but I'm also a singer." said Belyndica's dad.

"Our daughter Belyndica is a lover of music, but she's still interested in her dad's cop work." said Belyndica's mom.

"Hey you look familiar have we met?" said Fawn's dad to Calvis' dad.

"You guys have he's someone we went to school with until he graduated and moved to a more formal place like he said." said Walter.

"Oh yeah now I recall." said Fawn's dad.

"You remembered me and my big brother and the rest of us from when we went to school together?" said Nillia and Ariannie's mom.

"Yes I do even though none of us were friends no offense I just wasn't sure we had much in common." said Calvis' dad.

"It's okay we're not all alike." said Jaser's mom.

"Are you guys also the parents of Calvis?" said Jaser's dad to Calvis' parents.

"Yes that's us." said Calvis' mom.

"You guys' son is a real music and dance fan." said Jaser's dad to Calvis' parents.

"Yeah he is." said Calvis' dad feeling a little sad.

"What's wrong?" said Stacya, Lotusa, Jannia, Bentha, and Tarika's dad to Calvis' dad.

"Do you not like it that Calvis has a music and dance career my husband and I and our daughters Stacya, Lotusa, Jannia, Bentha, and Tarika have music careers, and we're very happy?" said Stacya, Lotusa, Jannia, Bentha, and Tarika's mom.

"No I am happy for him, it's just I feel like he's a lot different from me, I had us move here because I knew he fit in better here, and I'm wondering if he understands me and how I take care of him." said Calvis' dad.

"I'm sure he does, he should." said Nillia and Ariannie's dad.

Where Chrysalis is with her sisters and friends at the studio Ariel was playing with Trixie.

"Trixie's really adorable." said Ariel.

"Yeah we just got her back from the hospital today." said Raymen.

"Just in time for Chrysalis' birthday in a couple of days." said Cherrycake.

"Your birthday is in a couple of days." said Ariel to Chrysalis.

"Yeah do you guys, Ariel and Calvis, want to ask your parents for them and you guys and the rest of your family Ariel to come to my birthday party if my parents agree?" said Chrysalis.

"Sure." said Calvis.

"Uh." said Ariel not knowing if she wants to.

"You wouldn't want to miss going to Chrysalis' party." said Bessa.

"Yeah her parties are so fun." said Cleo.

"But we're not going to force you to come." said Falla who is Cleo's twin sister.

"Well I, uh, guess so." said Ariel.

"Okay." said Chrysalis.

"Hey Heviner what was it you were going to say about your parents meeting that lady earlier?" said Jaser.

"What lady?" said Ariel.

"Heviner's parents meet the lady who was mean to Chrysalis earlier." said Ridga who is Heviner's girlfriend.

"I already told it to my girlfriend Ridga here." said Heviner.

"That's me." said Ridga.

"They were taking a walk earlier and ran into her, they said hi to her, but she didn't say hi back, and then she tried showing off her singing to them but then they sang and everyone watching thought they did a better job and Falyby looked jealous." said Heviner.

"Whoa." said Candace.

"Oh yeah whoa." said Constance.

"Oh I just remembered I finished my formula for your parents. It glows in the dark has multiple mixed colors and glows for forty minutes but is able to glow again after you shake it." said Dilia who is a human/ alligator monster with blonde hair and is forty-two years old but a foot taller than her size in her human form to Heviner.

"I never heard of you." said Calvis to Dilia.

"Dilia's not a famous performer or star, but she is a nice and helpful friend." said Chrysalis.

"I recognize you I saw you and your family moving into that lovely house while I was taking a walk." said Dilia to Ariel.

"Oh really." said Ariel.

"And I'm Cassandra and these two twins are my older sisters Pennya and Mabel." said Cassandra.

"Hi." said Mabel.

"Hello." said Pennya.

"Hi, speaking of sisters which ones of you guys are Chrysalis' sisters?" said Ariel.

"That's us." said Natasha with the rest of Chrysalis' sisters.

"Oh okay." said Ariel nervously.

"Why are you nervous?" said Zadie.

"Sorry, I still need to be good at hanging out with other." said Ariel.

"Come with me there's an area in the studio I want to show you and Calvis." said Chrysalis.

So Ariel and Calvis followed Chrysalis with her friends and sisters, coming with them to a very big room in the studio where there is a circle stage up to the wall and the floor is a dance floor. Clearly, it was a party room.

"Wow," said Calvis.

"This is where we are having my birthday party at," said Chrysalis.

"Whoa," said Ariel.

"Definitely don't want to pass on Chrysalis' party now right?" said Swifta to Ariel.

"Yeah." said Ariel.

Just then, Butterscotch, Dakota, Fredricka, and Lalo saw Chrysalis' friends' parents and her grandparents and great-grandparents and friends of Chrysalis' great-grandparents since her great-grandparents were kids and Ariel's family going by, but once they saw Kylestone they ran over to him.

"Where are they going?" said Ridga looking at Butterscotch, Dakota, Fredricka, and Lalo leaving.

41

"Where are you girls going?" said Belyndica.

They all followed them.

"You know you guys are really good looking, you know," said Kylestone.

"So are your kids and other adult friends of yours. Where are your other adult friends anyway?" said Regina.

"They're with the kids, they like hanging out with them." said Ridga's mom.

"And thanks, a lot of others say that about us." said Ridga's dad.

"Yeah thanks," they all said.

"Those are nice monster forms of yours." said Ridga's mom.

Fredricka, Dakota, Butterscotch, and Lalo were running to Kylestone and stopped when they got to him.

"What the?" said Kylestone.

"Don't worry Kylestone we know these kids." said Rowshella's dad.

"Oh that's what they were following and wow." said Chrysalis who caught up to them with her friends and sisters.

"Dad have you met these kids?" said Ariel.

"No I never have in my life." said Kylestone.

"Hi." said Butterscotch.

"Cute they are happy to see someone." said Jindy, Tira, Irenie, and Candace's mom.

"Hey mom dad you guys and everyone else are having fun with who I'm guessing is Ariel's family and Calvis' parents?" said Mirabel.

"Yes we are." said Mirabel's mom.

"Good Ariel is her over there, (while Mirabel pointed at Ariel looking at her) I know you guys already saw Calvis." said Mirabel to her parents.

"Reminds me how I was with my father admiring staring at him." said Kylestone.

"Where is your dad?" said Butterscotch's mom who is a human/ pink poodle dog monster with no tail or sharp teeth or whiskers.

"You guys know what happened to him." said Walter.

"We do?" said Stacya, Bentha, Jannia, Lotusa, and Tarika's dad.

"Yeah you guys know what happened to Ivern." said Marleen.

All of them who didn't know that Ivern is Ariel's grandfather became shocked.

"Ivern!" said Butterscotch's dad, who is a human/ blue and a little bit of yellow colored collie dog monster with no whiskers or tail or sharp teeth.

"What!" said Pennya, Mabel, and Cassandra's mom who was holding a cup in her hand and accidentally splashed water on Jistopher's mom.

"Hey." said Jistopher's mom wet.

"Oh sorry." said Pennya, Mabel, and Cassandra's mom to Jistopher's mom.

"Don't worry hun you know I keep a towel with me." said Jistopher's dad.

Jistopher's dad gave Jistopher's mom the towel.

"Thanks honey." said Jistopher's mom.

"Your dad has been carrying around a towel." said Candace to Jistopher.

"Yep." said Jistopher.

"Ivern, hey mommy daddy isn't that the name of the singer you guys love to hear?" said Butterscotch.

"Yeah it is." said Butterscotch's mom picking up Butterscotch to hold her in her arms.

"But actually he's the same Ivern they're talking about." said Butterscotch's dad to Butterscotch.

"Oh yes it's true." said Butterscotch's mom.

"Whoa Kylestone didn't say your Ivern's son." said Amandie who is a senior citizen.

"I was going to, but I didn't think I needed to right away." said Kylestone.

"That's fine." said Amandie.

"Where is your dad?" said Dakota.

"Ivern is dead." said Shenatha.

"He is how?" said Nillia.

"He was killed by a lady who was jealous of him, and she pushed him into the street then a car ran over him and the lady made him go into the street was terrified that she did that." said Shenatha.

"Is that true?" said Fredricka who is a human/ cat monster who is white and light blue, has no claws, no whiskers, no sharp teeth, long fur that covers her limbs when she stands on all of them, five fingers on each hand, and five toes on each foot.

"What Shenatha said was true sadly." said Chrysalis.

"She was awful." said Ariannie.

"How dare she, I want to fight her." said Butterscotch.

"Now Butterscotch we don't do revenge on others." said Butterscotch's mom petting Butterscotch.

"It's true Butterscotch we prefer to do justice." said Butterscotch's dad petting her too.

"Okay." said Butterscotch.

"Yep." said Chrysalis.

Chrysalis' friends Loua, Dava, and Bemma, who are triplet sisters, each popped a confetti cannon while making happy surprised poses.

"Ah Loua, Dava, Bemma what are you guys doing?" said Darent.

"We thought we could use a more sprucing moment." said Loua.

"Fun right?" said Dava.

"Yeah." said Chrysalis.

"And shocking." said Ariel trying to feel not scared.

"Oh and you guys, I have your formulas to I told you guys I will give to you two when I've finished." said Dilia giving them to Heviner's parents.

"Thanks Dilia." said Heviner's dad.

"Thank you." said Heviner's mom.

Heviner's parents grabbed the formulas from Dilia.

"Oho pretty can you make me one?" said Nillia

"And me." said Ariannie.

"It will be great for the dark since I'm scared of it." said Nillia.

"I used to be scared of the dark too, but my father would sing to me about the dark not being scary and that always made me feel better." said Kylestone.

"Wow I feel better thinking about it too, but I still want that formula because it's pretty." said Nillia.

"I want to hear a song about the dark not being scary." said Ariannie.

"Well then your girls' mom and I will think of one." said Nillia and Ariannie's dad.

"Sweet thank you." said Nillia.

"Thank you." said Nillia and Arianie.

"You're good with my seven-year-old little cousins Nillia and Ariannie." said Fawn to Kylestone.

"Thanks." said Kylestone.

"Hey Dilia can you make one for me too?" said Cersanthama.

"Sure I can make more for you girls and by the way Ariel and Ariel's family I'm very interested in looking in your new house." said Dilia.

"Really well I think you will someday." said Regina.

"Thanks Dilia." said Cersanthama.

"Thank you." said Nillia and Ariannie to Dilia.

"So Dilia you make formulas are any of them used for medicine?" said Tarzan.

"Yeah some of them." said Dilia.

"Really I make medicines myself." said Tarzan.

"Cool you do." said Chrysalis.

"Are you a pharmaceutical scientist?" said Marleen to Tarzan.

"Yes I am." said Tarzan.

"What's a phar- phar- mace- something scientist?" said Darma.

"Someone who makes medicines." said Kert.

"Oh wow." said Darma.

Just then they heard a crashing sound and a groaning sound that frightened Kylestone, Regina, and Ariel and some of the others and the kids younger than thirteen all ran to hug Kylestone tightly because of them being scared.

"Whoa, that might be a bit too tight." said Kylestone.

"Sorry." the kids younger than thirteen hugging Kylestone said and then continued hugging him less tightly.

"What was that?" said Ariel.

"Oh don't worry that's just Fern." said Chrysalis.

"Oh man she did it again." said Belyndica.

"Who's Fern?" said Calvis' mom.

Fern came over and showed her face who is a human/ cat monster who is yellow, has no whiskers, no claws, no sharp teeth, five fingers on both hands, and five toes on both feet and with her is her husband Chet who is the same human/ yellow cat monster and their less than a year-old daughter Tafelena who is also the same human/ yellow cat monster in Chet's arms.

"Okay who got scared this time I heard some scared?" said Fern.

"They did." said Jistopher pointing at Ariel, Regina, and Kylestone.

"My boyfriend is right." said Trudy.

"Sorry about that why do I keep hitting and knocking stuff down and every time I groan everyone gets scared while some actually, those like Chrysalis, Zazannie, Constance, Bessa, Trudy, Mirabel, LuLu, LeLe, and LiLi are the kind that don't get scared." said Fern.

"I also get scared when you make those scary frog sounds." said Bentha.

"And I do when you make those scary elephant sounds." said Tinka.

"And I don't even try to make them scary." said Fern.

"You need to be more careful with your sounds." said Jistopher to Fern.

"Yeah you're right." said Fern.

"Ah that baby of theirs is so cute." said Ariel looking at Tafelena.

"Glad Tafelena didn't wake up." said Jistopher.

"Okay, but it's fine after you made that sound." said Kylestone to Fern.

"Don't worry about it." said Regina.

"Yeah but don't make your scary sounds when I'm around." said Ariel.

"Don't worry I'll try not to and same thing for everyone." said Fern.

"Tafelena is cute, who are you guys by the way?" said Chet to Ariel and her family.

"Oh yes we haven't seen you guys before." said Fern.

"Hey Fern and Chet guess who's here." said Dannya and Tinka's dad.

"Yeah dad, Fern, Chet guess who's here." said Dannya.

"First what's going on with him and them are those kids doing a hugging competition by hugging him?" said Fern pointing at Kylestone being hugged by the kids younger than thirteen hugging Kylestone.

"No but I do want my personal space back." said Kylestone.

"Javada, Zila, Lalo, and Darma and the rest of you kids can let go of him now." said Kert, Javada, Zila, Lalo, and Darma's dad.

"Sorry." said the kids younger than thirteen hugging Kylestone to him.

"We forgot we can let go of you since it was only Fern." said Candace.

So they stopped hugging him.

"Kert tell mom and dad about you being boyfriend and girlfriend with Slecks to calm them down," said Javada.

"Boyfriend and girlfriend," said Slecks' mom.

"Is that true Sleck?" said Slecks' dad.

"Well mom and dad, yes." said Slecks.

"It's true." said Kert.

"Nice." said Kert, Javada, Zila, Lalo, and Darma's mom.

"Very well then." said Slecks' dad.

"So what is it you want us to guess? I think it has something to do with you who I'm looking at." said Chet looking at Calvis' dad.

"Well that's part of it." said Dannya and Tinka's mom.

"After hearing what my mom said look for more than one thing to find out about." said Tinka.

"Oh I know who you are, an old schoolmate of some of our friends we saw photos of you in their yearbooks." said Chet.

"And them over there are Ivern's son and granddaughter." said Fredricka pointing at Kylestone and Ariel.

"Fredricka Fern and Chet were supposed to guess that." said Shiloh.

"It's okay I probably wouldn't have got that, but wow Ivern I'm a big fan of him." said Fern.

"Yeah me too and I'm also a big fan." said Chet.

"Good singer." said Zinnia.

"Sorry about what happened to him." said Fern.

"Oh yeah sorry about that." said Chet.

"Yeah." said Zinnia.

Just then Tafelena started to open her eyes.

"Ah she's waking up I'm glad she was able to sleep though that loud sound Fern made," said Ariel.

"Yes, I need to be more careful," said Fern.

"Now that you guys know." said Kert.

Kert got out his bright light music love bracelet and setted up his phone to play a rhythm and started singing to Slecks about how happy they are that they are a couple. Then Slecks joined in with her bright light music love bracelet and their bracelets lighted up while everyone loved watching them. Then they finished and removed their bracelets and Kert grabbed his phone and put it away.

"By the way, the building is finished, Sasha and Ard let me be the one to tell you guys that," said Chet.

"It is, so exciting." said Dakota.

"Oh finally I finished the map to put around the place so we'll know our way around." said Nillia and Ariannie's dad holding out the maps.

"What, building?" said Kylestone.

"There's a building next to one of the studios that's been redone for us who works for my great-grandma Sasha for us to have us all have each a room to do dressing, makeup, hanging out, and staying over when we do performances out there, but we're able to have others like you guys to come in or not with the makeup I don't do wearing makeup." said Chrysalis.

"Oh really thank you." said Pocahontas.

Ariel and the rest of her family thanked them too.

"I'm calling the building <u>HANGING STARS SPOT</u>." said Sasha.

"Come with us to see it. We are going to want you guys to come over with us." said Chrysalis.

"Wow, sure, but we can't be too long we still have unpacking and cleaning to do at our new house." said Regina.

"Oh you guys can stay longer there I can help you guys with your house." said Dilia.

"Thanks Dilia but didn't you have formulas to make for the girls?" said Zinnia.

"Oh I can make them there at the building, not your guys' house." said Dilia.

"Yeah there's a room there for Dilia to make her formulas." said Venelope's dad.

"There is." said Tarzan.

51

"Yeah there are other kinds of rooms there you'll see." said Venelope's mom.

"Well okay sure thanks Dilia." said Tarzan.

"Thanks Dilia looks like today you do get your chance to look into our house." said Regina.

Ariel, Kylestone, Pocahontas, and Zinnia thanked Dilia too.

"Hey mom dad, are you guys going to be only having you guys go stay the room you guys designed?" said Venelope.

"No, we just want a room we designed there anyone is allowed." said Venelope's dad.

"Well let's go." said Venelope's mom.

"Hey mom dad can I ask you guys about something about my party?" said Chrysalis.

"Sure." said Marleen.

So they left Chrysalis carpooled with Ariel and her family.

"So I told my parents about you, your family, Calvis, and his parents about coming to my party, and they said if you're allowed to and your family and Calvis and his family can you guys can come." said Chrysalis.

"Okay, hey Chrysalis' birthday party is in three days can we all go?" said Ariel to her family.

"Your birthday Chrysalis is in three days." said Regina.

"Yes I'm turning fifteen." said Chrysalis.

"Wow really well do we have anything happening that day?" said Regina.

"Not that I know of." said Tarzan.

"Are we all in?" said Zinnia.

They all agreed.

"Okay, we're all in for sure," said Regina.

"Yes," said Ariel.

"Okay, I'll text you guys the information." said Chrysalis.

In Dilia's car with some of Chrysalis' friends and their parents carpooling with her.

"Check out this new fetcher I added to my car," said Dilia.

Dilia pushed a button that made her car bump up like it ran over bumps.

"Whoa what was that?" said Shiloh.

"My new car fetcher." said Dilia.

"Your new car fetcher is making your car feel like it's riding over bumps." said Kiri.

"It would have been less scary if you told us before doing that." said Agnesa's dad.

"That's strange, like your butterfly hanging over your middle mirror that makes a lion roar sound." said Agnesa.

"I like it." said Justina.

Dilia pressed it, and it made it's roaring sound.

"Hey why am I smelling honey mustard?" said Jistopher.

"Oh that's me it's my new room fragrance spray." said Bessa.

"Oh I was thinking whoever brought that smell brought hotdogs with honey mustard on them." said Cleo.

"Oho you know what should have also got the hotdog one then it will smell like we're near hotdogs with honey mustard on them." said Zazannie who is Chrysalis' senior citizen friend.

"They make hotdog ones too?" said Falla.

In Ariel's family car.

"I hope you won't be too long with you guys finishing to pack. I was hoping later you would want to go to the GLAMOR PAL MALL with me and my sisters and friends. My friend Kiri's mom is a fashion designer, and they're having a sale on her clothes she designed, here's one of her designs." said Chrysalis.

Chrysalis showed Ariel the photo on her phone.

"Whoa that's beautiful," said Ariel.

"Yeah and I can buy your outfits for you. They do cost a lot," said Chrysalis.

"Oh my gosh thanks." said Ariel.

"And the mall is in the woods, but you can still see it without going into the woods." said Chrysalis.

"A mall in the woods cool." said Ariel.

"Wow check out that crazy horse." said Chrysalis looking out the car window.

Then they all saw it running around the field extremely crazy while driving by.

"Talk about a sugar high if that's it." said Tarzan.

"It's easy to believe that my friend Shiloh, Kiri's older cousin, that Shiloh's dad was Kiri's mom's first model because he's Kiri's mom's older brother, and he's known for being good looking." said Chrysalis.

"Are Shiloh's mom and Kiri's dad models?" said Ariel.

"Yeah they are." said Chrysalis.

"Were they at the studio?" said Ariel.

"Yeah they were they saw you and your family there." said Chrysalis.

"Oh okay." said Ariel.

In Calvis' family car.

"So mom dad are you guys okay with Chrysalis' party?" said Calvis.

"Well sure we'll go." said Calvis' dad.

"Sweet let me ask Chrysalis the information, and I'm going to ask Rowshella to dance at Chrysalis' party with me."said Calvis.

"How nice why don't you also ask her out?" said Calvis' mom.

"Sure I'll do that too." said Calvis.

"Oh do you need to be taught ballroom dancing for when you dance with Rowshella?" said Calvis' dad.

"Oh no I don't like ballroom dancing and neither does Rowshella we said that to each other when we met at the flea market. How come ballroom dancing is the only kind of dancing you dad?" said Calvis.

"Other dances aren't what's for me." said Calvis' dad.

"You're not saying my dancing is an issue?" said Calvis upsetly.

"It's not a problem if you want to do it then okay." said Calvis' dad.

"Well once again we don't have the same thing in common." said Calvis.

"Look Calvis we don't need to have a lot in common to get along." said Calvis' dad.

"Your dad's right Calvis." said Calvis' mom.

In Shenatha's parents' car.

"Nice new car," said Kathleenie.

"Thanks," said Shenatha and her parents.

"You know Darent, I'm thinking about what to do during my next radio broadcast." said Darent's dad.

"Oh nice." said Darent's mom.

"A mom dad can we not have that I'm concerned about it being too weird." said Darent.

"Okay I'll think of something not to weird." said Darent's dad.

"Oh good thanks." said Darent.

"I'm sure you'll do something good for your radio broadcast. They are hilarious." said Darent's mom to Darent's dad.

"Thanks hun, and I want it to be good I'm in such the mood to do it after getting this cool keychain." said Darent's dad holding out his new keychain.

"Wait dad where did you get that?" said Darent looking at the keychain his dad is holding.

"Oh I got it from that store that down the street we live at." said Darent's dad.

"What, dad you went to that weird store close to our house?" said Darent finding what his dad did odd.

"Yeah what's wrong with that?" said Darent's dad.

"Yeah Darent?" said Darent's mom.

"You know that store is crawling with ants you can clearly tell." said Darent.

"If the ants aren't dangerous then I don't care if I've stepped in there." said Darent's dad.

"Well if you didn't bring any in the house." said Darent.

"Relax you know how very careful I am with bring not good things in the house." said Darent's dad.

"So you're not scared of a bunch of ants, but you are scared of being a foot off the ground?" said Heviner to Darent's dad.

"Hey you can get hurt from fall a foot off the ground." said Darent's dad.

"I remember when we were kids when you were a foot off the ground you fear vomited." said Agnesa's dad to Darent's dad.

"Oh yeah." said Ridga's mom.

"Yes and that is a day I will remember to remind myself not to have myself a foot of the ground." said Darent's dad.

"You will also be having us be sure on that too." said Belyndica's dad.

"Hey hun why don't you do a saxophone introduction in that drum rhyme people do, you know duh da da da duh da da." said Darent's mom.

"Oho you're right." said Darent's dad.

"That's good." said Darent.

Just then they heard Belyndica playing her small saxophone.

"You brought that with you?" said Trudy.

"Yeah, why, you like hearing the triangle?" said Belyndica.

In Ariel's family car.

"Oh sweet Rowshella and Calvis are going on a date," said Chrysalis, looking at her phone.

"That's nice," said Ariel.

"There it is." said Chrysalis.

"Wow beautiful." said Regina.

"Oh look Epe's car's there." said Chrysalis.

"Epe drives a car and her older sister Poppy drives a motorcycle." said Chrysalis.

"A motorcycle wow." said Pocahontas.

They stepped out of the car and then everyone else who hadn't arrived yet arrived.

"Hey guys," said Shenatha, stepping out of her parents' car.

"Hi Shenatha," said Chrysalis.

"Come on let's go look inside. I'm so excited." said Shenatha.

Dilia's car showed up too. Then Dakota came out of the car.

"Hey guys do you guys like the smell of honey mustard?" said Dakota.

"It's okay." said Chrysalis.

"I don't mind." said Shenatha.

"Okay." said Ariel.

"Okay because Bessa might be using her new honey mustard room fragrance spray in her room and a room she'll be using it in a place like this." said Dakota.

"Bessa got a honey mustard room fragrance spray." said Chrysalis.

"Gosh I never thought about them having that." said Shenatha.

"Yeah neither did I." said Cersanthama who just walked over.

They went inside the building, and then they all headed into the room in the building, that's the party room where there were appetizers and refreshments.

"Hey what's that?" said Kylestone.

"Ard and I had this be set up for a welcome to our new building to hang out with the help for Fern and Chet." said Sasha.

"You're all welcome to join in including you and your family Ariel." said Ard.

"Thank you." said Ariel.

Ariel's family thanked them too, and they all gave in.

"This strawberry soup and macarons taste way better than before." said Chrysalis to Mirabel.

"Oh my gosh I know right, hey maybe I should write songs about them from my next show." said Mirabel.

"I feel like I want to hear that." said Chrysalis.

"Oh man." said Dannya upsetly.

"What wrong big sis?" said Tinka.

"Sorry guys I'm not feeling much like I want to party because I just can't get this line right for the music video I'm going to be in later today, I remember the line, but it's hard for me to say it right." said Dannya holding out the script.

"Go to the twirly worldly, twiller, skill berg, whirlwind woo, okay am I reading that right?" said Princeson reading Dannya's script.

"Yes you are in the video before the song Dannya plays a person who is so sad that she doesn't care about what words she's saying but then the song cheers the gal up." said Agnesa's dad to Princeson.

"Strange but interesting." said Princeson.

"But don't worry about it Dannya just have fun and if you can't say the line by the time we do the video I promise we'll figure something out." said Agnesa's dad.

"Okay yes I will now that that's settled." said Dannya.

Dannya got out her kazoo and Tinka did the same thing.

"Let's get out and party," said Dannya.

Then Dannya and Tinka blew through their kazoos dancing.

"They sure do look like they needed it out." said Princeson.

"Hey Kylestone, Regina, since Ariel didn't own a bright light music love bracelet until Chrysalis gave her hers. I'm guessing you guys don't have one." said Walter.

"Well my father had one, but it got destoryed because he had it with him when- well." said Kylestone.

"Oh, well do you guys want Marleen's and mine that way you guys can each have one for a light show while you guys sing in public?" said Walter while he and Marleen held theirs out.

"Oh well thank you, but I'm not willing to sing in public." said Regina.

"Or me." said Kylestone.

"Oh well okay but still you can have mine." said Marleen.

"And mine." said Walter.

"But are you guys sure you don't want to sing in public?" said Marleen.

"It's fun, here we'll show you guys, we'll give the bracelets to you guys after we sing." said Walter.

Walter and Marleen stood next to each other and started singing and dancing, and their bracelets lit up, making orange, blue, red violet, and white lights blasting out and everyone was loving it.

"Wow, that was amazing." said Kylestone.

Marleen and Walter took off their bracelets and gave them to them.

"Do you guys think now you want to try it?" said Marleen.

Regina felt like she wanted to, but once she felt she was about to, she stopped because she changed her mind.

"No I'm still not willing to." said Regina..

Kylestone stared at his new bracelet feeling upset that he's not singing in public to his new friends but he still felt too nervous to do it.

"Sorry I still can't do it." said Kylestone.

"It's okay." said Marleen.

"Yeah, you guys don't have to." said Walter.

"Thanks for the bracelets." said Kylestone.

"Yeah thank you." said Regina.

"Ah man why are there squeezed raspberries on this table?" said Kert, Javada, Zila, Lalo, and Darma's dad.

"I got it." said Kert, Javada, Zila, Lalo, and Darma's mom sliding it into her hand.

"That's from me those raspberries are soft and squishy please don't throw them out mom I'm going to use them again." said Darma.

"Use them, again what do you mean?" said Venelope.

"I put those raspberries under my armpit, and it felt good, and I'm going to do it again with those later." said Darma.

"Ah man." said Kert, Javada, Zila, Lalo, and Darma's mom dropping them on the floor feeling disgusted.

"El." said Princeson.

"Eww." said Kylestone.

"Is there a dust pan and a sweeper?" said Kert, Javada, Zila, Lalo, and Darma's mom.

"We had some be placed in the closet." said Ard.

"I'll get it." said Lamoria who is a senior citizen.

"I am so not touching a squished raspberry again." said Ratia.

"Oh wait, here's one of the maps." said Nillia and Ariannie's dad handing one of the maps to Lamoria.

"Thanks." said Lamoria.

"Darma don't be using raspberries like that." said Kert, Javada, Zila, Lalo, and Darma's dad.

"Come on now we're going to have to clean your armpit." said Kert, Javada, Zila, Lalo, and Darma's mom grabbing Darma's hand.

"Okay I'm done eating I got to go now." said Axa quickly who is a human/ bunny monster with no whiskers and is white and has no red eyes or tail.

"You're going already?" said Shenatha.

"It feels like a short time for you to be in this room." said Constance.

"It's actually something for the building in one of the rooms I'm going to be working in." said Axa quickly.

"A room, can I look at one of those maps?" said Chrysalis to Nillia and Ariannie's dad.

"Sure, here." said Nillia and Ariannie's dad handing Chrysalis another one of the maps.

"Which room?" said Chrysalis holding the map out.

"It's the one right here." said Sasha pointing at it on the map Chrysalis has held out.

"Baby are you sure you don't want the interor designers to finish that room for you?" said Axa's mom who is the same human to monster Axa is.

"I'm back with the dustpan and sweeper. What's going on by the way?" said Lamoria.

"You're about to find out," said Chrysalis.

"Your mom's right. We let you finish the room because you said you wouldn't rush yourself so hard and we thought you already did it." said Axa's dad who is the same human/bunny monster Axa is.

"I know I know but-" said Axa quickly.

"Axa talk slowly you're not going anywhere until we have a normal speed conversation." said Axa's mom.

Just then they heard a broken glass sound.

"Sorry I dropped my glass cup, I'm going to need the dustpan and sweeper next," said Mirabel.

"Forget it, make that right now." said Kert, Javada, Zila, Lalo, Darma's mom.

"I got it." said Joyce who, is a senior citizen who took the dustpan and sweeper from Lamoria she gave to her to help.

Joyce cleaned it up and handed it to Kert, Javada, Zila, Lalo, Darma's mom.

"Thanks Joyce," said Mirabel.

"Thanks Lamoria." said Kert, Javada, Zila, Lalo, Darma's mom.

"Okay and after that happening." said Axa's mom.

"I don't want the interior designers to do it because I wanted to set up the room to get me started on being an interior designer and I want to be sure the room looks exactly how I want it to and to be sure nothing has been ruined, but I forgot to do it and I ended up not finishing in time." said Axa.

"Axa that's not good and that's not the way to become an interior designer." said Axa's dad.

"And to think she was that excited to be working on that room." said Colleen.

"Huh go finish." said Axa's mom.

Axa ran.

"And still no rushing, you're more likely not to do a good job and it's not good for you," said Axa's mom.

"Okay," said Axa.

"You know what actually I should go with you to be sure you're not rushing." said Axa's mom.

"I'll come too for extra." said Axa's dad.

Axa ran again but stopped after she took a step because she remembered what her mom said. So Axa and her parents both went to the room Axa was supposed to finish.

"By the way, I found this in the cleaning supply room," said Lamoria, holding out a wind up toy scorpion.

"Who's wind is that?" said Sasha.

"Oh that's mine. I must have dropped it when I was helping Jindy, Tira, and Irenie move paper crowns into the cleaning supply room," said Swifta.

"I also helped with that too," said Nia.

"Oh, there were crowns in that room too," said Lamoria.

Jindy, Tira, and Irenie ran.

"Where are they going?" said Chrysalis.

"To get the crowns," said Nia.

"Wait hold on, you mean they actually-." said Candace.

Jindy, Tira, and Irenie came back with multiple crowns.

"And pop you get a crown." said Tira, placing crowns on Sasha and Lamoria's heads.

"Hey, you, place that hard, you know." said Sasha.

"Oho." said Lamoria.

Then they started doing it to others.

"You guys actually set up doing that crown thing you guys are doing." said Candace to her big sisters Jindy and Tira.

"Well yeah you didn't think we weren't to celebrate the opening of <u>HANGING STARS SPOT</u>." said Jindy.

"And pop you get a crown." said Irenie putting a crown on Candace.

Then they continued.

"You know I don't like wearing things in my hair," said Candace.

"I find that hard to believe," said Belyndica, since Belyndica likes to wear a blue headband.

In one of the dressing, makeup, hanging out, and staying over rooms three unknowns were in it and Chrysalis and her family and friends didn't know about them.

"Lovely place this is." said one of them grabbing her lipstick.

"I agree we're going to be in this building as often as we can." said another of them.

"Hey I hear someone." said another of them.

"Quick turn off the light and don't worry about them coming in I doubt they will." said the one who spoke first.

They turned off the lights. It was Axa and her parents walking past one of the doors to a dressing, makeup, hanging out, and staying over room, but after they went past them they didn't know that there was talking behind the door.

"See so far it doesn't look like I'm rushing." said Axa to her parents while they walked by the door.

"See I told you that whoever was coming won't be going in here." said a voice behind the door.

"Good now we can stay in here longer." said another voice behind the door.

"Oops." said another voice behind the door knocking down a stool.

"Ow you knocked that stool seat on my foot," said the first one who spoke behind the door.

"Sorry," said the one who spoke third behind the door.

Back in the party room of the building.

"I'm ready to look around more," said Chrysalis.

"Can I come along?" said Ariel.

"Sure," said Chrysalis.

"And pop you get a crown." said Jindy, putting crowns on Chrysalis and Ariel's heads.

"Hey that was hard." said Ariel.

"Yeah a little bit." said Chrysalis.

Chrysalis and Ariel took off the crowns on their heads. Then Chrysalis and Ariel went upstairs on the non-steps escalator to the floor where the voices behind the door were at.

"We're up searching the second floor." said Chrysalis after she and Ariel got off the escalator.

"I like the non steps escalator better than having an elevator." said Ariel.

"Me too, it's safer than taking an elevator, and so we don't have to take so many steps on the stairs here that are set for if we need them." said Chrysalis.

"Hey do you hear that?" said one of the voices behind one of the doors down the hall.

"Oh yeah I think we should go now." said another voice behind the door.

"What are the screens on the doors for?" said Ariel.

"Here, I'll show you by going into this room." said Chrysalis opening the door but not to the room where the voices were inside.

Chrysalis and Ariel went inside the room and there was a letter keypad on the wall by the door.

"What's this for?" said Ariel.

"Here watch and look at the door's screen." said Chrysalis.

Ariel looked at Chrysalis type on the letter keypad on the wall and then looked at the door screen while she was typing and saw Chrysalis' name on the door screen.

"Oh." said Ariel.

"It's so we know who's in the room and if it's being used none of us here own a certain room here." said Chrysalis.

"So all rooms are for all and always and no one keeps a room for themselves?" said Ariel.

"Yep." said Chrysalis.

"Cool then we can enjoy and explore every room here." said Ariel.

"Yeah fun right." said Chrysalis.

Ridga, Heviner, and their parents then came up the second.

"Hey guys," they said.

"Hey," said Chrysalis and Ariel.

Ridga's dad walked past the room Chrysalis and Ariel are in to go to the third room next to the one Chrysalis and Ariel are in. That was the room the three unknowns were in.

"Wow, nice room. Hey dad, why not look at this room first that Chrysalis and Ariel are in?" said Ridga.

"After this one, Sasha said there's a cheetah-pattern couch in this room that I want to look at." said Ridga's dad.

Ridga's dad opened the door and saw the couch in there, but no unknown guess.

"Ah man, check this couch out," said Ridga's dad.

Chrysalis, Ariel, Heviner, Ridga, Heviner's parents, and Ridga's mom entered the room Ridga's dad is in too.

"Hey guys," said Tarika coming into the room with Chrysalis' sisters and friends.

"Hi." they all said.

Axa came running back.

"Whoa Axa remember what your parents said," said Gaddy.

"I do, but they said don't run when I'm in a rush, and I'm not in a rush. I finally finished the room." said Axa.

"Good for you." said Chrysalis.

"You guys want to see it?" said Axa.

"After looking in this room." said Stacya.

The rest of them agreed.

"Okay, I'll look in this room too, oho is that a cheetah pattern couch?" said Axa.

Chrysalis looked into the bathroom and saw something on the floor that was a pink liquid.

"Odd," said Chrysalis.

"Hey, did anyone go into this room earlier?" said Chrysalis.

None of them said yes.

"Odd I found a drop of pink shampoo on the bathroom floor," said Chrysalis, showing it on her finger.

"That is odd," said Lotusa.

"Maybe Fern and Chet were using that bathroom before we were told about this building being done." said Gaddy.

"Maybe." said Zita.

In another room, Kylestone and Zinnia were exploring it. Just then Zinnia grabbed Kylestone's arm.

"You're alright with me bringing you to the bathroom with me to put lotion on your face?" said Zinnia.

"Um, sure." said Kylestone.

Zinnia took Kylestone into the bathroom and got out a squirt bottle of lotion she brought with her and placed some of it on Kylestone's cheeks.

"Um-why-are-you-putting-lotion on- me?" said Kylestone while having his face pressed by his mother's hand while she put lotion on his cheeks.

"I really wanted us to have a moment in the lovely bathroom together." said Zinnia.

Then Zinnia grabbed both of his hands and lifted them up a little.

"Ah man my baby boy," said Zinnia.

"You're not going to be wanting to do this in every bathroom are you?" said Kylestone speaking clearly now that his mother finished.

"Well yes but if you want to and not all in one day just whatever times." said Zinnia.

Zinnia was about to kiss Kylestone on the cheek but stopped herself because she realized he just had lotion placed on him, so she kissed him on the forehead, then placed him in a position for her to hug him without him getting lotion on her.

"Okay mother, thank you." said Kylestone.

Zinnia kissed him on the forehead again and then let go of him.

"Baby boy," said Zinnia, staring at Kylestone with delight.

"Can I take that lotion with me?" said Kylestone.

"What for?" said Zinnia.

"I want to put more on me in another bathroom to get to try in there." said Kylestone.

"Okay sure." said Zinnia.

So Zinnia handed Kylestone the lotion, then they opened the bathroom door and saw Walter looking around the room.

"Hey guys like this place so far?" said Walter.

"Well- oo!" said Kylestone, who accidently squirted lotion on him because he accidentally squeezed the squirt bottle of lotion on him because the lid wasn't closed.

"Whoa." said Walter.

"Are you okay baby?" said Zinnia.

"I'm fine but embarrassed." said Kylestone.

"Don't feel bad about it, here." said Walter.

Walter walked inside the bathroom and turned the sink on and filled his hands with water and then threw the water on his face.

"What, why did you do that?" said Kylestone.

"Now do you feel better and not embarrassed?" said Walter.

"Actually, yes I do feel better and not embarrassed." said Kylestone.

"Yeah see." said Walter.

Then they started to laugh, then Dilia came in and saw them like that.

"Sweet," said Dilia.

Dilia got out her lipstick and scribbled her face with it.

"Um, what are you doing?" said Walter.

"What, I thought we were messing up our faces?" said Dilia.

"Let me explain." said Kylestone.

Marleen and Regina and Tarzan and Pocahontas were looking in another room.

"This is nice strawberry soup," said Regina while eating some.

"So are the macarons." said Marleen, eating some.

"I am so glad we moved." said Pocahontas.

"Me too." said Tarzan.

Just then Beatrix's parents came into the room.

"Hey Pocahontas, Tarzan, can you two stand there face to me in a couple of passion. I would be great for photos to put in the magazine?" said Beatrix's dad.

"Oh you're a photographer." said Pocahontas.

"My husband is also a singer too." said Beatrix's mom.

"I love doing them both." said Beatrix's dad.

Regina started moving to where her parents were having a picture taken to watch, but she then looked at her bowl of strawberry soup and admiring it and not knowing how close she was slithering up to her parents.

"Don't get too close to Regina." said Beatrix's mom.

"Whoa." said Reginasfire stopping herself and slipping strawberry soup on her face.

Beatrix's dad snapped the shot well.

"Oh man Regina," said Pocahontas.

"Ah man, this is odd," said Regina.

"Oh, here look at me." said Marleen to Regina.

Marleen splat her macaron on her face.

"Why did you do that?" said Regina.

"To make you feel better, isn't it funny?" said Marleen.

"Yeah it is." said Reginsafire.

Then they started laughing. Then Dilia came in rubbing lipstick off her face with a wet towel with still some on and looked at Regina and Marleen.

"Are we really not making our faces messy looking?" said Dilia.

"Why is there lipstick on your face like that?" said Marleen.

"I'll explain and then you guys can explain why you guys look like that." said Dilia.

"Okay." said Marleen.

Falyby was outside the building next to it with her phone out, and she stopped and started talking through it.

"Yes it's me, you're there, you spend way too much time there. You know. Well, at least you're enjoying that time you're having I'm dealing with something with a singer, don't be complaining about it, I'm already hearing about you complaining, yes I know that's why I wish we didn't have this issue years ago with you!" yelled Falyby through her phone.

Inside the building in the party room.

"Hey, do you hear someone yelling?" said Ridga to her boyfriend Heviner.

Outside the building, Falyby put away her phone.

"How phony this has been!" yelled Falyby.

"Um, can you please keep it down out there?" said Hermalody, one of Chrysalis' senior citizens friends to Falyby.

Falyby looked by her and saw Hermalody behind an opened window with Chrysalis' great-grandparents and Chrysalis' other senior citizen friends.

"We're trying to have some friends pals time." said Hermalody.

"Well excuse me all you teenagers!" said Falyby angrily to them.

"Oh ah we're not teenagers we're actually seniors, senior citizens that is." said Hermalody.

"I told you guys we're always going to be mistaken for teenagers." said Grimia.

"Yeah I knew it too." said Amandie.

"We all did guys." said Sasha.

"Wait, what, well, whatever you guys are!" said Falyby still mad.

"Whoa still, tone it down." said Poppy.

"Yeah don't be upset about it you're not the only one a lot of others mistake us for teenagers I used to keep track of how often and my check lines went pass the page front and back." said Grimia.

"I knew it was right to guess that." said Texia.

"I know it because I lose track of the amount." said Hermalody.

"Just because you forgot how often doesn't mean it's that much." said Tersephone to Hermalody.

"Yeah you're right that was not a good sentence to use." said Hermalody.

"Ah Grimia I don't think that's what she's mad about." said Epe.

"Correct and I don't need to keep hearing you teenagers, I mean senior citizens." said Falyby.

Then Falyby walked away.

"Well, didn't calm her down, but she's gone now," said Poppy.

"What's her problem?" said Texia.

"Um are you guys going to be eating these macarons because I am tired of standing in this same spot." said Pennya, Mabel, and Cassandra's mom who was standing behind them with a tray of macarons.

"Sorry about that." said Ard.

Then they started to grab the macarons.

"So, Zazannie, you have a hotdog fragrance spray?" said Tersephone.

"Yeah interested?" said Zazannie.

"No thanks, I just didn't think they ever make that." said Tersephone.

"Okay then." said Zazannie.

Then Pennya, Mabel, and Cassandra showed up to them too.

"They were the last ones to grab macarons who didn't get any." Now can we have seconds?" said Mabel.

"Okay but not too many." said Pennya, Mabel, and Cassandra's mom.

"Sure thing mom and you guys should come see Axa's room she designed." said Pennya.

"If Axa can get herself to keep up on time she'll be ready to be an interior designer." said Cassandra.

"Really well let's see it." said Sasha.

So they left to go look at it Chrysalis and everyone else was looking at it, and they all admired it.

"Wow." said Ard.

"Yeah this is nice." said Sasha.

"Great job Axa." said Axa's dad.

"Yes at least you were able to decorate a lovely room." said Axa's mom.

"I promise I'll try to do things on time." said Axa.

"Okay good." said Axa's mom.

"Here's a crown for you Axa." said Tira putting a crown on Axa's head.

"Oh, um thanks." said Axa.

"Here's one each for you guys." said Jindy while she and Irenie placed crowns on Axa's parent's heads.

"Oh, thank you." said both of Axa's parents.

"Hey Fern Chet do you guys hang out here in the room with the cheetah pattern couch before you tell us about the building being done." said Gaddy.

"There's a room with a cheetah pattern couch, I've got to see that, but no we did not." said Fern.

"Well that doesn't explain the pink shampoo on the bathroom floor of that room." said Chrysalis.

"There was pink shampoo on the floor in that room." said Gaddy's dad.

"Was someone else in that bathroom?" said Gaddy's mom.

Still no one said yes.

"Maybe one of my construction workers was using that bathroom I'll have a talk to them all to warn them not to do that again." said Texia.

"Your construction workers, do you own the company?" said Ariel.

"As a matter of fact yes just like Sasha I choose not to retire too." said Texia.

"Wow." said Ariel.

"By the way we saw Falyby who was doing the yelling" said Sasha.

"Oh, Falyby again." said Chrysalis.

"She didn't say anything to you guys or did anything bad did she?" said Marleen to Sasha, Ard, and Chrysalis' senior citizen friends.

"Let me guess she mistook you guys for teenagers like a lot of others." said Chrysalis.

"Yep." said Poppy.

"Well she wasn't nice to us but we're okay." said Sasha.

"Hey Candace why did your sisters put crowns on me and my parents?" said Axa taking the crown off her head.

"Just something they wanted to do we all had a crown on our heads from them." said Candace.

"Okay." said Axa feeling a little odd.

"We should probably get going now." said Tarzan.

"Can't we look a bit longer?" said Ariel.

"Remember dad Dilia did say she will help us finish unpacking." said Regina.

"Well okay but also remember that we can come back here. Dilia, did you finish making the formulas for Nillia and Ariannie and Cersanthama?" said Tarzan.

"Oh yes I did." said Dilia.

Dilia hanged Nillia and Ariannie and Cersanthama the formulas she also made for Heviner's parents.

"The room for making my formula is great." said Dilia.

"Okay but Dilia is the room safe enough?" said Fern.

"Yeah it is." said Dilia.

"No item so close to you that they might knock you down while you are making your formulas?" said Fern.

"No." said Dilia.

"Got a smoke alarm in case there is a fire to warn you?" said Fern.

"Yes." said Dilia.

"Uh you know Fern you could go look at the room for yourself." said Shiloh.

"Oh yeah right I'll go do that." said Fern.

So Fern left to go look at the room.

"Dilia is a very good friend to Fern and Chet but Fern and Chet sometimes worry that something will happen to her." Chrysalis said to Ariel and her family.

"Huh." said Ariel.

"Well I'm going to go look around more." said Chrysalis.

"Ah Walter why is your shirt wet?" said Jimonthey.

Jimonthey said that before Chrysalis left the room, so she stayed to hear. At Ariel's house, Ariel and her family arrived back with Dilia to finish unpacking.

"Thanks for helping Dilia," said Regina while she, Kylestone, and Dilia were putting away dishes.

Just then they heard the doorbell which made the sound of a snake going ding-dong in snake hssing.

"I think I know who that is, a hint from Chrysalis," said Kylestone.

He, Regina, and Dilia went over to the door and opened it and saw it was Fern and Chet with baby Tafelena in Fern's arms.

"Hi Fern, Chet, and Tafelena." said Dilia.

"Hi guys so you guys' new house is on the way to the **GLAMOR PAL MALL** that Chet and I are helping our friend unload her clothes she designed for her big sale there for her clothes, and we wanted to stop by her to know if everything is going alright." said Fern.

"Oh it's going fine." said Dilia.

"Ariel is going to be going there too with her new friends when she's done unpacking." said Regina.

"Oh good." said Fern.

Then Fern got out a magnifying glass and looked through it looking around at the front of Dilia, Kylestone, and Regina.

"What are you doing?" said Kylestone to Fern.

"Checking to see if Dilia has a cut or you guys having a cut if you guys have a cut to be sure you guys are doing safe." said Fern.

"Okay, well better safe than sorry." said Kylestone.

"Exactly." said Dilia.

"Okay you guys are good, and I also do this to help me find out what fashionable outfits will be good for you guys,you guys should also go to the <u>GLAMOR PAL MALL</u> too there are many outfits for you guys there." said Fern.

"Yeah you guys come along too and with your parents if you want." said Chet.

"Oh we would but–." said Regina.

"What you guys can't buy so much we'll pay for you guys and your guys' new friends Marleen and Walter will be there." said Fern.

"Yeah we know how much you guys adore them." said Chet.

"Well we could go." said Regina to Kylestone.

"Yeah sure okay." said Kylestone.

"Ah man this is going to be fun." said Dilia.

"So this mall is really going to be in the woods?" said Kylestone.

"Yep." said Chet.

Just then, Tafelena started crying.

"Oh shot um can we go inside to change Tafelena?" said Fern.

"Oh sure," said Regina.

"Yeah, go ahead," said Kylestone.

So Fern and Chet and Tafelena went inside Ariel and her family's house. Ariel was unpacking her items, then she heard Tafelena crying and left to go where she was crying from which was in her parents' bathroom where Ariel saw her parents, Fern, Chet, and Tafelena.

"Are they here to help?" said Ariel to her parents.

"No by the way your dad and I are coming to the mall with you." said Regina.

"Would about-?" said Ariel.

"Your grandparents are going on motorcycle rides with Chrysalis' great-grandparents and Poppy and Epe and some of their friends for a while before going to the mall." said Regina.

"Oh okay." said Ariel.

Ariel looked at Fern, Chet, and Tafelena in the bathroom. Then Kylestone went up to Ariel and hugged her.

"Reminds me of when you were a baby." said Kylestone, lifting Ariel's head up to him while hugging her.

"Come on dad when I was a baby I was a lot of work." said Ariel.

"And we still love you the same and still always want you." said Kylestone.

"Yes." said Regina coming up to them.

Then she started kissing Ariel while she was being hugged by Kylestone. Then Dilia came into the room.

"Ariel, you didn't finish unpacking in your room. Do you want me to help you?" said Dilia.

"Sure" said Ariel.

Ariel left her parents' room to go to her room with Dilia to finish unpacking.

"Nice room this is, we're almost done then we can go to the mall." said Dilia.

"I hope no mean girls will be there." said Ariel.

"Don't worry about them and just have fun Ariel." said Dilia.

"Okay." said Ariel.

Later Chrysalis, Ariel, Chrysalis' sisters, their parents, friends, and Chrysalis' friends' parents arrived at the mall.

"Wow this is beautiful." said Ariel, holding up a dress.

"Hey guys." said Cherryette behind a cashing out counter.

"Cherryette what are you doing?" said Chrysalis.

"Wait she doesn't work here?" said Ariel.

"No." said Chrysalis.

"I heard Kiri's mom say one of the cashiers here had to go home because he got sick, so I'm filling in." said Cherryette.

"I'm pretty sure Kiri's mom did not have you fill in." said Chrysalis.

"And you're right Chrysalis." said Kiri walking up to them with Shiloh.

"Yeah Cherryette I don't think it's a good idea for you to fill in being cashier because everytime you're playing cashier you do something weird." said Shiloh.

"Hey Kiri, Chrysalis is right about your mom being an amazing fashion designer." said Ariel.

"Glad you like then oh and in a few minutes my mom is going to start her fashion show here." said Kiri.

"Oh wow." said Ariel.

"Come on guys I'm not going to do something weird. Hey Chrysalis Ariel are you girls going to get those outfits?" said Cherryette.

"Well yes but we're still looking around." said Chrysalis.

"Okay but still pretend to be paying for them now with me pretending to be the cashier." said Cherryette.

"Huh okay." said Chrysalis.

So Chrysalis and Ariel played along with Cherryette pretending to be a cashier.

"No need to tell me the price. I added it up before we saw you here." said Chrysalis.

So Chrysalis got out her money but dropped two dollars.

"Oops hold on there's still money on the ground." said Chrysalis.

"I'm sorry what?" said Cherryette.

"There's still money on the ground." said Chrysalis after moving her head up before going back down again to grab the last dollar.

"Sorry I still didn't hear that." said Cherryette.

Then Cherryette looked down where Chrysalis was and saw a flower-shaped chocolate candy unwrapped on the ground.

"Ahh still chocolate on the ground ahh!" said Cherryette.

Then she ran away from the cash register.

"Ahh!" said Cherryette.

"Whoa," said Ariel.

"Cherryette," said Shiloh.

"Cherryette, that's not what I said and calm down," said Chrysalis.

Chrysalis grabbed her money and put it back in her pocket, and then they went after Cherryette but they did not run out of the store and Chrysalis grabbed Cherryette by the shoulder and turned her around.

"Cherryette calm down." said Chrysalis.

"Yeah Cherryette you take loving candy way too serious." said Shiloh.

"Tell me about it." said Ariel.

"Cherryette you were yelling about chocolate on the floor again?" said Rowshella coming over with Chrysalis' sisters and other friends.

"Yeah sorry about that guys." said Cherryette.

"We told you you're weird when you're playing cashier." said Kiri.

"No one needs to be a cashier to fill in for the one who got sick because I will be after the fashion show so that area will be closed for a while." said Kiri's mom holding a closed sign.

Then she walked away but just then stopped and turned around to Chrysalis and her friends and sisters.

"Oh by the way, Ariel, you're definitely going to want to watch this fashion show," said Kiri's mom.

All of them got curious.

"Hey guys excited about the fashion show?" said Cersanthama's dad with Cersanthama's mom.

"Yeah we sure are." said Chrysalis while everyone else nodded their heads yes.

"Hey mom dad what was it that-?" said Cersanthama.

"What your friend Kiri's mom said to Ariel about definitely wanting to see the fashion?" said Cersanthama's dad.

"Yeah do you guys know about it?" said Cersanthama.

"Well yes, but we can't tell you we were told to keep it a surprise." said Cersanthama's mom.

"And by the way Cherryette a hint about being a cashier don't go crazy like that when you see chocolate in the ground." said Cersanthama's dad.

"You guys saw that." said Chrysalis.

"Yeah we did." said Cersanthama's mom.

"Enjoy the fashion show here at my mall." said Cersanthama's dad.

"Your mall?" said Ariel.

"Oh yeah I forgot to mention Cersanthama's dad owns this mall." said Chrysalis.

"Wow." said Ariel.

"Well no one should waste chocolate." said Cherryette.

Cersanthama looked where the chocolate was.

"Oh that's mine, I'll go get it," said Cersanthama.

"Yes go do that," said Cherryette.

"Calm down you take loving chocolate too much." said Cersanthama.

"Sorry Cersanthama." said Cherryette.

"It's fine." said Cersanthama while going to get her flower-shaped chocolate from the floor.

Just then, Ariel's grandparents, Chrysalis' grandparents, Chrysalis' great-grandparents, and Chrysalis' senior citizen friends arrived.

"Hey, you guys made it on time." said Chrysalis.

"Were the motorcycle rides good?" said Shenatha.

"Yep they were, and we sure did come in just in time to change for the fashion show." said Epe.

"Wait you guys are going to be in the fashion show too?" said Ariel.

"You don't have a problem with that, do you? Who says you're too old for something?" said Poppy to Ariel.

"No no no I don't even if you guys weren't senior citizens I would still have asked that." said Ariel.

"Don't worry about it and yeah we are, come on guys." said Poppy.

"Oho I have to go get my stuffed cat ready too." said Dakota.

Behind the stage of the fashion show.

"Hey guys are you all set up?" said Walter, appearing backstage with Marleen to their friends.

"Yes, we are all set up," said Shenatha's mom.

"Oh look they're here." said Shenatha's dad pointing at Chrysalis' great-grandparents and their friends.

"Hey guys." said Hermalody.

"You guys are on your way to get changed right?" said Shenatha's mom.

"Yes didn't worry." said Tersephone.

Dakota came running by.

"Dakota your stuffed cat isn't ready." said Dakota's mom, who is a human/ cat monster who's orange, has no whiskers, no sharp teeth, no claws, five fingers on both hands, five toes on both feet, and two feet taller than a cat on it's legs.

"Hi sorry but don't worry I can get her ready in a flash." said Dakota.

Dakota quickly ran again.

"Dakota be careful when you're running and rushing." said Dakota's dad, who is the same human/ cat monster Dakota's mom is but is black with brown on his face.

"Okay dad." said Dakota.

Kiri's mom appeared.

"Okay except for those who just got here, are we all set up?" said Kiri's mom.

"Hey sis, I'm going to need a minute or two my scarf has a rip." said Shiloh's dad.

"It does? Ah man okay." said Kiri's mom.

"You know since your big brother is having a delay why not have your new moods go up first?" said Walter.

"Um yeah, why not?" said Kiri's mom.

"Oh and why not we make an announcement about them while they are walking the runway to make it more interesting?" said Marleen.

"Oh yes." said Kiri's mom.

Later the fashion show started, and first to be walking the runway were Ariel's parents, Kylestone and Regina.

"Mom dad," said Ariel.

"Whoa," said Chrysalis.

"Oh, so that's what my mom was talking about to you, Ariel." said Kiri.

"These two one the runway are Kylestone and his wife Regina, Kylestone who is also the son of the dead singer Ivern." said Marleen through the speaker.

"Huh, oh my, oh my gosh, Ivern." said the audience.

"Wow sounds like everyone is interested in this." said Chrysalis.

Somewhere on TV in the <u>HANGING STARS SPOT</u>, someone who was watching felt mad and pounded the couch's arm rester.

"Oh, it doesn't sound like you like that couch." said Matilda who's the human/ monster who looks like a human with green skin, dark green spots on her face, purple teeth, and four fingers.

Matilda was also one of the unknown guests who was at the building earlier when Chrysalis and her friends and family first went in there.

"I don't think that's what she's mad about Matilda." said a lady with brown hair sarcastically.

"You think I don't know that Hailey." said Matilda to the lady with brown hair.

"Hey it's just sarcasm." said Hailey.

"You know I hate that." said Matilda.

At the fashion show, after Kylestone and Regina left the runway. Dakota came on the runway next with her stuffed cat wearing a cute pretty outfit.

"Aw, that is cute," said Ariel.

"Adorable," said Chrysalis.

"Aw, wow," said the audience.

After Dakota Sasha, Ard, and their senior citizen friends all walked on the runway together.

"Wow," said the audience.

"So now those teenagers are walking the runway." said Mesha, who's at the fashion show with Manora, and Mingmi.

"Hey who said that?" said Hermalody.

"Whoever said that for the last time we are not teenagers." said Grimia.

"Don't be saying for the last time Grimia this is clearly going to be going on forever." said Joyce.

"Yep Joyce is right." said Arb.

Chrysalis looked over and saw Mesha, Manora, and Mingmi in the audience.

"Oh man it's Mesha, Manora, and Mingmi." said Chrysalis.

"What are they doing here?" said Shenatha.

"Maybe they're here because they could help but want to see Kiri's mom's a.k.a. Shiloh's aunt's new outfits." said Agnesa.

"I'm hoping that's it and not for trouble and I also agree with what Joyce said." said Chrysalis.

At the <u>HANGING STAR SPOT</u> where Matilda and three other human/ monster ladies are.

"Calm down," said Matilda.

"I can't just look at them happy, makes me mad." said the unknown lady.

"Whoa you better calm down." said Nagaila who is a human/ monster who's purple light on the face, rest of her skin dark purple, bigger than her original height, and has a small bird beak.

"If you're going to be in a bad mood be careful not to leave anything that will make them think someone was here." said Tuckles who is a human/ monster that looks like a green frog tall taller than her original human height, no long tongue, big flat lips, and five fingers hands.

Nagaila and Tuckles were also the other unknown guests who were at the building when Chrysalis and her friends and family arrived in the <u>HANGING STAR SPOT</u> for the first time.

"Ah right," said the unknown lady.

Matilda looked at the TV and noticed Ariel in the background that really caught Matilda's attention.

"Matilda, did you not hear what I said?" said Tuckles.

"What do you say?" said Matilda.

"I said what are you looking at." said Tuckles.

"I know that look you're admiring that cute looking pink human/monster snake girl." said Nagaila.

"Oh you know me see well Nagaila." said Matilda.

"Cute looking?" said Tuckles confused.

"It means adorable." said Matilda.

"Oh right." said Tuckles.

At the <u>GLAMOR PAL MALL</u> the fashion show ended.

"Wow mom and dad that was amazing seeing you guys up there." said Ariel while hugging them.

"Yes that was a good surprise." said Tarzan.

"Yeah." said Kylestone.

"Ah man I remebered when your dadda stared in fashion shows." said Zinnia to Kylestone.

"You know they asked me to star in a fashion before but I was too nervous to do it which I still am so don't ask me to be in one." said Zinnia.

"Well we saw the whole fashion show." said Carlica coming with her friends Mesha, Manora, Mingmi, and Vargoe.

"You guys did like the show right?" said Agnesa to Carlica and Carlica's friends.

"You guys better not cause mischief I am a cop here." said Belyndica's dad.

"Look cop to cop." said Mesha.

"I don't believe you're a cop." said Chrysalis to Mesha.

"Well I'm a fashion cop." said Mesha.

"So in other words you're a fake cop." Mirabel.

"I don't have time for this." said Mesha.

"And by the way we know you're the fashion designer of the clothes that were shown during the fashion show and here is something for you." said Mingmi to Kiri's mom giving Kiri's mom a sheet of paper Mingmi wrote something on it.

"A police fashion ticket for not having any one of you girls checking how good the clothes are before being revealed during the fashion show." said Kiri's mom.

"Remember the ticket is a fake so don't mistake you for being in trouble." said Mirabel to Kiri's mom.

"Luckily the fashion show was a good one but still you have that ticket there for a warning." said Vargoe.

"Don't be acting like you need to show off." said Kiri's mom to Carlica and Carlica's friends.

"By the way since we heard that Ivern's son and his son's wife are your parents, you must be his granddaughter." said Vargoe staring at Ariel.

"Yes." said Ariel.

"What is your name?" said Vargoe to Ariel.

"Ariel." said Ariel.

"Um how long are we going to keep talking for because I am starving?" said Manora.

"Calm down Manora we'll go eat now." said Carlica.

So Carlica and her friends left.

"I thought the fashion show was great. I also feel inspired to sing now," said Chrysalis.

"Oho sing Chrysalis." said Nia.

"Yeah," said others who were looking around the mall store, Chrysalis and her family and friends were in.

"Okay guys," said Chrysalis.

Chrysalis then got up on the fashion runway and started singing with her bright light music lover bracelet on and set up her phone on the instruments choose follow along to someone singing music app and sang while her bracelet made gold, silver, red, yellow, green, and pink color and the audience loved her singing and color showing then Chrysalis stopped and put her phone and bracelet back in her pocket.

"Hold on there's something I want to say." said Vargoe.

She went up to Kylestone and grabbed him by the arm.

"You, why are you hanging out with singers? Isn't your father being a singer is what got him dead? If he wasn't one he never would have gotten killed" said Vargoe.

Just then, Cleo dropped her milkshake by them.

"Oops sorry," said Cleo.

So Vargoe moved her and Kylestone further from Cleo's dropped milkshake.

"It wasn't because of his singing, it was because of that lady's jealousy." said Kylestone.

"Don't be listening to him Kylestone, she just wants you to leave us because she knows it will make us upset." said Chrysalis.

"I know." said Kylestone.

"I have had it with you and your friends." said Walter to Carlica and her friends who walked back into the store.

"So have I now let go of him now, or you'll be banned from this mall for a while." said Cersanthama's dad to Vargoe.

"And you'll also be under arrest for a while too." said Belyndica's dad.

"Uh fine." said Vargoe.

So she let go of Kylestone's arm.

Just then, Falla dropped her milkshake by them.

"Oops sorry," said Falla.

So they move farther away from Falla's dropped milkshake.

"You girls need to be careful." said Falla and Cleo's dad to Falla and Cleo.

"On huh." said Falla and Cleo's mom.

"Right mom and dad." said Cleo.

"Carlica why don't you do your thing if they get on our nerves more?" said Manora.

"I don't need to so let's go." said Carlica.

Carlica walked away with her friends.

"Ah man those guys." said Walter.

"What is their problem?" said Lotusa.

"What did they mean about Carlica doing a thing?" said Chrysalis.

"Probably talking about being tough." said Tira.

"Maybe." said Chrysalis.

"By the way Hermalody if you're still wondering who mistaked you and your senior citizen friends for teenagers, again, it was Mesha who you just saw." said Fawn.

Later, Ariel and her family started having lunch at the mall food court.

"Okay, here's everything that we ordered," said Kylestone, bringing a tray with what they ordered, with Regina bringing another tray of what they ordered.

Just then, Carlica, Mesha, Manora, and Mingmi came up to them.

"Hey you guys didn't take it the wrong way with us to you guys," said Carlica.

"What are you talking about?" said Kylestone.

"Yeah Carlica, that sentence you said doesn't sound clear." said Mesha.

"Whatever, I mean even though we're not close still follow our skills if you guys at least want to be better. So we're willing to be open for that to teach you guys, so if we're going to be dealing with you guys, at least have more style." said Carlica.

While Carlica spoke, Mesha put a note next to Ariel that, on top of it said TO: ARIEL DON'T TELL YOUR PARENTS.

"I believe we're good, how we are," said Tarzan.

"Mistake." said Mingmi.

"Look we shouldn't be near you guys can you all at least go if you ladies aren't going to be nice?" said Kylestone.

"Okay, okay fine we'll go." said Mesha.

So they left, but left the note for Ariel behind.

"I just don't get them," said Pocahontas.

Ariel saw the note next to her and opened it without having her family know about it and inside it said to meet them at the <u>PEACH SWEET</u> store at the mall.

"Hey mom dad I think I left my phone at where Kiri's mom did her fashion show. Can I go get it?" said Ariel.

"Okay, but be quick, we don't want your food to get cold," said Kylestone.

"Okay, yes I will," said Ariel.

"I hope if she does find her phone and it's not broken like mine was when I lost it at a mall when I was younger than her age." said Pocahontas.

Ariel quickly left but to go to the <u>PEACH SWEET</u> store in the mall. Then Ariel arrived there and saw Carlica, Mesha, Manora, and Mingmi, there.

"Hey Carlica, Mesha, Manora, and Mingmi I got your guys' note, but I can't stay long my parents want me back quickly, and they don't know I'm here." said Ariel.

"Oh well then we'll wait for you to get back here we wanted to try to get you to change yourself." said Carlica.

"Myself why?" said Ariel.

"Well clearly you don't have style or skills." said Mesha.

"That's not true I do." said Ariel getting mad.

"Well why don't you come with us around this mall and prove it later that is because of what you said." said Carlica.

At the table where Ariel's family are at.

"I hope she found her phone at least if she comes back when her food got cold." said Kylestone.

Back at the <u>SWEET PEACH</u> store in the mall.

"Okay sure yeah I'll come back and show you all." said Ariel feeling mad at them.

"But still don't let your parents know or anyone else pretty sure there will be issues if they knew." said Carlica.

"I won't." said Ariel.

Ariel left and returned to her family at the mall's table feeling mad.

"Baby what's wrong?" said Regina.

"It's nothing." said Ariel.

"Baby girl something is wrong with you." said Kylestone.

"Oh Ariel did you break your phone? It's okay we'll get you a new one." said Pocahontas grabbing onto Ariel's hands.

Ariel pulled her hands out of Pocahontas' hands.

"Baby you need to tell us what's wrong." said Kylestone.

"I just bother by mean words that were said to me." said Ariel.

"What word do you mean what those mean people were saying after the fashion show?" said Regina.

"Yeah." said Ariel.

"They're just words don't listen to them baby." said Kylestone.

Then Kylestone kissed Ariel on the head and it made her feel better. At another store at the mall where Chrysalis and her family and friends are looking at clothes.

"Ah man I love this outfit thanks for helping me find it Chrysalis." said Dakota.

"Sure thing Dakota." said Chrysalis.

"My Dakota that is beautiful." said Dakota's mom.

"Thanks mom." said Dakota.

Constance came over with her parents while they each held an outfit.

"Hey guys look at these outfits my mom, dad, and I picked out." said Constance.

"Wow." said Chrysalis.

"Thanks that's what we were going with." said Constance's mom.

"My dad picked them out." said Constance.

"Well actually I suggested we pick them but I wasn't sure but you and your mom agreed for us to get them Constance." said Constance's dad.

"Oh my gosh you're right my mom told me to bring over the necklace she forgot to buy she told me get for her for her photoshoot which she is paying me back for." said Slecks holding out the necklace.

"Is she really sure she didn't want to have a milkshake in her hand during her photoshoot?" said Cleo.

"I didn't know who's weirder with sugar foods you two or Cherryette." said Kathleenie to Cleo and Falla.

"Well we don't go crazy when we see chocolate on the ground." said Falla holding out her milkshake.

"Yeah." said Cleo while bringing out her milkshake to hold out.

But Cleo accidentally knocked down her and Falla's milkshakes on the floor.

"Oops." they both said.

"Really again." said Justina.

"Okay maybe we are a little weird with sugar foods." said Cleo.

"On huh." said Falla.

"Oh hey there's Ariel I'm going to ask her if she wants to come." said Chrysalis.

When Ariel slithered by the store entrance.

"Hey Ariel you want to come with us to see Sleck's parents' photoshoot?" said Marge.

"Oh, ah, sorry can't there's somewhere I need to be." said Ariel slithering to them.

Just then they heard a loud crash in the store which was a lot of clothes holders that fell on the floor with Pennya on top.

"Sorry I fell on them." said Pennya.

"Where are you going?" said Chrysalis to Ariel.

Just then clothes were flying in the air making Chrysalis and Ariel ducking and move themselves to avoid them from hitting.

"What are you guys doing?" said Chrysalis to Pennya, Mabel, Tarika, Swifta, Dayla (who is a human/ bunny monster just like Axa), Butterscotch, and Stacya digging through the clothes throwing them in the air.

"Oh Tarika lost her key somewhere and we think they're under the clothes." said Stacya.

"Oh oh we'll help you, we're also big fans." said a lady with a lot of people behind her.

Then the lady and people ran to the clothes pile and dug through the clothes too but made there be more clothes being thrown in the air making Chrysalis and Ariel duck and move themselves more.

"Whoa." said Chrysalis.

"Do you know those people who just came and are throwing more clothes?" said Ariel to Chrysalis.

"I don't know their names but know they are fans and this isn't my first time seeing them." said Chrysalis.

Just then Chrysalis notices Tarika's key on the floor close to her then she picked it up.

"Hey Tarika I found your key." said Chrysalis holding it out.

"Oh good thanks." said Tarika.

Chrysalis tossed Tarika's key into her hands and then the fans all applauded around Chrysalis.

"Thanks everyone but can you all please keep it down so I can talk to my friend Ariel?" said Chrysalis.

"Oh sorry, sorry, my bad, big fan of you Chrysalis Loom, big fan, big fan of you Chrysalis Loom." said the fans.

"Thank you." said Chrysalis.

But Ariel slithered away quickly out of the store in the mall but Chrysalis went after her with her friends and sisters behind her.

"Ariel, is there something wrong?" said Chrysalis.

"I'm just not so good with being near so many others because well you know what happened to my grandfather." said Ariel.

"Oh okay but at least you're doing better around others." said Chrysalis.

"Yeah." said Ariel.

"But what are you doing that you're not coming with us?" said Chrysalis.

"I just want to look around the mall more." said Ariel.

Just then Carlica and Veza came over to them.

"Hey you guys, friend of mine here her name is Veza." said Carlica pointing her hands at Veza.

"Not good seeing you guys." said Veza.

"Rude." said Chrysalis.

"Can you stop staring at me?" said Ariel to Carlica.

"Okay Carlica stop freaking Ariel out." said Chrysalis.

"Don't be telling me what to do, even though you're incredibly beautiful, an amazing singer, dancer, and other things you're not in charge of me." said Carlica to Chrysalis.

"Well yeah you're right I'm not in charge of you but it's still mean what you're doing to Ariel." said Chrysalis.

"Oh man please stop saying those true amazing things about Chrysalis. I don't want to hear it, so you know what I'm going to leave in a cool way at least, through this door." said Veza.

"Ah Veza, that's just an outside of the store display door for that hardware store by it, it doesn't go to another room or outside." said Pennya.

"Whatever I still want to go through it in a cool way." said Veza.

Veza opened the door.

"Ha ha." said Veza laughing at them looking back at them with her head down backwards.

"Look out we're coming by the door with a janitor's cart." said Cleo pushing the janitor's cart with Falla by the door Veza is about to walk through.

Just then when Veza walked through the door she crashed into the janitor's cart Cleo and Falla were pushing but because she didn't listen to them or looked where she was going.

"Whoa." said Veza.

Carlica hit her face with her hand feeling bothered.

"Oho." the rest of them said.

"Why are you guys pushing a janitor's cart?" said Jerrica to Cleo and Falla.

"Well we told the store owner we will clean up the mess we made with the milkshakes and we asked the janitor and he let us use his cart." said Falla.

"But since you caused this mess Veza you clean it while Falla and I clean ours." said Cleo giving Veza a mop while Veza got up.

"Don't worry we'll be quick." said Falla while she and Cleo each grabbed a mop and a mop bucket.

"Well I got to go see you guys later bye." said Ariel.

"Bye Ariel." said Chrysalis and her sisters and friends.

Ariel arrived at the <u>SWEET PEACH</u> store where Mesha, Manora, and Mingmi were waiting for her. Just then Carlica came into the store.

"Hi guys I took a different way in the mall to get into this store so no one will get suspicious about us meeting." said Carlica.

"Clever move Carlica." said Mingmi.

"Well I'm ready." said Ariel.

"Well then let's see how your style skills are." said Carlica.

"Okay sure." said Ariel.

"So what do you think goes with this shirt?" said Carlica, holding out a shirt.

"That pink shirt over there." said Ariel, pointing at it.

"Uh lame but I do like the gems on that skirt with this shirt." said Carlica.

"Well at least I was right about those going with it." said Ariel.

"Try something else." said Mingmi.

"And you better not make it lame again." said Mesha.

At an area outside where Slecks' parents are having their photoshoot being taken by Beatrix's dad where Chrysalis' other friends' parents are at too.

"Okay, a little more dermatic." said Beatrix's dad to Slecks' mom while she was laying on a tree.

Slecks' mom looked more dermatic while lying on the tree. Then Beatrix's dad took the photo. Then Chrysalis and her sisters and friends came over.

"Hey guys." Slecks' dad.

Then Chrysalis and her sister and friends waved back.

'Hi mom dad, here's the necklace mom you wanted me to get. It's it too late?" said Slecks, holding out the necklace to her mom.

"No you're right on time." said Slecks' mom, grabbing the necklace from Slecks and paying her back.

"You guys didn't bring Ariel." said Mirabel's mom.

"No she had something else she wanted to do." said Jaser.

"Oh." said Beatrix's dad.

"Okay we're ready for the photos of us wearing lots of jewelry." said Slecks' mom, wearing a lot of jewelry and her husband wearing a lot of jewelry too.

Just then Vargoe and her friends Veza and Neevya were coming up to them while Veza was walking looking at a camera Neevya was recording Veza on her phone.

"And now you see me walking in this area in this highly nice outfit." Veza said Neevya's phone.

Veza stopped once she saw Chrysalis.

"Oh hey you look just like Chrysalis Loom and those guys over there doing that photo shoot looks like her friends." said Veza.

"I am Chrysalis Loom thee Chrysalis Loom and those guys are my friends who you think are look a likes of them." said Chrysalis.

"Oh you are and- wait how come you're here and them?" said Veza.

"To do and watch a photo shoot of my friend Slecks' parents." said Chrysalis.

"What, I didn't think any of them would be smart enough to do a photo shoot here." said Veza.

"Okay your being mean Veza." said Chrysalis.

"Chrysalis is right, and are you guys on the air?" said Dilia.

"Get away gator gal." said Veza to Dilia.

"Hey no one talks to Dilia like that." said Fern.

"No one talks to Dilia like that." said Cherryette, holding up a sign saying that.

"You have a sign that says: No one talks to Dilia like that." said Calvis.

"Yeah I also have a box here next to me of signs." said Cherryette pointing at the box.

Calvis stared at it.

"Okay." said Chrysalis to Cherryette.

"Well I don't agree with you guys." said Veza.

Veza changed into a monster without using the human to monster formula that's called a yovola that has dark pink bumpy skin, black triangle finger nails, blonde hair, a pointy nose, four fingers, fangs, and a triangle green bump on her head.

"I disagree while I am in this form too." said Veza.

"You're a human/ yovola the kind that when you use the human to monster formula that you have the ability to change back to human without the reverse formula." said Chrysalis.

"I can't believe someone would want to look like that." whispered Whitneya to Chrysalis.

Veza changed back to her human form.

"Hey look at my buggy stuff animal." said Nillia showing it up to Chrysalis.

"Cool." said Chrysalis looking at it.

Veza saw it too.

"Ah!" said Veza scared of it.

Then Veza fainted.

"Oho that's not good." said Chrysalis looking at Veza.

"Well we're off." said Vargoe.

But when Vargoe walked away she didn't watch where she was going and bumped into Cersanthama blowing a bubble and got gum her hair.

"Oha, what." said Vargoe.

"Oh my, got to be careful Vargoe." said Marleen.

"Sorry." said Cersanthama to Vargoe.

"We're still cool ones." said Neevya before she and her friends left.

Ariel, Carlica, Mesha, Manora, and Mingmi were still at the <u>GLAMOR PAL MALL</u>. Mesha held green nail polish with an orange dress.

"If you wear that green nail polish on you with that orange dress you should wear a green necklace with fuschia and yellow so you can look like you're dressing up like an orange flower." said Ariel.

"Well you are right on that." said Carlica.

"So far after fifty tries you've done you only did a good job at three." said Manora.

"Actually it was forty-six tries." said Mesha.

Mesha got out a sheet of paper with line checks in them.

"I kept track." said Mesha.

"Good for you." said Matilda who appeared.

Matilda came up to Ariel.

"Oh aren't you adorable." said Matilda staring at Ariel.

Matilda tried to grab Ariel's cheek but once Ariel felt her she pushed Matilda's hand away and went away from Matilda.

"Don't touch my face." said Ariel.

"Aaw you're so cute." said Matilda coming closer to her.

"Who are you?" said Ariel moving away from Matilda.

"Ariel, be nice around our friend Matilda." said Carlica.

"Yeah, Matilda loves adorable things." said Mingmi.

Ariel tried to get away from Matilda slithering backwards but bumped into a clothes rack behind her that's four racks attached to each other shaped like a square with a square board on top of them.

"Well can you please tell her to go or leave me alone." said Ariel while Matilda tried to grab her cheek again.

Once Matilda touched Ariel's cheek Ariel went under and over Matilda's arm and moved away.

"Ariel, we don't tell our friends to go and she's clearly not going to listen to us about leaving you alone so you're just going to have to deal with it." said Carlica.

"What I'm not having her trying to grab or touch me." said Ariel while Matilda put her arm around Ariel and her other hand under Ariel's chin up to her face.

Ariel got out just in time before Matilda fully had her.

"Well Ariel if you want to get away from her you're going to have to drop out of the game even though there's still most of the store here we didn't go through yet." said Carlica.

"Which means you lose and you barely have good taste." said Mingmi.

"Well if you are going through this you would be wanting to leave but don't you want to have another chance to prove me wrong again even though I'm sure I can prove you wrong." said Ariel trying to not be near Matilda.

"Well you're right about that not about you proving me wrong again but okay how about next time we'll try again but at the <u>BLOSSOM SPA</u> let's see how your style is with spa supplies like lotions, makeup, nail polish, and other things." said Carlica.

"And it's just going to me and the four of you there that is you, Mesha, Manora, and Mingmi?" said Ariel while she was grabbing onto the clothes racks that looks like the one she bumped into and while on top of it on her stomach while Matilda was pulling on Ariel's tail to get her to let go of the rack to come to her.

"Yeah sure we can make that happen." said Carlica.

"Hold on a second." said Mingmi.

Mingmi went up to Ariel and whispered something to her.

"That's the time when I should come over there, fine." said Ariel.

"And didn't even think about us having you have any spa treatments there." said Carlica to Ariel.

"Okay fine but can you at least tell your friend Matilda to let go of me? I'm starting to lose my grip." said Ariel.

"Okay fine Matilda let's go of Ariel." said Carlica.

But Matilda didn't let go.

"Told you she wouldn't listen." said Carlica.

Then Carlica and Mesha, Manora, and Mingmi left.

"Wait you can't leave me with her." said Ariel.

"We told you she wouldn't listen to us." said Mingmi where Ariel couldn't see her or Carlica, Mesha, and Manora.

"Yeah what's the point?" said Manora.

"Ah." said Ariel feeling like she was about to lose her grip.

Ariel tried to think of something and she did she grabbed a handful of hangers of clothes from the racks she's grabbing on to and threw them at Matilda that covered her face and made her let go of Ariel so Ariel very quickly got off the clothes racks' top and very quickly slithered away.

At one of Sasha's studios Agnesa's parents were recording a music video of Colleen and Ratia's parents doing a video of their new song while Chrysalis and her friends and family watched but they did not have their bright light music lover bracelets on.

"And cut, great job guys." said Agnesa's dad.

"Thanks." said Colleen and Ratia's parents.

"You know that song reminds me of something." said Fawn's mom.

"What's that mom?" said Fawn.

"Like how two of you guys first meet, falling from a tree couragement rising up and coming true in your guys' song which is like when you guys first met, when you guys first meet he dropped his sketchbook while sitting in a tree and almost hit you and he tried to make it up to you for almost hitting you and then you encourage him to go to the same school we did and then addition in front of Sasha to become a singer and all of those things happened." said Fawn's mom to Colleen and Ratia's parents.

"Okay yes you're right good job finding that out." said Colleen and Ratia's mom.

"I'm surprised we didn't think that we knew the story too." said Colleen.

"Don't feel bad about it girls." said Colleen and Ratia's dad.

Just then Regina, Kylestone, Tarzan, Pocahontas, and Zinnia arrived.

"Hey." they all said to each other.

"That's nice." said Regina.

"Do you sing Kylestone?" said Fredricka's mom who is a human/ cat monster that's pink, has no claws, no teeth, no whiskers, five finger on each hand and five toes on each foot.

"Not to someone who doesn't live with me." said Kylestone.

"Why are you nervous?" said Fredricka.

"Well yeah." said Kylestone.

"Okay then you don't have too." said Cassandra.

"No Ariel?" said Chrysalis.

"No she's somewhere else." said Kylestone.

"Where's that?" said Jerrica.

"She wanted to spend some me time at the <u>GLAMOR PAL MALL</u> and we trust her that she will be fine." said Kylestone.

"That's okay." said Chrysalis.

"Well it's less bad being there since we saw a friend of Carlica who is a human/ yovola named Veza cleaning a mess she made with the janitor's cart." said Fredricka.

"Those girls don't do anything to you guys did they?" said Fredricka's dad who is a human/ cat monster who's brown, has no whiskers, no claws, no sharp teeth, no tail, light brown on his face, five fingers on both hands, and five toes on both feet.

"Besides saying mean things nothing." said Chrysalis.

"No feelings got hurt?" said Fredricka's dad.

"No we're okay." said Aaron.

"Chrysalis are you promising me they didn't do anything to you? They dislike you the most because of their jealousy." said Fredricka's dad putting his hands on Chrysalis.

"Don't worry I'm fine." said Chrysalis to Fredricka's dad.

"Okay, okay." said Fredricka's dad.

"Honey calm down." said Fredricka's mom.

"Huh, you're right honey, I'm fine." said Fredricka's dad to Fredricka's mom.

"Yeah you worry sometimes about what's happening to Chrysalis as much as Fern and Chet worry about Dilia sometimes, no offense Fern and Chet." said Heviner's dad.

"Oh no I understand." said Fern.

"So do I." said Chet.

"I thought they were acting familiar." said Regina to her husband.

"I know but Chrysalis here is a dear friend and those girls have issues, but you guys are right I don't need to worry." said Fredricka's dad.

"Well now that that is done is everyone ready for the next music video?" said Butterscotch's mom.

"Hey Dannya are you finally ready to say your lines?" said Jaser.

"Yep I am." said Dannya.

"All set." said Jannia dressed up as a poor person.

"Um Jannia why are you dressed up as the poor person you're supposed to be the sad clown?" said Chrysalis.

"Oh I'm filling in for Ridga's dad. He's running a bit late and told me to fill in for him if he doesn't make it." said Jannia.

"So you're going to be both?" said Axa.

"Yes I am." said Jannia.

"Hi guys, sorry, I'm late but I'm back with the new spot light." said Ridga's dad trying to catch his breath while holding the new spotlight.

"Let me take that honey." said Ridga's mom grabbing the new spotlight from him.

"Thanks hun." said Ridga's dad.

"Wow dad looks like you don't need to jog for tomorrow." said Ridga.

"Ah man." said Regina.

"I hope that no one will steal this nighttime window stick poster." said Agnesa holding it out after grabbing it out of her pocket.

"Agnesa why do you have that? It's for one of our scenes for a movie later." said Agnesa's dad.

"You said it will be okay for me to look at it if nothing bad happens to it." said Agnesa.

"Well since it's okay, alright but ask for permission when you take something." said Agnesa's dad.

"Thanks dad and I will." said Agnesa.

"We're going to get going now, Chrysalis remember you're suppose to meet us at our house later." said Taffada.

"Don't worry I will." said Chrysalis.

Just then the lights turned off.

"Huh?" they all said.

"What's going on with the lights?" said Jistopher's dad.

"Introducing my outfit for the video." said Justina's mom but without anyone seeing her.

Everyone looked over where her voice was coming from and saw and saw at the entrance Dannya and Tinka's mom next to the lights by the entrance then Justina's mom appeared at the entrance and then Dannya and Tinka's mom turned the lights back on.

"Wow." they all said looking at Justina's mom's outfit.

"Thanks with the lights." said Justina's mom to Dannya and Tinka's mom.

"No problem." said Dannya and Tinka's mom.

"Wow that's beautiful." said Chrysalis.

"I'm glad we stook around long enough to see your entrance." said Raymen to Justina's mom.

"Thank you." said Justina's mom.

"Wow mom." said Justina after going up to her mom.

"Wow your outfit is honey." said Justina's dad.

Butterscotch came up too.

"Well?" said Butterscotch.

"Well what?" said Justina's mom.

"Aren't you going to name it?" said Butterscotch.

"Since when do we give dresses a name?" said Justina.

"Well it's so pretty and I figured we should give it a name." said Butterscotch.

"Okay Butterscotch what name?" said Justina's mom.

"Sparkle spotlight." said Butterscotch.

"I like it." said Justina's dad who came up.

"Me too, okay then we'll call it that." said Justina's mom.

Later at one of Sasha's studios Cersanthama's dad did a genuflection then Cersanthama's mom did a flip where she landed standing on her hands on her dad's shoulders and kissed each other in that position.

"Okay and cut." said Agnesa's dad.

"Wow." said Chrysalis.

"Hey guys check out how big of a hit our video is that we just posted went." said Colleen and Ratia's dad holding out his phone.

"Whoa." they all said.

"Wow I know the video was great." said Sasha.

"We all do." said Chrysalis.

Ariel was slithering by the studio and went inside because she knew her family was in there. Inside the studio a bunch of red marble spilled all over the floor.

"Whoa whoops." said Mirabel's dad who just knocked down a box of marble that spilled everywhere on the floor.

"Whoa dad." said Mirabel.

"Alright everyone be careful picking up the marbles and watch your step." said Mirabel's dad.

But Cleo and Falla's dad moved very quickly.

"Whoa slow down with the pasteing." said Kiri's dad to Cleo and Falla's dad.

"I can't help it I'm terrified of marbles." said Cleo and Falla's dad feeling scared.

"Relax honey." said Cleo and Falla's mom slowly going to him so she doesn't slip on the marbles.

"Chrysalis you can just go to the door since you have to go to Taffada and Raymen's house." said Walter.

Chrysalis was now holding Tafelena in her arms because Fern and Chet left and had Chrysalis watch Tafelena for them. Just then Ariel came into the room but didn't notice the marbles.

"Whoa." said Ariel falling from the marbles and fell on the floor.

"Oh, oh man." said Cleo and Falla's dad nervously.

"Calm down." said Cleo and Falla's mom rubbing Cleo and Falla's dad's shoulders.

"Yeah okay." said Cleo and Falla's dad calming down.

Ariel's family went to Ariel. Ariel's mom Regina got to her first.

"Are you okay baby girl?" said Regina helping Ariel up by grabbing Ariel around her chest.

"Ow." said Ariel while her mom was helping her get up.

"Baby I sent you a text about the marbles." said Kylestone.

"Sorry dad I ignored it because I thought it was going to be a text about me almost being here." said Ariel.

"Did you have a nice time at the mall?" said Pocahontas.

"Yeah, mom can I have a kiss from you?" said Ariel.

"Of course baby." said Regina.

Regina kissed Ariel on the head and it made Ariel smile.

"Did something bad happen to you?" said Regina.

"I'm okay mom, don't worry." said Ariel.

"Okay." said Regina.

Regina snuggled with Ariel.

"Parten I need to get through." said Chrysalis to Ariel and Regina.

"Oh you're leaving I was hoping we could hang out now." said Ariel to Chrysalis.

"I'm leaving to go babysit my new baby friend Trixie at her house and with Tafelena here. If you want I can ask her parents if you can come." said Chrysalis to Ariel.

"Taffada and Raymen?" said Ariel to Chrysalis.

"Yeah that's them." said Chrysalis.

"Um sure okay. Can I mom and dad?" said Ariel.

"Sure Ariel." said Kylestone.

"Okay." said Regina.

"Thanks." said Ariel.

"Great come with me, oh but first do you want to hold Tafelena after you wash your hands that is?" Chrysalis said to Ariel.

"Sure." said Ariel.

"Okay let's go to the bathrooms here." said Chrysalis.

So Ariel followed Chrysalis while Chrysalis got her phone out to text Taffada and Raymen that Ariel is coming with her.

"Okay everyone back to collecting marbles." said Arb.

"So far I'm having a hard time collecting them with these boxes around, they keep rolling back to me when I place them on the floor on the marbles to grab more of the marbles because some of them went behind the boxes." said Swifta kneeling on the floor.

Chrysalis and Ariel walked (well Ariel actually slithered instead) to Trixie's house and Ariel was holding Tafelena in her arms.

"It's nice they let me come over." said Ariel.

"Yeah and Tafelena really seems like she likes you Ariel." said Chrysalis.

"She does, doesn't she. You know this is my first time holding a baby." said Ariel.

Just then they ran into Cherryette, LuLu, LeLe, LiLi, Zita, Lumia, Colleen, Ratia, Dava, Loua, and Bemma standing in front of a red and white target on the building wall while having a bunch of pies with them.

"Hey guys you guys are done picking up the marbles?" said Chrysalis.

"Yep." said Dava.

"Hi what are you guys doing?" said Ariel.

"Well these pies are made from whip cream that's expired so we're going to make a use with them by throwing them at the target." said Cherryette.

"But are you allowed to do that here on that building?" said Ariel.

"Yeah I spoke with the lady who owns the building if it's okay and she said yes and she is also my mom." said Cherryette.

"Well if you're allowed." said Ariel.

They then each threw a pie at the target.

"It's fun to be funny, so get up and be a clown." said Cherryette.

Just then Swifta splat her head into a pie and smiled at them when she took her head out.

"Why did you do that?" said Ariel.

"What Cherryette said be a clown so I'm being a clown don't worry I didn't have my mouth open." said Swifta.

"It is kind of funny, ha ha ha." said Chrysalis.

Then the rest of them started laughing.

"Okay let's continue on." said Chrysalis.

"Actually the rest of us are coming down this path too." said Zita.

"Why's that Zita?" said Chrysalis.

"You'll see." said Dava.

Ariel and Chrysalis and everyone else ran into Chrysalis' friend Shenatha.

"Hey Shenatha." said Chrysalis and Ariel.

"Oh hey." said Shenatha who is feeling a little upset.

"What's wrong?" said Chrysalis to Shenatha.

"Yeah Shenatha didn't feel uncomfortable about this because of all of the attention." said Loua.

"Why Shenatha is here is why we're also here too." said Bemma.

"Well I got roped into having to drive them around." said Shenatha pointing at Chrysalis' other friends.

"Hey guys." said Chrysalis while Ariel waved back at them.

"Oh hi Chrysalis." said Jaya who is a human/ white cat monster with golden colored ears, no tail, no whiskers, no claws, five fingers, five toes, and is a foot tall and her parents are the same human/ monster she is but three feet tall.

"Oh man you guys are going to love what we're doing." said Jaya.

"Dava told us." said Chrysalis.

"Oh so Dava told you guys that my husband, Sue, Jaya, and I and everyone else are going to drive around in that green paint splattered topless bus." said Jerrica with Sue in her arm and using her other hand to point at the bus.

"And that also not being all." said Jaya.

"We're also going to be playing Ariel's grandfather Ivern's songs while driving around very out loud." said Aaron.

"Wow." said Chrysalis.

"Yeah us and everyone else over here." said Aaron pointing at Chrysalis' friends.

"Yeah we're so excited that Ivern's family are now living closer to us and that we're friends with them." said Jerrica.

Dayla moved closer to Ariel excitedly.

"I'm here next to the granddaughter of the dead singer Ivern." said Dayla talking into a microphone.

"Sometimes Dayla likes to pretend she's a reporter." said LeLe.

"And here I'm next to Ivern's granddaughter Ariel." said Cherrycake.

"Um." said Ariel.

"Hey Cherrycake don't interrupt me." said Dayla.

"Sorry I couldn't help it. I still can't believe we're here with Ivern's granddaughter." said Cherrycake.

"But I'm not a famous singer like my grandfather." said Ariel.

"True but you are his granddaughter so at least we're seeing you since he's dead now." said Navia.

"You guys clearly know I'm a fan of Ivern since I was a kid I've been listening to his songs while I swung on the swings and I was shocked when I found out how he died a little while after I started doing that." said Lumia.

"Yep she did." said Chrysalis.

"Wow there are so many big fans of my grandfather I've met today." said Ariel.

"Nice right." said Trudy.

"Yeah and we're going to be having ourselves taking turns being buckled to the pole over the bus to make it easier to do back flips." said Lumia.

"It would look more like to me like you guys are being roasted." said Ariel.

"I told you guys someone would think that." said Darent.

"So what it's their fault for not understanding." said Fawn.

"Yeah I'm not calling it off." said Beatrix putting herself into the buckles of the pole.

"Oh but before you guys go there's something we wanna show you girls in the bus, come with us." said Kathleenie.

So Chrysalis and Ariel went into the bus and saw an evidence board on the bus wall.

"An evidence board." said Chrysalis.

"And to find the lady who killed my grandfather." said Ariel.

"Yes, how dare that lady kill him." said Jaser who came into the bus.

"Oh man I wish I was an actual reporter with a camera man to show her face to everyone that she has been caught if that happens." said Dayla who came into the bus too.

"You guys aren't planning on doing harm to her are you?" said Chrysalis.

"No no we're just going to have her be put behind bars." said Kathleenie.

"Okay that's good not to cause harm." said Chrysalis.

"So far you guys have no clues on where she is or what exactly she looks like." said Ariel upsetly looking at the evidence board.

"Yeah we're afraid so." said Slecks who came into the bus too.

"Yeah no one's exactly sure on what she looks like she always went around wearing a big hat that covered most of her head and she wore a long trench coat but there are a few hints about what she looks like she's a lady, she has black hair, and she was around twenty years ago." said Chrysalis.

"Yeah and that's all we got about her." said Heviner.

Chrysalis and Ariel and everyone else got out of the bus.

"I didn't really want to be a part of this but I do love Ivern and his music but they said if I drive they'll come with me in the bus to explore the dark alleys." said Shenatha.

Just then Belyndica came over with a manikin lady.

"Hey guys sorry I'm late." said Belyndica.

"Belyndica you're coming with them too?" said Chrysalis.

"Yeah, and I came here to bring this manikin for Shenatha. She feels like this plan draws too much attention so I brought this manikin lady with me for you Shenatha to hide behind." said Belyndica.

"Ah well that is better." said Shenatha.

"I knew it would be with this gal around." said Belyndica high fiving the manikin lady with after she lifted it's hand up.

"Well we're going to get going now." said Jerrica.

"Where are you girls going anyway?" said Jaya to Chrysalis and Ariel.

"We're going to Trixie's house. I'm supposed to babysit her while bringing Tafelena to babysit them both and Ariel wanted to come along." said Chrysalis.

"Oh okay and listen out for the music." said Jaya.

"We will Jaya." said Chrysalis.

Then Jaya and everyone else but Chrysalis, Tafelena, and Ariel went into the bus and started driving while playing Ivern's music and while Marge, Kathleenie, Princeson, Venelope, and Beatrix were flipping buckled to the pole over the topless bus.

"Huh, I wish I could see my grandfather sing. He sounds so wonderful." said Ariel.

"Me too." said Chrysalis.

So Chrysalis and Ariel continued going to Trixie's house.

"Uh Chrysalis, are the dark alleys scary?" said Ariel.

"Well nothing serious has happened in them but sometimes some people hear surprising sounds like bumping into something and it is dark." said Chrysalis.

"Okay but I say they made a better decision going in a bus into there." said Ariel.

"Me too." said Chrysalis.

At Trixie's house.

"I found your hand mirror honey." said Raymen.

"Oh thanks hun I can't believe I missed placed it." said Taffada holding Trixie.

"Yeah me too." said Raymen.

Just then Chrysalis, Tafelena, and Ariel came in through the door.

"Hi Raymen, hi Taffada." said Chrysalis while they smiled and waved.

"Oh we're glad you girls are here, here's Trixie." said Taffada handing Trixie to Chrysalis.

"Thanks for helping us out we'll be back later, bye." said Raymen.

Then they all waved good-bye. Then Trixie started smiling in Chrysalis' arms.

"You two seem close." said Ariel.

"Trixie is a happy baby." said Chrysalis.

"Chrysalis is a really cool friend." said Ariel to Trixie.

Just then they heard another one of Ivern's songs.

"Hey that's another one of Ivern's songs." said Chrysalis.

Chrysalis and Ariel went outside to see the bus while Trixie and Tafelena were still in Chrysalis and Ariel's arms. When they got out there they saw it and waved to them while they waved back.

"I saw that Kathleenie traded places with Trudy so she can use the turning pole." said Chrysalis.

Chrysalis, Ariel, Tafelena, and Trixie went back into the house.

"He sure did sing some good songs." said Chrysalis.

"Huh yeah he did." said Ariel.

In the bus Shenatha's driving Dannya, Tinka, Cherrycake, Lumia, and Darent were flipping buckled to the pole over the bus during one of Ivern's songs then the song was over.

"Okay guys the song's done can we call it done now?" said Heviner.

"I agree with Heviner guys." said Trudy.

"Yeah I think we're good now." said Tinka.

So they stopped the pole and everyone buckled on it unbuckled off.

"Okay off to the alley." said Shenatha.

So Shenatha drove into the alley and removed the manikin lady away from her.

"Um, Shenatha I think we should think this through." said Belyndica sitting next to Shenatha.

"Hey you guys said right after being done with this Ivern thing we'll go straight to the alleys." said Shenatha.

"We did, can someone hand me my manikin? I think I wanna hide behind it too." said Belyndica.

"Here you go." said Lumia handing Belyndica the manikin.

"Thanks Lumia." said Belyndica grabbing the manikin and then putting it on her lap ready to hide behind it.

"What do you guys think about this being in this alley?" said Zila to Jerrica and Aaron taking a selfie together while Jerrica held Sue in her arms.

"It's fine with us no one ever needed to go to the hospital or to a doctor because of going in there." said Aaron while he and Jerrica were taking more selfies with Sue in Jerrica's arms.

Shenatha kept driving.

"Hey look over there on the left it's the big house." said Marge.

"Oho nice." said Shenatha.

At Trixie's house.

"Your great-grandma bought another big house." said Ariel.

"Yeah in case she gets a lot more famous workers to use that place for the same reasons as the <u>HANGING STAR SPOT</u>." said Chrysalis.

"So what do you guys want to do?" said Ariel.

"Well you guys want to go out to eat now?" said Chrysalis.

"Okay let's go." said Ariel.

So they left the house while Chrysalis and Ariel carried Trixie and Tafelena in their arms. At Ariel's house Kylestone was looking at old photos sitting on his mother's bed in her room just then Regina came to the doorway.

"Honey are you ready to go?" said Regina.

"Yeah I am." said Kylestone.

Regina slithered into the room and sat next Kylestone and laid on him snuggling.

"Oh that's you and Ariel when she was a baby." said Regina looking at the photo Kylestone is holding.

Next Kylestone switched to another page.

"Oh that's you and your, dad." said Regina.

"Yeah." said Kylestone.

"It was nice what those guys did earlier playing his music on that odd bus." said Regina.

"Yeah and weird." said Kylestone.

"Yeah." said Regina.

"You know what, maybe I should sing in public." said Kylestone getting up.

Regina got up too.

"Well, would if we sang a song in public together if we get embarrassed at least we won't be alone?" said Regina.

"Yeah." said Kylestone while he and Regina hugged each other while snuggling.

Just then Zinnia came into the room.

"Aw so sweet reminds me of the time I accidentally opened the door and went into the room where you guys were kissing and made me find out you guys became a couple." said Zinnia.

Regina and Kylestone laughed looking back at it.

"Oh Kylestone, remember to put the photos back when you're not looking at them, I don't want them getting lost or ruined." said Zinnia slithering over to collect them and put them away.

"Sorry mother." said Kylestone.

Zinnia stopped and looked at the photo that Kylestone was looking of him when he was a kid with his father. Kylestone and Regina knew what was going on with her and Kylestone whispered something to Regina and nodded her head agreeing.

"Mother let's go now I'm sure you'll feel better when we go out to eat." said Kylestone holding his mother's hands after having her turn around to him.

Zinnia kissed Kylestone on the head.

"Hm, my baby boy." said Zinnia.

In Mirabel's family car aren't just Mirabel's parents in the car but also Fern, Chet, and the parents of Agnesa, Trudy, Fawn, Nillia and Arianie, Gaddy, Swifta, Cherryette, and Shenatha.

"Thanks for having us carpool." said Trudy's dad to Mirabel's parents.

"No problem." said Mirabel's mom.

"I'm glad I remembered this for Fawn." said Fawn's dad holding up something.

Everyone seeing it thought it was strange.

"Is that an accordion with a clown face and wig on it?" said Shenatha's dad to Fawn's dad which is what Fawn's dad was holding up.

"Yep it's for her clown performance at the restaurant's big performance night." said Fawn's dad.

"Of course she wanted to join Cherryette's pie throwing." said Fawn's mom.

"That daughter of ours is hilarious." said Cherryette's mom to Cherryette's dad.

"She sure is fun." said Cherryette's dad.

Just then Chet was getting a phone call so he got out his phone.

"Oh." said Chet looking at who was calling him.

"Is that Spencer calling?" said Trudy's mom.

"Yep." said Chet.

Chet answered his phone.

"Hey Spencer." said Chet.

"Hey Chet my wife Emily and our baby daughter Batie and I are going to be going on the plane very soon so so far we'll make it in time for the big show at <u>BRING IT IN</u> restaurant." said Spencer who is the same human/ monster Tafelena is but orange and same thing with Emily and Batie their less than a year old daughter.

"Oh okay that's good, and there's something we think we should help you guys out with when you get back." said Chet.

"Hold on a minute there's something we want to ask you guys about like something about meeting the family of a deceased singer." said Spencer.

"Oh you mean Ivern." said Chet.

"AAAAAAHHHHHHHH!" said a lot of loud voices through Chet's phone that everyone in the car heard that bothered their ears.

"What the heck?" said Agnesa's dad.

"Oh man." said Cherryette's mom.

"Ow, was that you guys who yelled like that ow?" said Chet back talking on his phone.

"Ow, no actually I was the people and people/monsters who are also at the airport they're all big fans." said Spencer while the people and people/ monsters who screamed through the phone were starting at them.

Just then Batie started crying because of the big yells.

127

"Oh shot Batie's getting up and now starting to cry hold on." said Spencer.

Spencer moved farther away to be able to hear Chet.

"Okay yes him we saw them on the TV of the fashion show his son and his son's wife were models and how come you guys didn't tell us you guys were meeting them?" said Spencer.

"Well that's what I wanted to tell you guys and we were hoping when you guys get back we can help you simmer down better when you meet them. We know that you guys are big fans of Ivern too." said Chet.

"Oh man Ivern!" said a lady at the airport.

"Oh man, I wanna hear a song from him right now." said a man at the airport.

"Well at least now two of those fans aren't shouting but yeah you're right we could use that Emily and I are big fans too bad he passed away before we were born because he was killed by a wicked bad lady." said Spencer.

"Oh yes that lady oh man." said Chet.

"Hey honey I got Batie back to sleep." said Emily while rocking Batie to sleep in her arms.

"Oh good." said Spencer.

Just then another lady who screamed earlier through Spencer's phone got out a speaker.

"What is the lady doing?" said Spencer.

"I think I know what she's doing." said Emily.

The lady then attached the speaker to her phone and played one of Ivern's songs out loud.

"Whoa what the?" said Chet hearing the music loudly through his phone and everyone else in the car too.

"Oh whoa!" said Fern.

"Oh man, that is loud." said Ridga's mom.

"See you guys at the restaurant!" said Spencer.

Then Spencer hung up his phone and Batie started to cry again.

"Oh man." said Emily.

So Spencer and Emily tried to cover Batie's ears. In Mirabel's family car.

"Man what is going on at that airport?" said Gaddy's dad.

Chrysalis and Ariel arrived at the restaurant with Trixie and Tafelena but are now being held by Natasha and Gege who are at the restaurant too with the rest of Chrysalis' family and friends except for those who were in Mirabel's family car and Spencer, Emily, and Batie.

"Hey where's Pennya, Mabel, and Cassandra?" said Pennya, Mabel, and Cassandra's dad.

"Oh there they're." said Chrysalis pointing to them sleeping at the restaurant tables in sleeping bags.

They all went up to them and then they woke up after their parents shaked them.

"Hey mom and dad." said Pennya.

"You girls were sleeping there." said Chrysalis.

"Yep we wanted to be sure we got here on time so we came an hour early and then fell asleep, but don't worry they let us." said Cassandra.

"Girls up and don't worry about getting here on time." said Pennya, Mabel, and Cassandra's mom.

Marleen came up while looking at her phone because she got a text message.

"Bring over Spencer, Emily, and Batie." said Marleen looking at her text.

"Oho Spencer, Emily, and Batie are coming here." said Chrysalis.

"And trying to get them to keep it cool with meeting the family of Ivern so far doing good but we might need a little more time. Is it okay if they stay outside of the restaurant for a while?" said Marleen continuing reading her text.

"Are you guys okay with that?" said Pennya, Mabel, and Cassandra's mom to Ariel and her family.

"Um sure." said Ariel.

The rest of Ariel's family agreed.

"But even if they still can't handle it still we want to join you guys here not just because Regina and I really want to do something here." said Kylestone to them.

"Of course we wouldn't want to leave you guys out." said Walter.

"We'll let you guys know." said Jistopher's dad.

"Thanks." they said while leaving.

"So you guys are planning on doing what you guys did earlier on that bus again playing Ivern's songs tomorrow." said Cleo and Falla's dad.

"Yes we are to give everyone a second chance in case they missed it like Spencer, Emily, and Batie." said Cleo.

Outside of the restaurant where Ariel and her family are.

"Baby why did you say that you and Regina wanted to be in the restaurant for?" said Zinnia.

"Sorry mother I can't tell you it's a surprise." said Kylestone.

"Okay as long as it's nothing bad." said Zinnia.

"No of course not it's something for you and everyone else to enjoy it's something that someone like you could use." said Kylestone.

"What do you mean?" said Zinnia.

"Look mother, Regina and I know how you were feeling while you were looking at that picture of me and father when I was a kid and I don't want you feel lonely." said Kylestone.

"But baby I'm not alone I do wish he was here but I still have a family and friends and it's because I had you with me to bring more others in my life." said Zinnia putting her hand on Kylestone's face.

"I know and I get that but I don't want you to feel sad you've been with me my whole life." said Kylestone.

"And I appreciate you care but I promise I'm fine." said Zinnia.

"Yes but still let me try to make you feel better." said Kylestone.

"Okay." said Zinnia.

Then she kissed him. Inside the restaurant Spencer, Emily, Batie, and everyone else who was in Mirabel's car to be taken to the restaurant arrived and Tafelena and Trixie were given back to their parents.

"Okay I believe we're ready to meet Ivern's family." Spencer.

"Good and I can't wait to bring these up with me." said Dannya removing a red covering and lifting up to her chest a terrarium of snakes.

"Whoa." said Tinka.

"You're going to bring those snakes with you when you go up on stage?" said Chrysalis.

"Yeah I'm going to walk up there and introduce these snakes being in this terrarium going good with my outfit, I'm also going to do the same thing next time when we walk the red carpet." said Dannya.

"If anyone wants you to cover them up do that so you don't scare them. Not everyone is okay around snakes." said Dannya and Tinka's dad.

"Don't worry dad I will." said Dannya.

"Cool, hey can I do the same thing with newts?" said Tinka.

"If you promise to be careful and do the same thing I told Dannya to do." said Dannya and Tinka's dad.

"Sure thing I will." said Tinka.

"I'll text them to come back in the restaurant." said Cherryette's mom.

So that's what Cherryette's mom did and then Ariel and her family got her text.

"Oh well let's go." said Regina.

Then they left to go inside the restaurant. Inside the restaurant.

"Well it is very nice to meet you guys." said Emily to Ariel and her family.

"If it's okay with you guys I like to sing." said Emily.

"Right now?" said Regina.

"Yes." said Emily.

"But you're going to go on soon during the show for us to perform in." said Amelia.

"I know but still." said Emily.

Emily got up on top of the table next to them while she set up her phone to play the instruments she wanted, then she put on her bright light music lover bracelet and started to sing. She sang really good pleasing everyone while her bracelet lit up fuchsia and silver lights and then when Emily was done she took her bracelet off and grabbed her phone.

"Wow, that was amazing." said Kylestone.

"What a delight." said Ariel.

"Thank you." said Emily.

Sasha got out her phone and looked at the time.

"Oh guys we got to start now." said Sasha.

"Okay, I'm up first." said Colleen and Ratia's mom.

"Okay mom get up." said Ratia.

Colleen and Ratia's mom went up on stage and began to sing while Shiloh's mom, Rowshella's mom, Axa's mom, Dakota's mom, Heviner's mom, and Ridga's mom were her background dancers. While she sang she didn't have her bracelet on her but she did have big moving swirling lights happening on stage.

"Wow." they all said after Colleen and Ratia's mom was done singing.

Everyone applauded while they left the stage.

"Okay I'm up now." said Joyce.

Rowshella's mom came over to Rowshella and Rowshella's dad.

"Great good job mom I can't wait to see you sing later too." said Rowshella.

"Yeah same thing with me hun." said Rowshella's dad.

"Oh thanks." said Rowshella's mom.

"Hey hi great good job and I know you'll do well when you sing." said Calvis to Rowshella's mom.

"Thanks Calvis." said Rowshella's mom.

"By the way Calvis since you're dating Rowshella I think my wife and I should be hanging out with your parents." said Rowshella's dad.

"My parents, are you sure you want to do that?" said Calvis.

"We knew your dad when we were kids, we should do fine." said Rowshella's dad.

"We were never friends with your dad but we weren't enemies." said Rowshella's mom.

"I'm not worried about you guys arguing with my dad I'm worried about him being too boring around you guys." said Calvis.

"Excuse me young man but you know I'm right here." said Calvis' dad.

"Calvis don't talk like that about your dad." said Calvis' mom.

Just then the lights went down again.

"We'll have to talk later dad the music will be too loud." said Calvis.

Joyce started to appear on stage without her bright light music lover bracelet and started singing until she stopped.

Matilda, Tuckles, and Nagaila saw Joyce on TV at the <u>HANGING STARS SPOT</u>.

"That teenager did a great job designing the background on stage." said Tuckles.

"Um she's a senior citizen." said Nagaila.

"Oh right." said Tuckles.

"You know a little of her hair is gray." said Matilda.

"Yeah but I keep thinking she's wearing gray hair dye." said Tuckles.

"Oh that makes sentences." said Matilda.

At the <u>BRING IT IN</u> restaurant up on the stage after Joyce finished singing and people applauded for her singing Dannya walked up with the snake terrarium of snakes she has held up in her hands up to her chest.

"We are about to show our next performer soon and enjoy these snakes of mine that can go good with an outfit, oh but not as in skinning them I mean what I'm doing with them now you know like an accessory." said Dannya.

"Calvis I'm upset about how you're being, and don't worry I paid for the table." said Calvis' dad.

"Don't worry you paid for the table, what are you talking about?" said Calvis to his dad.

Calvis' dad did a karate chop and broke the table apart and everyone saw it.

"Whoa." said Calvis.

"Your dad's not boring he's cool he took karate you know." said Calvis' mom.

"You didn't know your dad took karate?" said Rowshella.

"Actually I do know but he stopped taking lessons when I was three and I haven't seen him do any moves since." said Calvis.

"That's because I haven't been needing it too often." said Calvis' dad.

"I get that but still I thought you would have forgotten right now." said Calvis.

"Well no I have not." said Calvis' dad.

"Now do you think that your dad is too boring for us?" said Rowshella's dad.

"No, not anymore I'm sorry dad." said Calvis.

"Well it's better now." said Calvis' dad.

"Okay I'm going to announce the next performers." said Sasha.

"I hope Kylestone and Regina will make it back in time." said Tarzan.

"Oh don't worry about that, trust me." said Sasha.

Sasha walked up on stage.

"Everyone the ones about to sing are Regina and her husband the son of Ivern Kylestone." said Sasha.

"OH MY, AAHH, IVERN'S OWN SON AND HIS SON'S WIFE!" said the audience excitedly.

"So this is what my baby Kylestone was talking about." said Zinnia.

On the stage Kylestone and Regina looked a little nervous but they were about to sing from getting themselves to feel like they received a lot of courage to sing so that's what they did and the audience loved it so did Chrysalis and her family and friends and the audience thought they were great singers. Then they got off the stage when they were done and hugged Ariel.

"Wow!" said Chrysalis.

"Hold on everyone we have something to say!" yelled Carlica with her friends.

"What is it Carlica?" said Chrysalis.

"You guys know Falyby who is a friends of ours." said Vargoe.

"Yeah, what about her?" said Ocieana.

"These are cool snakes." said Zila holding one of Dannya's snakes while Slecks, Dakota, Lumia, and Candace were doing the same thing.

"Oh man, oh my gosh snakes!" said Veza disturbed.

Carlica's friends were all discussed by the snakes but not Carlica.

"Oh my gosh." said Vargoe.

Vargoe fell down discussed but she didn't pass out.

"Oh great now I have a singer down, medic." said Carlica.

Two people wearing medic clothes came to Vargoe and put her on a stretcher and carried her out.

"You actually have doctors with you?" said Ocieana.

"Yes they're like our school nurses except they don't work at a school and they follow around by the way Falyby wanted me to give you this note she also said it's for all of you singers and every other singer to hear and she got that from someone." said Carlica grabbing the note from her pocket and handing it to Sasha.

Sasha opened to note after she grabbed it from Carlica.

"What does it say?" said Chrysalis.

"Don't bother singing and the words since Ivern was a singer are crossed out." said Sasha reading the note.

"Whoa, someone who hates Ivern." said Gege.

"Hah!" said the audience surprised with upsetness.

"We know everyone we're surprised too!" said Zadie yelling to the audience.

"Well now I'm going to go before I need my medic crew to carry me out in a stretcher because of those snakes, el." said Mingmi.

Just then the rest of Carlica's friends started to feel like they were going to do the same thing Vargoe did but they kept on walking.

"That was weird." said Jindy, Tira, Irenie, and Candace's mom.

"I want to be our medic." said Darma.

"You do?" said Lalo.

"Yeah let me check your heart beat Lalo." said Darma getting out her toy stethoscope that has a drawing sticker on the bell.

"Hey who's that on your stethoscope's bell?" said Ariel.

"That's Darma's made up character Bearman." said Chrysalis.

"I drew it for her." said Javada.

"Uh-huh." said Darma.

At the <u>HANGING STARS SPOT</u>.

"Okay who wants a slice of cherry cake?" said Nagaila.

"I do, you don't make a mess right?" said Hailey to Nagaila.

"Oh will you stop saying that no I didn't look for yourself." said Nagaila.

Hailey walked into the kitchen of one of the rooms with Nagaila behind her and Nadeline(who is a human/ monster who looks like a human with blue skin, a yellow neck, five feet taller than her original height, small half circle ears that stick out you can see the earholes, and white eyes with blue swirls that start from the black dot in the middle) and the kitchen looked clean to her.

"See." said Nagaila.

"Oh yeah then what's that on the ground?" said Nadeline pointing at a cherry on the floor.

"What that wasn't there I promise." said Nagaila.

"Hey what's that on your hand?" said Hailey looking at Nadeline's hand.

"Hey that's cherry juice, you grabbed a cherry and just threw it there." Nagaila said to Nadeline.

"Hey I'm still mad you started making the cake first I'm the one with the better cooking skills." said Nadeline.

"Oh really well if you don't want to enjoy my cake then have the cherries." said Nagaila.

Nagaila opened the fridge and got out a cherry jar and opened it and threw it on to Nadeline's face

"Okay now you made a mess." said Hailey talking like she doesn't care.

At the **BRING IT IN** restaurant.

"Oh man here comes Chrysalis." said Ariel.

Chrysalis appeared on stage and started to sing. Everyone loved it. It was their favorite song of the performances at the restaurant today. Later Ariel and her family were heading home in their car.

"That was amazing." said Regina with Ariel laying on her.

"Hey look it's that horse again." said Pocahontas pointing at it through the window.

"Wow still acting like it's on a sugar high." said Regina.

"That was wonderful singing you two did." said Zinnia while driving the car.

"Does that mean that you two are going to sing out in public more often?" said Tarzan.

"Regina and I loved it and we talked to Sasha and let us work for her." said Kylestone.

"Oh you guys are singers now, good for you." said Tarzan.

"Oh man my baby is a singer now just like his dadda." said Zinnia.

"Hmm hm." laughed Kylestone with his mouth closed blushing.

"Would if Falyby is the one who killed grandfather twenty years ago? I know who did has black hair but she could be wearing a wig or dye her hair." said Ariel.

"Baby we don't know for sure her ever having that mean note doesn't prove that even though it was supposed to be about your grandfather." said Regina.

Later they arrived at their house and got out of the car.

"Dad, grandmother you two feel suspicious about Falyby right?" said Ariel grabbing onto Kylestone and Zinnia's hands.

"Well look it is possible but she might not be so we shouldn't accuse her." said Zinnia.

"It's true baby girl." said Kylestone.

Ariel let go of their hands upsetly because they didn't agree with her.

"Look Ariel we know you're upset that you don't get to see your grandfather." said Zinnia bending down a little having her hands placed on Ariel's shoulders.

"And that you love learning about him but he wouldn't want you to feel so miserable about him being gone." said Kylestone.

"So can you try staying more focused on having fun?" said Zinnia.

But Ariel still felt upset. She pushed her grandmother's hands off her angrily but her dad grabbed her and placed her laying on him while he had his arm around her and the other over her head and his head over her head and closed his eyes.

"Calm down baby, calm down." said Kylestone.

Ariel did start to calm down and gave in to her dad's hug while a tear fell down her eye and then her dad kissed her on the head.

"Let's go inside now." said Kylestone.

So they slithered inside while Kylestone and Ariel slithered inside still in the hugging position. After Kylestone and Ariel entered through the doorway their family were all staring at them, and Regina came up to them, and Kylestone let her take Ariel and hugged her in her arms.

"There there my baby." said Regina.

Later Ariel and her family sat in the living room. Ariel sat on the couch leaning on her mom with her mom's arm around her.

"Oh my sweet baby, remember how your grandfather would want you to feel." said Regina.

Pocahontas came into the living room with a tray of hot chocolate Ariel's grandparents and dad each grabbed a mug.

"Ariel don't you want some hot chocolate?" said Regina.

"Here Ariel." said Kylestone holding out a mug for her.

"Remember Ariel you will see your grandfather when you go where he is in heaven." said Pocahontas rubbing Ariel's shoulder.

Ariel felt more better and grabbed the mug from her dad and he kissed Ariel on the head then her mom kissed her on the head too. Then they started drinking. Ariel finished her's the quickest.

"I'm going to get ready for bed now." said Ariel.

Regina knew she felt a little sad still.

"Do you want me to come with you to comfort you?" said Regina.

"Sure mom." said Ariel.

So Regina went with her to Ariel's room. There Regina helped Ariel a little by putting on her pajamas and watched her put herself to bed. Then Regina sat by her on her bed and rubbed her shoulder.

"Oh you." said Regina smiling at Ariel.

Then she kissed Ariel and left her room. Later Kylestone and Regina were in their room in bed with the blanket over them while they were kissing each other while hugging too. Then they were hugging and snuggling with each other.

"You're so sweet." said Regina while she and Kylestone hugged and snuggled together.

"I love you and I always will." said Kylestone.

"I promise I to do the same with you." said Regina.

Then Kylestone kissed Regina on the head. Then Regina lifted the blanket over them more while she and Kylestone slowly laid down then they fell asleep. The next morning at Chrysalis' house Chrysalis walked up to her great-grandparents.

"Did you call to find a place where to relocate the plants?" said Ard to Sasha.

"Don't worry I did, they found a few places to relocate those plants." said Sasha.

"What plants and why do they need to be relocated?" said Chrysalis.

"The plants from the other new house I bought next to the one I bought earlier." said Sasha.

"You mean the one that's covered up by a bunch of green vines?" said Chrysalis.

"Yep that's the one." said Ard.

"I thought I should buy another place for the same reason as the other big house I bought next to it." said Sasha.

"Is it ready to have people and people/monsters to stay over?" said Chrysalis.

"Not completely and not just because there are a bunch of vines covering such as the backyard including the pool." said Sasha.

"Yeah even the inside of the house is covered with vines." said Ard.

"That's what happens when a house's previous owner was a major plant lover." said Sasha.

"Whoa." said Chrysalis surprised.

"But we loved the plant vines a lot and we didn't want them destroyed to be thrown out to the dump so we're looking for new houses for them." said Sasha.

"What places have been found so far for the vines?" said Chrysalis.

"Greenhouses, plant stores, zoos, other places where plants are kept alive or useful." said Ard.

"Have any of them been removed yet?" said Chrysalis.

"No not until a while?" said Sasha.

"Can I explore it?" said Chrysalis.

"I don't see why not." said Sasha.

"After all the house is still all sturdy." said Ard.

"Thanks." said Chrysalis while leaving.

At Ariel's house in the kitchen.

"Okay I made Ariel's favorite waffles blueberry waffles." said Zinnia.

"I'll check to see if she's awake." said Regina.

Regina slithered upstairs to Ariel's room and knocked on her door. Ariel heard her mom knocking on her door while she was finishing up getting dressed while looking at her dressing mirror.

"Yeah?" said Ariel.

"Ariel are you ready to eat?" said Regina.

"Yeah mom I'm coming out." said Ariel.

Ariel opened the door and went downstairs with her mom to the kitchen.

"Hi Ariel look at what's at the table." said Zinnia.

"Oh wow." said Ariel rushing over to the table.

At Lumia's house in the living room.

"Hey honey breakfast is ready." said Lumia's dad walking into the living room to Lumia's mom.

"Hawn what?" said Dilia.

"Dilia?" said Lumia's mom.

"What are you still doing here?" said Lumia's dad.

"Oh sorry guys I must have suddenly fallen asleep while you guys had me over for dessert and I ended up sleeping when you went to bed and let me hang downstairs awhile longer." said Dilia.

"That's okay Dilia." said Lumia's dad.

"Okay then I'll tell Lumia." said Lumia's mom.

Just then Lumia's mom turned her head and stared directly at a cheetah statue's head while she was exiting the living room.

"Whoa." said Lumia's mom that she accidently fell backwards trying to avoid bumping into it but Lumia's dad caught her.

"Lumia." said Lumia's dad bringing her mom up.

Lumia was the one holding the cheetah statue over her shoulder.

"Sorry mom and dad." said Lumia while eating a strawberry frosting sprinkled donut.

"Lumia no eating sprinkled donuts in the living room they make messes." said Lumia's dad.

"Oh sorry." said Lumia.

"Wow that looks so real I thought you were holding a cheetah." said Dilia.

"Whoa Dilia you're still here." said Lumia.

"Yes I am." said Dilia.

"I got the cheetah statue ready for the movie scene at Sasha's studio that's the closest to here I've been keeping it clean and together." said Lumia.

"Agnesa is excited for the movie to be done not just because she wants to watch it but also because she's allowed to keep the night image for the window when they're done." said Lumia's mom.

"That's fun for her." said Dilia.

Lumia's parents whisper to each other.

"Well Dilia, since you're here do you want to have breakfast with us?" said Lumia's dad.

"Sure thanks." said Dilia.

So they all walked into the dinning room. At Kert, Javada, Zila, Lalo, and Darma's house Kert was sitting on the couch looking at his phone while his sisters were coloring on the floor just then their parents came in.

"Okay kids ready to go out for breakfast?" said Kert, Javada, Zila, Lalo, and Darma's dad.

"Yeah." said Javada, Zila, Lalo, and Darma.

"Sure thing." said Kert.

"Well let's get going." said Kert, Javada, Zila, Lalo, and Darma's mom.

"Yeah, don't want to miss the singing flower bus, oh and by the way on the bus they're playing Ivern's songs all day because they're excited that Ivern's son Kylestone and Regina are now singers like him." said Kert, Javada, Zila, Lalo, and Darma's dad.

So they head for the door. Cherryette and her parents were walking to the bus station too and on their way they heard one of Ivern's songs playing and they looked over at where it was coming from and they saw it was coming from the sing flower bus.

"Sweet." said Cherryette.

"Let's go quicker." said Cherryette's mom.

So they did and made it to the bus and met up with Kert, Javada, Zila, Lalo, Darma, and their parents. Chrysalis was walking to the vine covered house her great-grandma bought. Just then Chrysalis ran into her friends Spencer, Emily, Batie, and other human/ cat monsters just like Spencer, Emily, and Batie but brown who Chrysalis is friends with Jared, his wife Sutton, and less than a year old daughter Gidget who is Jared and Sutton's daughter being held in Sutton's arms.

"Hey guys." said Chrysalis.

"Hey Chrysalis." they said.

"Where are you guys going?" said Chrysalis.

"We're going to go play laser tag at the <u>GLAMOR PAL MALL</u>." said Sutton.

Just then they heard one of Ivern's songs playing and saw the singing flower bus drive by and their friends inside the bus waving while they waved back outside.

"Fun." said Chrysalis.

"But first we have to drop off Batie and Gidget to Rowshella and her parents." said Emily.

"Yep you can't bring a baby into laser tag." said Spencer.

"But we are going to come back for them right after and go back to the mall because we want to spend more time there with them." said Jared.

"Oh okay well have fun." said Chrysalis.

"By the way where are you going?" said Emily.

"I'm going to go check out the big house my great-grandma bought that's covered in vines." said Chrysalis.

"Oh Sutton and Gidget and I were in that house when your great-grandma and great-grandpa were looking around it." said Jared.

"Oh wow well, see you guys later." said Chrysalis.

So they left to go where they said they were going. At Ariel's house Ariel was sitting on the couch with her mom Regina while Regina hugged Ariel while Regina snuggled behind Ariel's neck and back.

"Excited for eating at the <u>DANCEFLOOR RESTAURANT</u> and then go to the new <u>FASHION BALL MALL</u> later?" said Regina to Ariel.

"Yeah." said Ariel, but not smiling.

"What's wrong Ariel?" said Regina.

"Nothing." said Ariel.

"You seem so sad about something, did you do something?" said Regina.

Ariel was still thinking about the lady who killed her grandfather and was feeling guilty about if she accused Falyby for nothing.

"No it's just, well I, about Falyby-." said Ariel.

"You're not still accusing her are you?" said Regina.

"No but I feel bad if I've been wrong to blame her." said Ariel.

"Just don't blame her for something unless you know for sure." said Regina.

"Okay." said Ariel.

Regina kissed Ariel on the head. Kylestone was in another living room looking at a picture frame with a photo of his father Ivern in it. While he was looking his mother Zinnia came over to him.

"It's so sweet you and Regina are singing now, by the way you're going to be needing this" said Zinnia, holding out a microphone.

"Father's mic." said Kylestone looking at it.

"Uh-huh, finally it can stop collecting dust." said Zinnia.

Kylestone stared at the mic looking back when his father Ivern used it to sing his sang out loud pleasing the crowd like crazy while Kylestone when he was a kid was being held by his mother in the V.I.P section while they both loved his performance too Kylestone loved it a lot that he was laughing. Then Kylestone was done thinking about it when his mother shaked him.

"Baby boy are you okay you freezed for a while looking sad." said Zinnia.

"Sorry I was just looking back when he used it." said Kylestone.

"Oh I understand." said Zinnia.

Then Kylestone hugged the mic and Zinnia hugged him and then Kylestone snuggled against her. Just then Kylestone looked back at the time he last saw his father before he died.

In Kylestone's flashback it was taking place at night Ivern was sitting on the couch watching TV with eleven year old Kylestone laying on him watching TV with him with his father's arm over Kylestone just then Zinnia slithered into the living room.

"Oh, you guys are watching that." said Zinnia twenty years ago looking at the TV showing one of Ivern's music videos.

"Once again you made another great music video and song father." said eleven year old Kylestone.

"Thanks Kylestone." said Ivern twenty years ago when he was alive.

"Mother, have you ever taken a singing class or dance class?" said eleven year old Kylestone.

"Well no I was more of a person/monster who does arts and crafts but I've always loved music and dancing." said Zinnia twenty years ago.

"And your mother is a very great jeweler haven't seen anyone who has made better jewelry than the best ones she had made." said Ivern twenty years ago when he was alive holding Zinnia twenty years ago's hand.

Then Zinnia twenty years ago and Ivern when he was alive kissed each other. Then Zinnia twenty years ago kissed eleven year old Kylestone and rubbed her hand on his face then Ivern twenty years ago when Ivern was alive kissed eleven year old Kylestone too then eleven year old Kylestone hugged his father Ivern twenty years ago when Ivern was alive.

"Aw, I've been sitting long enough I'm going to go for a slither outside." said Ivern twenty years ago when he was alive getting up.

"Okay honey." said Zinnia twenty years ago.

Then eleven year old Kylestone got off the couch too and hugged Zinnia twenty years ago.

"Oh." said Zinnia twenty years ago surprisingly being hugged by eleven year old Kylestone.

"Aw sweet baby of ours he is." said Ivern twenty years ago when he was alive, with the door opened.

"A treasure he is." said Zinnia twenty years ago.

Then Ivern twenty years ago, when he was alive, went out the door and closed it. Kylestone stopped his flashback then started feeling like he was about to cry a little. Then he thought of another flashback.

In Kylestone's other flashback that happened later on after he last saw his father alive, eleven year old Kylestone was playing in the living room on a balance beam then Zinnia twenty years ago came in.

"Aw you're doing good are you sure you don't want to take gymnastics?" said Zinnia twenty years ago.

"No thanks mother I'm more of a singing and dancing person/monster." said Kylestone eleven years old.

"Okay my baby." said Zinnia twenty years ago.

"Did father come back from his walk?" said Kylestone eleven years old.

"No not yet, aw you know seeing you keeping your balance on that balance beam it keeps reminding me when you were a baby and you were taking your slithering standing up more instead of down like crawling, because you were going over to your dadda singing because you loved hearing the song he was singing." said Zinnia twenty years ago touching eleven year old Kylestone's cheek and grabbing on to him so he doesn't fall off the balance beam.

"It made father come up with a song for younger kids that he sold to a show for younger kids." said Kylestone eleven years old.

"Uh-huh." said Zinnia twenty years ago.

Then Zinnia twenty years ago kissed eleven year old Kylestone on the head. While she was kissing him they heard the doorbell (which makes a splashing wave sound).

"That can't be father." said Kylestone eleven years old.

"No he wouldn't be ringing the doorbell from his walk." said Zinnia twenty years ago.

"Can you lift me off mother?" said Kylestone eleven years old.

Zinnia twenty years ago did lift him off the balance beam and they both went to the door. When they got there Zinnia twenty years ago opened the door while eleven years old Kylestone put his arms around his mother and behind the door there were three police officers standing out crying and trying to keep it together.

"Zi- Zi- Zinnia we know." said an officer trying to hold back his tears.

"Yes what is it?" said Zinnia twenty years ago.

152

"We are so sorry and so- upset." said the second officer trying to hold back his tears.

"What is it?" said Kylestone eleven years old.

"Yeah what's wrong?" said Zinnia twenty years ago.

"We're sorry but Ivern your son's dad is dead." said the third officer who cried crazy right after he told them.

"What, no." said Zinnia twenty years ago shocked with sadness.

"No mother, no it can't, father he." said Kylestone eleven years old.

"We're so sorry there was a lady he ran into who was mad at him and pushed him into the street and accidentally in front of a moving car that went over him, the lady who was driving the car saw the whole thing such as that lady's expression who pushed him after she did that." said the second officer.

"He's over there on that stretcher under that tarp." said the third officer pointing at the stretcher with the blue tarp over it.

"Oh man I'm so going to get a lot of tissues after this." said the first officer before him and the other officers started crying out loud.

Just then they heard and saw a clown themed truck driving by playing a sad song.

"Yep that clown truck found out about Ivern's death too so now it's playing sad songs instead of happy ones." said the second officer.

Zinnia twenty years ago was about to cry but then eleven year old Kylestone got all upset and quickly slithered to his room crying.

"Kylestone, I have to go to him." said Zinnia twenty years ago.

Eleven year old Kylestone quickly slithered into his room and slammed the door shut and went into his bed crying into his blanket.

"Kylestone baby boy please let me come in don't you think you want your momma with you." said Zinnia twenty years ago behind the door to eleven years old Kylestone's room.

"Sm-sm-ye-sm." said Kylestone eleven years old trying to talk while crying.

"I can tell you're saying yes." said Zinnia twenty years ago behind the door to eleven years old Kylestone's room.

So Zinnia twenty years ago opened the door to eleven year old Kylestone's room and sat next to him on his bed.

"Baby boy." said Zinnia twenty years ago touching his face.

"Father's dead, sm-I don't want to go on without him." said Kylestone eleven years old crying.

"I know me too but look momma's with you." said Zinnia twenty years ago.

Eleven year old Kylestone still kept crying but put his hand on his mother's hand that she's touching his face with.

"Now, I'm not going to let you out of my arms until you're done crying. I'll even be carrying you around." said Zinnia twenty years ago covering eleven year old Kylestone in her arms while he cried.

Eleven year old Kylestone gave in being in his mother's arms but still cried.

"Now I want you to say momma is here for you." said Zinnia twenty years ago.

"Mother is here for me." said eleven year old Kylestone while tears kept falling from him.

"Good." said Zinnia twenty years ago.

Then she kissed him on the head.

"Mother is here for me, mother is here for me." said eleven year old Kylestone.

Then Kylestone's flashback stopped and was still doing the same thing with his mother before his flashbacks.

"Mother is here for me." said Kylestone out loud quietly.

"What?" said Zinnia who surprisingly heard him.

"Oh I-." said Kylestone with a tear coming down from him while getting out of his mother's arm.

"Is that a tear? You were thinking when you found out your dadda died didn't you? Now I just remembered what you said was something I told you to say when I was comforting you." said Zinnia.

Kylestone slowly put the mic down sadly and then turned to his mother Zinnia.

"Yes, I was." said Kylestone.

"You really look like you were feeling the motion and momma is going to comfort you again." said Zinnia coming over to Kylestone with her arms opened.

"No mother, thank you but no you don't have to." said Kylestone stopping her.

"But why not?" said Zinnia.

"I'm not going to sob as much as I did when I found out he was gone it's just the one tear." said Kylestone.

"Okay baby." said Zinnia.

Ariel was coming into the room.

"Dad grandmother, I heard what you guys were saying and it did make me sad, can you-?" said Ariel while Zinnia and Kylestone went up to her.

"Oh, come here baby." said Kylestone putting his arms around Ariel.

Zinnia rubbed Ariel's back and kissed her on the head.

"You know what I'm in the mood for a smoothie. You want to help me make some for us?" said Kylestone grabbing onto Ariel's hands and holding them out.

"Sure dad." said Ariel.

So they left to go to the kitchen. Chrysalis already arrived at the big house covered in vines. It was true what was said about it, it really was covered in vines. Chrysalis went to the back of the house and saw that the pool, the big porch that even the pool is built into the porch floor, and the giant trellises that goes around the porch were all covered in vines.

"Wow, yep this guy was a major plant lover." said Chrysalis.

Chrysalis went inside where there were more vines on the walls, the stairway, inside doors (that are all wide open), and there was a big hole through the upstairs floor where a bunch of vines were coming through. Chrysalis liked the house then she put on her new bright light music lover bracelet on and setted up her phone to play the rhythm she wanted and started singing while moving around admiring the place. Then she stopped her phone and took off her bracelet and put them in her pocket again and went upstairs where there were more vines up there.

"Knew it was going to look like this upstairs." said Chrysalis.

Chrysalis explored the upstairs then she saw a red lipstick tube on the ground. Chrysalis picked it up and wondered who left that. At Ariel's house Ariel and her dad were making smoothies and they were both chopping fruit.

"Excited about checking out the <u>FASHION BALL MALL</u> and where we're going to eat dinner at?" said Kylestone to Ariel.

"Yeah." said Ariel.

Regina came up to them.

"Aw, Ariel, you look like you're having fun and good also because you said you were feeling bad about accusing Falyby yesterday." said Regina.

"That's good Ariel." said Kylestone.

Kylestone put down his knife and wrapped his arms around Ariel's arms and laid his head on her. Meanwhile, Chrysalis was walking from the vine covered house holding the lipstick tube she found.

"Hey Chrysalis we were told you went to the big house covered in vines." said Fern with Chet and Tafelena in her arms having their pictures taken by a bunch of photographers whose cameras are not on flash because of a baby present.

Fern and Chet came up to Chrysalis with Tafelena in Fern's arms and the photographers following them taking pictures.

"Yeah and I want to go ask my great-grandparents if anyone else besides them and Jared, Sutton, and Gidget have gone into that house before me because I found this lipstick tube in there." said Chrysalis, holding out the lipstick tube.

"Huh it could be Sutton's she doesn't wear lipstick but she does put it on when she kisses autograph pictures of herself." said Fern.

"Yeah that could be it." said Chet.

"Well I'll find out." said Chrysalis.

Just then Dayla came over walking backwards spraying perfume in front of her but not at her.

"Dayla what are you doing?" said Chrysalis.

"I accidentally spilled a bottle of perfume on me because the lid wasn't on tight enough at the beauty shop that's the closest to here and a bunch of fans loved the family song I sang with my parents and now they're following me around and easily finding me because of the perfume scent on me so I'm using this different perfume to cover my tracks." said Dayla.

"That explains the strong perfume scene." said Chet.

"And why your clothes are wet too." said Chrysalis.

"Which is why I'm on my way home to change my clothes and get this scent off. Well see you guys." said Dayla.

"See you Dayla." they all said.

At one of Sasha's studios where Chrysalis' great-grandparents are watching a movie being made.

"Okay is the set all set up?" said Pennya, Mabel, and Cassandra's mom.

"Okay we're all set." said Agnesa's mom.

Just then they heard a big explosion in the hallway. Cleo and Falla came walking out of the hallway covered in glitter and coughing.

"Sorry I accidentally set some of the glitter bombs while walking in the hallway, but don't worry there's still enough for the movie." said Cleo.

Chrysalis walked out of the hall where Cleo and Falla walked out of but Chrysalis only had a tiny speck of glitter by her head in her hair.

"Glad I was not that close to you guys." said Chrysalis.

Chrysalis walked up to her great-grandparents.

"Hey great-grandma, great-grandpa." said Chrysalis.

"Chrysalis you got a little of glitter there." said Sasha, pointing on her own head where it is on Chrysalis' head.

"Oh." said Chrysalis clawing it off.

After the glitter came off.

"Has anyone else been in that vine covered house before me beside you guys and Jared, Gidget, and Sutton?" said Chrysalis.

"I like to call it the jungle vine house." said Agnesa.

"No not that I know of." said Sasha to Chrysalis.

"Why's that?" said Ard to Chrysalis.

"I found this lipstick tube in the house and I am trying to find who it belongs to." said Chrysalis showing it after taking it out of her pocket.

"Oh." said Ard.

Chrysalis saw Rowshella holding Calivs' hand and Rowshella's parents at the studio.

"Hey guys did Spencer, Emily, Jared, and Sutton pick up Gidget and Batie?" Chrysalis said to them.

"Yeah they did." said Rowshella's mom.

"Oh so they must be at the mall now not playing laser tag thanks." said Chrysalis leaving to go there.

Just then Chrysalis almost ran into Ariel and her family entering the room.

"Whoa, sorry Ariel." said Chrysalis.

"It's okay Chrysalis are you leaving?" said Ariel.

"Yeah I'm going back to the GLAMOR PAL MALL." said Chrysalis.

"Oh." said Ariel.

"Do you want to come with me?" said Chrysalis.

"Sure." said Ariel.

Ariel looked at her parents.

"Can I go with Chrysalis?" Ariel said to her parents.

Ariel's parents agreed.

"Sure." said Regina.

"Thanks." said Ariel.

"Hey you guys." said Jaser's mom, talking through an open window of one of the sets for the movie being made.

"Whoa, mom." said Jaser, who was standing by her on the side where her head was popping out surprised.

"Sorry Jaser." said Jaser's mom.

Chrysalis and Ariel both laughed a little quietly.

"You know because of you guys now being singers loads of people and people/monsters have been asking me when will you guys sing again they say it feels like Ivern's back because someone who shares his DNA is now singing to crowds." said Sasha to Ariel's parents.

Regina and Kylestone both laughed a little quietly.

"Hey Sasha." said Ariel.

"Yeah what is it?" said Sasha.

"Well I- I- feel glad that it happened." said Ariel.

"You wanted to sing in front of me but you started to feel too nervous to do it." said Sasha.

"Yeah, that's exactly it and sorry." said Ariel.

"It's okay even though you don't work for me or sing in front of me. I like having you as a friend." said Sasha.

"Thanks." said Ariel.

"Let's go." said Chrysalis.

Then Ariel and Chrysalis left the studio to go to the GLAMOR PAL MALL. At the HANGING STARS SPOT Hailey was walking down the hall and saw Geena (who is a human/mouse monster who is white, is her normal human height, half of her face is green on the left but not her left ear, regular human teeth, and regular human eyes) going into a room with the lights off and having her flashlight on going in there.

"Again you're using your flashlight who is scared of the dark especially this much?" said Hailey to Geena.

"Hey I can still be scary." said Geena.

"Tell me when." said Hailey walking away not believing it would happen.

"I'll show her how me owning a flashlight will be scary, I have it built." said Geena looking at her flashlight up to her face.

Chrysalis and Ariel arrived at the <u>GLAMOR PAL MALL</u> and were already inside. Chrysalis and Ariel arrived at a candy store in the mall half of it was under the sea theme while the other half wasn't and in there they saw Jared, Sutton, Gidget (in Sutton's arms), Emily (with Batie in her arms), Spencer, and Batie.

"Hey guys." said Chrysalis.

"Hi." said Ariel.

"Hi." said Jared, Emily, Spencer, and Sutton.

"I know this isn't your first time in this mall." said Jared to Ariel.

"Yeah and I believe you guys know about the fashion show at this I attend but I haven't been in this candy store before. Does it alway have the half of this store under the sea theme?" said Ariel.

"Yep." said Emily.

"Hey Sutton, is this your lipstick tube from the house cover vines?" said Chrysalis showing the lipstick to her.

"Oh yes thanks I was wondering where that was." said Sutton.

Chrysalis handed Sutton the lipstick tube.

"That guy sure did love vines and plants." said Spencer.

Ariel went looking around the candy store and admired the clear glass colorful candy lollipops shaped like fish. Ariel picked one up and then Sutton holding Gidget came up to her.

"Fun lollipops those are, Gidget likes it when we do this with them." said Sutton.

Sutton grabbed a fish shaped lollipop and moved it up and down staring at Gidget like it was swimming to her while Sutton made fish faces at her that made Gidget laugh.

"Aw, so cute." said Ariel looking at it happening.

Just the Chrysalis' friends and family came into the candy store too.

"Hey guys." said Walter while everyone else waved.

"Hi." said Chrysalis and Ariel and the others.

Lalo was sucking a fake lollipop.

"Lalo no sucking on that that's not even a real lollipop." said Kert, Javada, Zila, Lalo, and Darma's, dad grabbing her.

"But it looks so pretty." said Lalo, while being held up.

"No." said Kert, Javada, Zila, Lalo, and Darma's dad.

Belyndica, Fredricka, Agnesa, Bemma, Loua, Dava, and Kiri were going crazy and quickly through the candies.

"Girls what are you doing?" said Loua, Dava, and Bemma's dad, with Loua, Dava, and Bemma's mom next to him.

"Well mom and dad we're looking for the candies here shaped like bugs." said Dava.

"Yeah I will be like eating bugs but less odd." said Fredricka.

"Just don't make a mess." said Loua, Dava, and Bemma's mom.

"I don't care if it's real bugs they eat either way, I've actually seen some people eat bugs." said Sutton.

"On accident?" said Mirabel.

"Nope." said Sutton.

Just then Joyce came over to the candy store on a topless pink six pole sedan chair.

"Hey everyone, sorry I'm late they were doing a commercial with me in it riding this sedan chair and told me if I was running late they would bring me here on this thing." said Joyce, getting off the sedan chair.

"Wow Joyce that's a cool entrance." said Dilia.

"And pretty." said Whittneya.

"Thanks for bringing me here." said Joyce to the people that carried her on the sedan chair.

"No problem bringing over a teenager on this sedan chair." said a guy who carried Joyce on the sedan chair.

"Why does everyone keep saying I'm a teenager?" said Joyce, after the people who carried her on the sedan chair left.

"I know how you feel Joyce." said Hermalody, touching her on the shoulder.

"Hey I found a bug shaped lollipop." said Kiri, holding up the bug shaped lollipop shaped as a centipede.

"Oh, a, huh that's unusual." said Princeson, feeling weird about the lollipop in Kiri's hand.

Fredricka and Agnesa were looking in one of the candy holders and accidentally made a chocolate shaped car fall on the ground.

"Hey, be careful with the chocolates." said Cherryette after picking it up off the ground standing on her knees.

"Ha ha again Cherryette take it easy with chocolate." said Fern laughing a little while holding Tafelena by Cherryette.

"I'm going to pay for it now." said Kiri.

"Um you might want to continue looking around the store Kiri." said Swifta.

Kiri looked at the line to the cashier and saw it was long.

"That line over there looks pretty full." said Zazannie pointing at it.

Chrysalis and her family and friends continued looking at the candies. Bemma, Dava, Loua, Fredricka, and Belyndica each found a bug shaped lollipop.

"Hey I found another bug shaped lollipop, oh what this is tick shaped lollipop but it's good enough for me." said Agnesa holding up a tick shaped lollipop.

"Yeah I would prefer the bug shaped ones." said Kert feeling odd near Agnesa's lollipop.

"Hey no line." said Fredricka pointing at the cash out.

So Agnesa, Belyndica, Loua, Dava, Bemma, Kiri, and Fredricka went to go buy their lollipops.

"You know Calvis your parents are fun." said Rowshella's dad.

"I can believe that now." said Calvis.

"So Texia you had a meeting with all of your construction workers and none of them admit that they were hanging out in the HANGING STARS SPOT after it was done?" said Lamoria.

"Yep but I gave them all a warning." said Texia.

"Attention mall guests the family and friends singing stage at the HALF SEA CANDY STORE will be starting in five minutes." said a lady through the P.A. system.

"Oho glad we bought our lollipops in time." Loua.

"Come on let's go." said Zila pulling her dad's arm.

"Yeah Zila, Javada, Darma and I had been looking forward to us singing to everyone." said Lalo putting her mom's arm.

"Don't worry girls we've been looking forward to you girls singing." said Kert, Javada, Zila, Lalo, and Darma's mom.

"Ah man Kert this is going to be the first time seeing two of your sisters sing." said Sleck while they walked to the room where the stage is.

"Yep." said Kert.

They all arrived at the stage in the candy store Javada, Zila, Lalo, and Darma both went up with microphones and set up what instruments they wanted to be played to their singing on their dad's phone they were about to sing but stopped from being nervous and stood quiet for a few seconds.

"Uh oh looks like they got butterflies in their stomachs." whispered Sleck's dad.

"I think we should get them down." said Kert, Javada, Zila, Lalo, and Darma's mom.

"Hold on a minute." said Chrysalis who had an idea.

Chrysalis started to singing everyone was looking at her then Chrysalis got on stage with Javada, Zila, Lalo, Darma and tried to make it look fun to them and it work they started singing along too the Chrysalis had them sing by themselves but they wanted Chrysalis to sing along too so she did and everyone was loving it. Carlica, Veza, and Vargoe came to see what was happening and saw them on stage having a great time making everyone love their singing and it made Carlica, Vargoe, and Veza jealous of Chrysalis' singing. Finally they stop.

"Uh unbelievable, why is Chrysalis Loom such an amazing singer." said Carlica.

"Tell me about it." said Veza.

"So unbelievable." said Vargoe.

So Carlica, Vargoe, and Veza left angrily.

"Hey guys I saw Carlica, Veza, and Vargoe here that heard Chrysalis singing and they were jealous." said Jaya.

"Whoa I didn't want them to be like that." said Chrysalis.

"I heard it too when I was going over to see if they are setting up the milkshakes, by the way they are." said Swifta, who just stopped running over.

"Oh man yes." said Chrysalis.

"Come on guys, on me." said Butterscotch's dad.

"Yeah." they all said.

So they all went to the part of the candy store where the milkshakes were happening.

"And here's one for you." said a lady handing a vanilla milkshake to Blinda.

"Thank you." said Blinda.

"This is so good." said Ariel, after sipping some of her vanilla milkshake.

"Yep, the farmer is very good at running her farm where this candy store got the milk from." said Chrysalis, while drinking her vanilla milkshake.

"Do you know the farmer?" said Ariel to Chrysalis.

"Yeah, and she's over there." said Chrysalis, pointing at the lady behind the counter helping serve the milkshakes and smiling at Ariel.

"Where is the farmer?" said Ariel, looking at the same lady.

"You're looking at her." said Chrysalis, still pointing.

"That's me." said the lady who Chrysalis was pointing to.

"You're the farmer." said Ariel.

"Yeah I'm Noodle." said the lady Chrysalis was pointing at.

"Oh." said Ariel.

"What you think because I don't dress like I own a farm I'm not a farmer?" said Noodle.

"Well, yeah I can clearly tell those are designer clothes you're wearing." said Ariel.

"Yeah they do look expensive but still I am a farmer." said Noodle.

"Her farm is the farm where we saw that crazy running horse." said Chrysalis.

"Yeah that horse is crazy because of how it has been eating, it's why we have it have it's own pen." said Noodle.

"Whoa." said Ariel.

"Her farm isn't just huge but she has a lot of workers who work for her there." said Chrysalis.

"Yeah, but still I help out there." said Noodle.

"Sometimes my parents help out there too." said Dakota.

"It's true." said Dakota's mom.

"Great farm it is." said Dakota's dad.

"Oh nice." said Ariel.

"Hey Ariel do you and your family want to see Noodle's farm?" said Walter.

"You guys should it's a really fun farm." said Jaser's mom.

"And even if you work there you're very much not going to get dirty." said Beatrix's dad.

"Are we able to keep ourselves away from the horses the whole time?" said Zinnia.

"Sure same thing with all the animals." said Noodle.

"Okay I'm in." said Zinnia.

"You don't like horses?" said Swifta.

"No I just don't want to be near them. A horse once sneezed on me when I was a kid." said Zinnia.

"Eww." said Tarson.

"If a horse did that to me I would feel the same." said Natasha.

"Hey Noodle is it okay if my family and I bring Ariel, Kylestone, Regina, Pocahontas, Tarzan, and Zinnia to see your farm for the first time?" said Elsa.

"Sure you guys are always welcomed. I'll also come with you guys too." said Noodle.

"So you guys want to come?" said Nessia to Ariel and Ariel's family.

Ariel and her family all agreed to come.

"Okay we'll go when we're ready to leave the candy shop in the mall." said Tarson.

They all agreed. Later Chrysalis and her family were on their way to Noodle's farm with Ariel and her family in their car.

"Well this is the biggest car I have been in." said Tarzan.

"Of course it's big when you have ten girls." said Marleen.

"And want to fit the whole family and extras." said Tarson.

"You know my dad had ten older siblings and my mom had twelve older siblings." said Sasha.

"Whoa big family." said Ariel.

"It feels strange comparing that to being an only child." said Regina.

"I feel that same way." said Kylestone.

"I'm pretty sure they would have felt the same thing with you guys only the other way around." said Sasha.

"If you guys want we have a blanket drawer." said Zadie.

"You guys do where?" said Ariel.

"It's by where you're sitting." Tiana said to Ariel.

Ariel saw the slot and opened it and there were blankets in there. Ariel got out a blanket with jungle leaf patterns on it.

"Oh my gosh it's so soft." said Ariel snuggling in it.

"Yeah it's made from silk. We got that one from our trip to China." said Chrysalis.

"Wow, feel it." said Ariel holding it out for her family to touch.

"Careful Ariel blanket on me makes me feel sleepy." said Pocahontas touching the blanket but trying not to have too much of it on her.

"Hey what's this doing in here?" said Ariel holding out a bullhorn speaker she grabbed from the drawer of blankets.

"Oh there's my bull horn speaker thanks." said Gege.

Ariel handed the bullhorn speaker back to Gege. At Noodle's farm Noodle already arrived and was looking out for Chrysalis and her family and Ariel and her family to arrive. Finally they did and they got out of the car.

"Hey guys." said Noodle.

"Hi Noodle." they all said.

They then looked at the crazy horse because they were hearing the crazy horse by them still running crazy by the fence.

"Does that horse ever stop?" said Kylestone.

"Not often, the pigs sometimes go crazy like that too." said Noodle.

"The pigs?" said Pocahontas.

"Yeah I'll show you, oh and stay five feet away from them." said Noodle.

So they followed Noodle and they saw she was right about the pigs and they were splashing mud so no wonder why Noodle said stay five feet away from them.

"Whoa that is crazy." said Ariel.

"Careful if you don't want mud on you but don't worry these guys are only like this when they are hungry." said Noodle.

Noodle grabbed some pig food and quickly gave them some. She did get a little bit of mud on her but she didn't care. Ariel looked over and saw words over a doorway into a barn that said: CRAZY FREAK CENTRAL (BUT NOT SCARY HONEST). Noodle saw what Ariel was looking at.

"Oh you're looking at my barn name for one of my barns, I like to name my property somethings." said Noodle.

"So it's not scary but why is it crazy and freaky?" said Ariel.

"Some of the animals in there are odd looking and do weird things, come with me." said Noodle.

So they all followed Noodle into the barn inside where there were animals and workers helping out with the animals.

"Whoa." said Ariel surprised when she saw the cow.

"Careful around that cow." said Noodle.

"Is it crazy too?" said Ariel.

"No its blind." said Noodle.

"Whoa." said Regina looking at the cow and walking over to it.

What Regina was looking at next and came to was a three tailed lizard in a terrarium in the barn. Everyone else came over to it too.

"Is that an actual three tailed lizard?" said Kylestone.

"Yeah and lucky we got one they are extremely rare." said Noodle.

"Whoa I didn't expect this." said Ariel.

Just then they heard horses coming into the barn.

"Oh the horses." said Ariel.

"Oh whoa." said Zinnia.

"Don't worry Zinnia you're at an okay location if any of them sneeze." said Noodle.

"Well that's good." said Zinnia.

Everyone else went to the horse to pet them.

"Copy what I do petting them." said Noodle demonstrating.

So they all did the same thing. Just then Pocahontas notice that the horse she is petting is wearing an eye patch.

"Hey this horse is wearing an eye patch." said Pocahontas.

"Yeah it only has one eye." said Noodle.

"Whoa." said Pocahontas surprised.

"And check out over here in this room." said Noodle walking over to a door.

Everyone followed her and Noodle opened the door and inside was a big room with a big terrarium of cobras where workers were feeding them.

"Wow you got more cobras to place in here." said Chrysalis.

"Yep these cobras also have their venom removed to make it safer." said Noodle.

"You have cobra snakes here just for fun just like that three tailed lizard?" said Ariel.

"No we have the cobras here to milk them." said Noodle.

"But snakes don't make milk unless you're a mutant snake like I am for your baby that is." said Regina putting her arms around Ariel.

"Okay mom you don't need to bring that way of having attention to me." said Ariel getting out of her mom's arms.

"True but we don't milk them for milk we milk them for their blood." said Noodle.

"Did you just say blood?" said Kylestone feeling odd about what Noodle said.

"You look weird out just like how the boys got when they found out about what Noodle said." said Chrysalis.

"Yeah I believe that." said Kylestone still feeling odd.

"If you guys want I have a gallon of snake blood in my hou-." said Noodle before being interrupted by Ariel and her family.

"No no." said Ariel and her family.

"If you guys are worried about there being venom in it I promise you we have their venom removed before we blood milk them for their blood and we do a positive check right after they have been de-venom." said Noodle.

"I think we're still good." said Kylestone.

"Snake blood is actually healthy." said Chrysalis.

"Are you guys vegetarians or vegans?" said Noodle to Ariel and her family.

"No." Ariel and her family said.

"So you guys eat something that comes from an animal well why not this?" said Noodle.

"It just feels too different okay." said Tarzan.

"Suit yourselves by the way there was a lady who came to a store where I sell my snake blood to and she destroyed a whole set of it." said Noodle.

"Whoa really what did she look like?" said Ariel.

"No one was exactly positive she was wearing a big hat that covered most of her head." said Natasha.

"And she was wearing gloves to hide her fingerprints." said Chrysalis.

"Odd." said Ariel.

"Here's another area for you guys to see, follow me." said Noodle.

They Noodle outside to what looked like a terrarium for people to go into.

"That really was a crazy freaky barn." said Ariel.

"Sure was baby." said Regina.

They all entered the terrarium but instead of butterflies they saw ladybugs.

"Ladybugs." said Ariel.

"Yeah they come in handy on the farm to get rid of bugs." said Noodle.

"Oh okay." said Ariel.

"How did you end up owning this farm?" said Pocahontas to Noodle.

"My parents got it for me for my birthday ten years ago." said Noodle.

Ariel had her finger out for the ladybug to crawl on her just then a ladybug flew and landed on her cheek. Ariel felt startled a little. Chrysalis came walking up to her and saw the ladybug on Ariel.

"There's a ladybug on me isn't there?" said Ariel.

"Yeah cool." said Chrysalis.

"Oho, hey Chrysalis can you move? I want to take a picture of Ariel and the ladybug." said Regina holding out her phone to take Ariel and the ladybug's picture.

Chrysalis moved and Regina took Ariel's picture with the ladybug on Ariel's face.

"Wow, a ladybug has never landed on my face before." said Tinka who popped out of the bushes between Regina and Ariel.

"Whoa!" said Ariel and Regina being scared by Tinka popping out.

Zinnia was slithering into a plastic pebbles path that looked like plants were covering it from above just then Zinnia fell over from slithering into Dannya who was hiding in the plants on the path, and Zinnia landed on her and Dannya landed on some plants.

"Ow." said Dannya.

Dannya lifted her head up and saw who was on her.

"Oh hey Zinnia." said Dannya who was actually smiling with delight.

"Dannya, Tinka." said Chrysalis after everyone in the terrarium had now standed up.

"Hey." both Dannya and Tinka said.

"What's going on here?" said Dannya and Tinka's dad coming out of an area of the ladybug terrarium with Dannya and Tinka's mom.

"Is everything okay?" said Dannya and Tinka's mom.

"We're fine." said Dannya.

"You okay Zinnia?" said Regina, going over to her.

"I'm fine heck I even landed on Dannya." said Zinnia.

"Oho a ladybug." said Mirabel, slamming herself into the glass wall of the outside of the terrarium by Zinnia and Regina.

"Whoa." said both Zinnia and Regina.

"Mirabel loves ladybugs a lot." said Chrysalis.

"Oh." said Navia, slamming into the glass wall of the outside terrarium too by Regina and Zinnia.

"Whoa." said both Regina and Zinnia.

"But Navia doesn't do that because she loves ladybugs." said Chrysalis.

"Ow, it's because I tripped." said Navia.

"You okay Navia?" said Navia's mom with Navia's dad.

"Don't worry mom and dad and everyone else I'm fine." said Navia, getting up.

"The nine of us carpooled." said Princeson, coming up with his parents.

Princeson then kissed Navia on the cheek where she hitted herself on the glass wall.

"Knew our son found a match." said Princeson's dad to Princeson's mom.

"Uh-huh." said Princeson's mom.

The nine of them who came into the ladybug terrarium then were Navia, Mirabel, Princeson, Navia's parents, Princeson's parents, and Mirabel's parents.

"Oh wow I love ladybugs." said Mirabel.

"Wow she seems like she loves ladybugs as much as Cherryette loves chocolate." said Ariel.

"You know guys earlier gave Texia some advice about her keeping an eye on her construction workers since they seem to be the ones who were hanging out in HANGING STARS SPOT unexpectedly." said Mirabel.

"Really what did you tell her?" said Chrysalis.

"To look out for trails." said Mirabel.

Mirabel started grabbing a magnifying glass out of her pocket.

"So look for clues." said Mirabel after grabbing out her magnifying glass and placing it over her eye.

Mirabel bent down looking through it to the floor and while walking.

"Uh, what are you trying to find here?" said Princeson to Mirabel.

"Nothing I just really want to use this magnifying glass." said Mirabel.

"If you guys think detective stuff with her is weird one of Texia's construction workers keeps detective movies locked up in a safe." said Noodle.

"Oh whoa." said Regina finding that strange.

Ariel and the rest of her family thought it was strange too. Later Ariel and her family were hanging out at Chrysalis and her family's house. Chrysalis and Ariel were both hanging out with each other on the big balcony on one of the floors of Chrysalis and her family's house that has big tree branches partly above it you can sit on them. The two of them were talking and laughing while sitting on the wooden bench at the edge.

"I'm so glad to have come here." said Ariel.

"I'm glad you came here too. So excited about the **DANCEFLOOR RESTAURANT** and going to the new **FASHION BALL MALL** after we have dinner." said Chrysalis.

"Yeah, you know Chrysalis you're an amazing friend who I'm close with, and my first one." said Ariel.

"Aw thanks Ariel you're the same thing to me except for being my first one that is." said Chrysalis.

Chrysalis and Ariel hugged each other, after they let go Ariel got the courage to do something.

"You know Chrysalis." said Ariel, getting up.

"What?" said Chrysalis.

"I don't want to do this in front of others but my family but I will in front of you." said Ariel.

"Are you going to sing?" said Chrysalis.

"Yes." said Ariel, feeling nervous but still going to do it.

Ariel got out her bracelet that Chrysalis gave her and took a deep breath before putting it on and set up her phone to play the instruments she wanted. Ariel started singing and still felt kind of nervous because she was singing clearly but her bracelet didn't light up. Chrysalis was smiling liking it and it made Ariel sing louder and with more joy and then her being nervous went away and her bracelet did light up this time lights of yellow, white, and fuschia in exploding sparkle works very close to each other. Kylestone and Regina were slithering close enough that they could hear Ariel singing and went to her by following her voice and saw her doing it. Finally Ariel stopped and Chrysalis adored the whole thing.

"Wow awesome I knew you had a good singing voice." said Chrysalis.

"We told her that too." said Regina after she and Kylestone entered outside.

Regina and Kylestone came up to Ariel and they gave her a hug.

"Mom dad, even though I was willing to sing in front of Chrysalis and I know she liked it still I don't think I can do it in front of Sasha or a crowd." said Ariel.

"It's okay baby girl we understand." said Regina, rubbing Ariel's back while hugging her.

"Are you girls ready to go eat?" said Kylestone.

"Yeah, are we leaving now?" said Chrysalis.

"Yeah it's why we came up here and to see our baby." said Regina.

"Well then let's go." said Chrysalis.

So off they went to the restaurant and everyone arrived there.

"Wow this is so cool." said Ariel.

"Hey guys." said Fawn.

"Hi Fawn." said Chrysalis and Ariel and their families.

"Hey guys ready to go into the <u>DANCEFLOOR RESTAURANT</u>?" said Fawn.

"Sure it's so fun there." said Chrysalis.

"Yeah it's pink in there and the dance floor lights up and there's a big screen where you can pick what background you want it to be." said Gege.

"So sweet." said Chrysalis.

"Do you see the biplane?" said Nillia.

"Whoa, oh sorry Nillia you startled me." said Fawn.

"Hey guys, the bipane is about to fly by." said Navia's dad.

They all stand outside to look out for it.

"You know the banner on it out to Ivern." said Stacya, Lotusa, Jannia, Bentha, and Tarika's mom.

"Hey there it is." said Dakota's dad pointing at it.

They saw the biplane go by and on the banner it said I LOVE CATS.

"I love cats, shouldn't it say I love Ivern?" said Heviner.

"Actually I ran into the guys who's flying the biplane because he wanted an autograph from me, and he said that the banner was meant to say that because Ivern came up with first hit song when he was twelve because he was inspired by the cats he was helping take care of at a cat care." said Fawn's dad.

"Ah man I love cats." said Chrysalis.

"Oh yeah that's right." said Slecks.

"Yeah and then he screamed with excitement." said Fawn's dad.

"At least you weren't at an airport where there were a bunch of Ivern fans who all scream with excitement when you say his name." said Spencer.

"Then they played his music so loud it also woke Batie up while she was sleeping there." said Emily, holding Batie.

"Whoa surprising." said Stacya, Lotusa, Jannia, Bentha, and Tarika's dad.

"Shall we go eat now?" said Ard.

They all headed inside to go eat at <u>DANCEFLOOR RESTAURANT</u>. They all went into the restaurant and sat down and ordered what they wanted then the waitress left after they ordered.

"Okay let's get back to dancing on the dancefloor." said Chrysalis.

All of them dance on the dancefloor then Chrysalis wanted to do something.

"Hey let's stop the music." said Chrysalis.

"Stop the music?" said Ariel.

"I think I know why Chrysalis wants to." said Jaya.

"I'm on it." said Dilia.

The music stopped then Chrysalis got out her phone set it up and bright light music lover bracelet and started to sing out make everyone adore it and her bracelet made a green light with small dark green wavy lines that shine out bright to go over her body having everyone in the restaurant love it then the music went back on went she was done and she put her phone and bracelet away and continue dancing on the dancefloor with everyone else.

"Awesome." said Ariel to Chrysalis.

Then Ariel and Chrysalis hugged each other. They all got their food and started eating.

"You're enjoying your food Puppety alright." said Arianie, pretending her puppet is eating.

"Arianie stay more focused on you eating your food than your puppet if you want to dance on the dancefloor more after eating." said Nillia and Arianie's mom.

"Okay mommy." said Arianie.

Poppy and her little sister Epe were eating at their table while Dilia walked by them.

"Hey guys I finished eating now I am going to dance." said Dilia.

"Dilia you better not dance where that sign is a waiter spilled juice over there." said Poppy.

"You also have Fern and Chet over there trying to keep themselves sure you're alright." said Epe looking at Fern staring at Dilia while Poppy and Dilia were looking at them too.

"Don't worry." said Dilia stepping forward.

But Dilia didn't realize that she was stepping too close to the juice puddle and slipped but Poppy and Epe caught her.

"Oh man thanks, good thing for you guys being fast runs in the you guys' family." said Dilia to Poppy and Epe.

"I was about to say the same thing." said Fern rushing over with Chet and Tafelena in Chet's arms up to Poppy, Epe, and Dilia.

"Nice catch." said Chet.

"Dilia being with you two, we shouldn't worry." said Fern to Poppy an Epe.

The waitress came over to clean the mess but then slipped but Poppy caught her.

"Oh thanks." said the waitress now standing up right.

"Well let's get back to our table baby." said Fern to her husband Chet.

Fern kissed Chet on the face. Just then Darma ran by them to the middle of the restaurant.

"Everyone quick listen up keep away from the juice spot you might slip." said Darma out loud.

"What, ah man slipper juice, I'm going to slip." said Dayla while hugging her mom scared.

Both of Dayla's parents at the table with her are both the same human/ bunny monsters Dayla is.

Chrysalis and her family laughed.

"Dayla just relax it's nothing to panic about." said Chrysalis.

"Okay, okay." said Dayla letting go of her mom calming down.

"Dayla, you need to watch how tight you squeeze someone." said Dayla's mom.

"You're mom's right you're like that with me sometimes too." said Dayla's dad.

"Sorry mom and dad." said Dayla.

Later they left and went to the FASHION BALL MALL and they were all inside.

"Hey guys check out what they have here, I'm also pointing at it." said Cherryette in a pit of foam rubber in the shape of music notes and that a slide goes into them.

Cherryette was also in there with up to her arms out of the foam rubber in the shape of music notes pit on the floor.

"And you're in it too." said Chrysalis.

"And you are also partly laying on the ground and staying in there for a long time." said Cherryette's mom walking up to Cherryette.

"Oh right sorry I find this pit relaxing." said Cherryette getting up.

"Cool I'm going on." said Ariel going to the slide.

"Me too." said Chrysalis going to the slide too.

Ariel went down first. Then Chrysalis.

"Ow." said someone in the foam rubber music note pit who Chrysalis accidently hit with her feet.

"What?" said Ariel partly in the pit before fully getting out.

"Lumia (who Chrysalis thinks is in the pit)?" said Chrysalis.

"Hi." said Lumia who was in the pit that Chrysalis hit.

"What are you doing in the music note pit you're supposed to be getting out after you slide?" said Chrysalis.

"I know and thanks for waking me up I fell asleep because these music notes are relaxing." said Lumia.

Then they got out. Raymen, Taffeta, and Trixie in her mom's arms came by walking by the music note pit.

"Oh this looks fun." said Taffada looking at it.

Trixie got her arms out at it because she wanted to go in.

"Oh you want to go in Trixie?" said Taffada.

"Aw, hey can I slide down with her?" said Ariel.

"Well okay but be careful." said Taffada.

"Oh and one last thing." said Raymen.

Raymen got out a water bottle and soap.

"Bring your hands out." said Raymen.

Ariel did bring her hands out and Raymen squirted soap on Ariel's hands and water from the water bottle on to Ariel's hands to clean them.

"This stuff is better than hand sanitizer and hand sanitizer is bad for babies." said Raymen.

Then he handed Ariel a towel and then Raymen used it to clean up the water on the floor.

"Got to be sure your hands are clean before carrying a baby." said Taffada handing Trixie to Ariel.

"Aw she's really cute." said Ariel while holding Trixie.

Ariel then slid down the slide with Trixie while Trixie laughed.

"Aw that was fun to watch." said Chrysalis.

"Taffada and I are going to be going down too." said Raymen.

Zinnia came over and saw Ariel holding Trixie.

"Aw that reminds me of when I saw your mom and dad holding you when you were a baby." said Zinnia to Ariel.

Then Zinnia kissed Ariel on the head. Raymen and Taffada went down the slide into the music note pit.

"Here's Trixie back." said Ariel, handing Trixie back to her parents.

"Thanks Ariel." said Taffada, after Ariel gave Trixie back to her.

"Wow fun looking slide I'm going to go on it." said Zinnia.

Zinnia went on the slide with Lumia behind her.

"I get to go on next ek." said Lumia, excitedly.

"Hey guys." said Bessa, eating a big long fruity shish kabob with white chocolate on the fruit.

"Hey Bessa." they all said.

"That's a big shish kabob and fruit." said Trudy.

"Ah man where did you get that kabob?" said Shiloh.

"Over there." said Bessa, pointing at the spot.

"Sweet." said Shiloh.

"It looks like Cleo, Falla, Pennya, Mabel, and Cassandra could each use one." said Shenatha, pointing at them sucking the giant fake fruit.

Chrysalis and her sisters and friends went to go remove them from the fake giant fruit.

"Guys really." said Cersanthama, helping remove them.

"Sorry they look so good." said Mabel, being removed.

"Wow after seeing that I am never sucking on a fake lollipop again." said Lalo.

"Guys those fake fruits are just there for fun display." said Trudy.

"Yeah guys would you rather be having what Bessa's having over there?" said Jaser, pointing at Bessa eating her shish kabob.

"Oh yeah." said Cleo, Falla, Pennya, Mabel, and Cassandra.

Cleo, Falla, Pennya, Mabel, and Cassandra's parents came over to them.

"Hey mom dad can get those shish kabobs over there?" said Pennya.

"Sure." said Pennya, Mabel, and Cassandra's mom.

"Can we have those shish kabobs too?" said Cleo to her and Falla's parents.

"Okay girls and don't be sucking on fake fruits again." said Cleo and Falla's mom.

"What a minute, you guys know that?" said Mabel.

"We were close enough to hear and see you guys when you were doing that." said Pennya, Mabel, and Cassandra's dad.

At a diner Carlica was eating dinner. Just then Carlica got a phone call (that makes a thunderstorm ringtone).

"Oh man was that thunder?" said a lady, startled who put Vargoe on a stretcher earlier sitting at a table with Carlica.

"No it's my phone, I have to go outside." said Carlica.

Carlica went outside and answered her phone which was Mesha calling her.

"Hey Carlica." said Mesha, calling through her phone.

"Oh hey Mesha." said Carlica.

"So how is it going?" said Manora, calling through Mesha's phone.

"Hey wait your turn." said Mesha to Manora.

"Did you guys find Ariel?" said Carlica.

"No, we haven't even entered the mall yet." said Mesha.

"Well I believe you guys will find her there, be sure she doesn't forget seeing us at that <u>BLOSSOM SPA.</u> That girl Trudy who they're friends with her mom is the mall's owner." said Carlica.

Chrysalis and her friends and family were still enjoying the mall.

"Oh my gosh these cupcakes are amazing." said Marge.

"These shish kabobs are great." said Cleo, eating her's.

Chrysalis and Ariel later took a ride in a cube shaped boat ride in a path of water inside the mall for another way to go to areas in the mall beside the walking path in the mall and they were about to go into a tunnel that looks like a jungle inside.

"This is fun." said Ariel.

"Hey guys." said Zita, who came out of the water and held onto the floating cube shaped boat Chrysalis and Ariel are riding in wearing goggles with a snorkel

"What the heck?" said Ariel.

"Zita, are you even allowed to do that?" said Chrysalis.

"I spoke with Trudy's mom and she said since the water is always clean she's okay with it." said Zita.

"You're wearing your clothes too." said Ariel.

"So what it's just water." said Zita.

Zita put her goggles and snorkel back on and went under water again.

"That was weird." said Ariel.

Zita swam up to another floating cube shaped boat.

"Hey, oh." said Zita, realizing her parents were in that one.

"Zita." said Zita's mom.

"What are you doing in there? You tell us you were at the mall's flowery garden walk path outside behind the mall." said Zita's dad.

"Oh oops I forgot but I do have permission to be allowed to swim in here, uh bye." said Zita, quickly swimming back in the water to get away from being in trouble with her parents.

"Zita." said Zita's dad.

"Zita you get back here right now." said Zita's mom.

"Oho man she's in trouble." said Shenatha, in a floating cube with Kathleenie and Marge in front of Chrysalis and Ariel.

Chrysalis and Ariel got off the ride.

"So where to now?" said Ariel.

"I'm going to go to the mall's flowery garden walk path area behind the mall." Chrysalis said.

"Okay I'll be go there too." said Ariel.

So Chrysalis and Ariel headed over there. At the mall's pet store.

"Wow, look at that snake so cool." said Beatrix.

"Hey is that snake poisonous?" said Belyndica to Cherrycake.

"No it's not but-." said Cherrycake, before Belyndica interrupted her.

"Cool I'm going to pet it." said Belyndica.

"Belyndica wait." said Cherrycake.

But Belyndica's mom put her hand over the terrarium lid before Belyndica put her hand in it.

"Belyndica you don't do that to this snake." said Belyndica's mom.

"You didn't let me finish talking. That's not a venomous snake but it still bites when it is being touched." said Cherrycake.

"Oh sorry." said Belyndica.

"Belyndica you could have gotten into serious trouble." said Belyndica's dad.

"You better listen to your parents plus your dad is a cop." said Jaser to Belyndica.

Colleen and Ratia were behind them and laughing.

"You can't argue with that." said Ratia.

"Hey guys check this out." said Constance coming to them excitedly.

"What is it Constance?" said Colleen.

"Well I was think about this when I was playing with the cats earlier at the cat care about ever wanting to add something to there and I found this." said Constance.

Constance went over to grab a big green cat scratcher shaped like a flamingo clown juggling balls and carried it over to show them.

"Great huh cats eat birds and they play with balls." said Constance.

"Wow okay good idea." said Constance mom with Constance's dad by her.

"Uh why is there a sheet there?" said Constance's dad pointing at a sheet on the floor.

"Not ours." said Colleen.

Constance picked it up.

"Hey who's sheet is this!" shouted Constance.

Dilia came into the store.

"Oh there's my sheet thanks." said Dilia while Constance handed it to her.

Chrysalis and Ariel were loving the beautiful flowers at the mall's flowery garden walkway.

"These are so beautiful." said Ariel looking at the flowers.

There they saw two ducks with twelve ducklings.

"Hey Ariel look." said Chrysalis pointing at the ducks.

"Oh what a nice duck family." said Ariel.

"Wow those ducks have more kids than my parents do." said Chrysalis.

The ducks waddell up to Kert, Javada, Zila, Lalo, Darma, and their parents.

"Oh hey look ducks kids." said Kert, Javada, Zila, Lalo, and Darma's mom.

"Oh." they said except for Zila.

Zila dumped a bag of mashed bananas on some of the ducks.

"Whoa." said Chrysalis and Ariel watching.

"Why did you do that?" said Javada.

"I thought the ducks needed more color on them." said Zila.

"Did you smash your banana slices on purpose?" Kert, Javada, Zila, Lalo, and Darma's dad.

"Yeah to spread them on the ducks better." said Zila.

The ducks were all eating the mashed bananas.

"Well good thing the duck can eat the bananas." said Kert, Javada, Zila, Lalo, and Darma's mom.

"Well now we know why she did that." said Chrysalis.

Chrysalis and Ariel continue going. Meanwhile Mesha, Manora, and Mingmi were searching for Ariel and arrived at the mall and started at the mall's flowery garden walk path outside.

"I don't see her here." said Mingmi.

"Neither have I." said Manora.

"I told you guys we should have started inside." said Mesha.

The duck family from earlier that Chrysalis and Ariel saw were by Mesha, Manora, and Mingmi and they shook themselves and got mashed bananas on them.

"Eww." said Mesha.

"Duck snot." said Manora.

Mingmi scooped some from her leg and sniffed it.

"No wait, it's bananas." said Mingmi.

"Oh that's better." said Manora.

Chrysalis and Ariel were still in the flowery garden walk path. Ariel saw a big white and fuschia house on a tall hill not far from the mall.

"Wow that's a great house." said Ariel.

"Yeah it is you can ask to see it if you want." said Chrysalis.

"Really who's house is that?" said Ariel.

"It's my house." said Shenatha behind them.

"Your house yeah you want to see it after the mall if my parents say yes?" said Shenatha.

"Yeah sure." said Ariel

"Okay you ask your parents and I'll ask mine and Chrysalis can you and your family for you to come to chapter one?" said Shenatha.

"Sure I'll tell them." said Chrysalis.

"Great." said Shenatha.

Mesha, Manora, and Mingmi spotted Ariel but Chrysalis also spotted them.

"What are you three doing?" said Chrysalis.

"What we can't admire a garden." said Manora.

"You guys better not cause trouble." said Shenatha to Mesha, Manora, and Mingmi.

So Chrysalis and Ariel both went inside and went separate. Ariel found her parents waiting to use the photo booth.

"Hey mom dad." said Ariel behind them.

"Oh hi baby." said Regina.

"Are you having a good time?" said Kylestone.

"Yeah and I wanted to know how you guys were doing." said Ariel.

"Well we're doing good and we were about to take pictures of ourselves, do you want to join us?" said Kylestone.

"No thanks I want to look around more and Shenatha wanted me to ask you guys if we can go to her house after the mall. It's the big white and fuschia one up on that tall hill." said Ariel.

"Okay." said Regina.

"Why not." said Kylestone.

"And baby but be careful while looking around." said Regina.

"Okay mom and thanks." said Ariel.

"Hey Regina, Kylestone you guys can use the photo booth now just got to take off this boa." said Dayla removing it.

Just then Dayla stopped.

"Uh-oh." said Dayla.

"Is it stuck?" said Dakota.

"Oh-huh." said Dayla.

"Ah here." said Dakota grabbing onto it.

Both Dakota and Dayla pulled on it and they knocked down the table with the accessories for the photo booth.

"Whoa." said Kylestone.

Finally they got it off Dayla's hair.

"Oww, oh hey it's off." said Dayla.

Ariel was far in the mall looking at a TV in the mall of singers such as Fern and Chet both singing together. Ariel felt like she wanted to be a part of being a singer but she didn't think she was ready to sing more besides Chrysalis and her family. Just then Mesha, Manora, and Mingmi found Ariel.

"Well it's you we are seeing now." said Manora.

"Is there something you girls want to tell me?" said Ariel.

"Yes and if you're thinking that Carlica and us have been messing up the rooms we promise you we did not." said Manora.

"Really us and Carlica were surprised too when we found out." said Mesha.

"Remember the time is 7:30 for you to be at the BLOSSOM SPA." said Mingmi.

"Here." said Manora handing Ariel a brochure.

"A brochure for the BLOSSOM SPA?" said Ariel.

"Yeah to be sure you know where it is and have directions to slither there." said Manora.

"Yeah by the way you must be upset you're not a singer like your parents are?" said Mingmi.

"Yeah I'm not jealous of them. I'm just upset with myself for not being brave enough to do it but I do know how to get that spa so don't worry about that." said Ariel.

"Carlica said to prepare yourself for both impressment you'll do or for disappointment you'll do but she believes in disappointment you'll do the most." said Mesha.

"Lucky for you you get a second chance." said Manora to Ariel.

"But don't be telling anyone for the same reason why Carlica didn't want you to tell anyone earlier when you were at the other mall with show her your style with clothes." said Mesha.

"Well tell Carlica she should think that through." said Ariel.

"We'll tell her and we're sure she'll still think the same thing and we'll agree with her." said Mesha.

They walked separately. Kylestone and Regina were done taking pictures of them spending time at the photo booth. They took their photo booth accessories off then Regina spotted an area where they were serving candy apples with red sticky coating and rainbow sparkles Regina went over there and grabbed one.

"Kylestone we should get our little baby girl one she likes these and they're pretty and sweet like her." said Regina, hugged one up to her face.

"Yes I agree, where is our baby girl anyway?" said Kylestone, looking out for Ariel.

At the pet store.

"A flamingo clown for cats." said Slecks, touching it.

"You know Constance I was thinking the cat care could use a cat scratcher while I was feeding bugs." said Lumia.

"You're not talking about fleas on cats right?" said Kert.

"Of course not they bug cats, ha. Heard what I just said? Ha, but no I was feeding bugs I saw while I was taking a walk with apple pieces." said Lumia.

"That's a relief." said Jistopher.

"Hi guys say hello to the hedgehogs." said Bessa, coming into the pet store with hedgehogs on leashes.

"Whoa Bessa when you said you were giving the pet store's hedgehogs a walk I didn't think you meant all of them at once." said LiLi.

"It's fun." said Bessa.

Princeson notices something moving and coming out of Bessa's pocket.

"Hey Bessa, something's moving in your pocket." said Princeson, pointing at it.

"Oh that." said Bessa.

"Is that another hedgehog?" said Princeson.

"Yep." said Bessa.

"Why?" said Marge.

"I wanted to try carrying one like this." said Bessa.

In another part of the mall outside the pet store.

"So mom and dad did you guys finish finding where to relocate the vines from that big house?" said Elsa.

"Yeah we did but they're not going to have them removed until later tomorrow." said Sasha.

Just then they heard Falyby singing out loud in front of everyone on the bridge inside the mall. After she finished she left.

"Well we know that Falyby does like singing." said Noodle.

"Ha." laughed Falyby while leaving.

Ariel was looking at her brochure in one of the mall's stores wanting to show how cool she can be to Carlica, Mesha, Manora, and Mingmi. Then Ariel folded the brochure, and put it in her pocket then her parents and Chrysalis showed up to her.

"There you are baby." said Regina.

"We got this for you." said Kylestone, handing Ariel a candy apple.

"Thanks." said Ariel.

"Oh by the way my family and Shenatha's parents agreed for us to come to Shenatha's house." said Chrysalis.

"That's great." said Ariel.

"Do you want to go now after Loua, Dava, and Bemma's surprise?" said Kylestone.

"Okay." said Ariel.

"We can." said Chrysalis.

"Then alright then let's go find everyone else." said Regina.

They went to find the rest of Ariel's family and Shenatha and her parents.

"Hey guys look I'm juggling candy apples." said Irenie to Chrysalis and Ariel and Ariel's parents.

Seven people by them all applauded at Irenie. Then Shenatha and her parents came up to them.

"Hey guys, you want to go now after Loua, Dava, and Bemma's surprise?" said Shenatha.

"We were actually going to ask you guys that." said Chrysalis.

"Hey guys, you guys are in a good spot." said Loua on the second floor balcony with her sisters.

"What are those things you guys have?" said Regina to Loua, Dava, and Bemma.

"You'll see." said Bemma.

Loua, Dava, and Bemma turned on the blasters that made sparkly confetti come out that were up there with them on the balcony poles.

"Wow this is a great spot." said Chrysalis.

"Sweet." said Swifta.

Swifta opened her mouth and caught a sparkly confetti on her tongue.

"Ah ha caught one." said Swifta with her tongue out.

"Swifta they're sparkly confettis not snowflakes." said Dakota.

"Still I want to catch one this way." said Swifta with the confetti off her tongue.

Later Chrysalis, Ariel, Ariel's family, Shenatha, and Shenatha's parents arrived at the bottom of the hill of Shenatha's house where there was a non gas run small car attached to a pole going straight up the hill.

"This is here so you can ride up the hill inside of walking if you want to leave the house without a car." said Shenatha's dad.

"Oh." Ariel and her family said.

Just then they saw by them a group of people and people/monsters who are all photographers taking pictures of them about to go into the non gas run small car.

"Whoa." said Ariel.

"Yep, the paparazzi comes to where we are sometimes." said Chrysalis.

"It was like that with my father Ivern." said Kylestone.

"Aah Ivern!" said the paparazzi.

"And also them yelling his name when it is said." said Chrysalis.

They all got into the car and it got turned on and drove up and they got out and into the big house. Chrysalis, Ariel, and Shenatha went into Shenatha's room.

"Wow you and your parents sure do own a lot of big long curtains, they're even too much for the windows." said Ariel.

"I like the curtains. I like to wrap them around me to make it look like I'm in another world and being protected." said Shenatha.

Ariel and Chrysalis went and did the same thing.

"This is fun." said Ariel surrounded by the curtain.

Ariel's family were with Shenatha's parents.

"Here's our balcony." said Shenatha's dad.

"Wow." said Ariel's family.

"This is amazing." said Pocahontas.

"Well you all are welcomed here anytime so you are able to see this view often." said Shenatha's mom.

Chrysalis, Ariel, and Shenatha came over to the balcony while Ariel's family and Shenatha's parents were still there. Ariel quickly slithered up to the balcony with excitement.

"Oh wow." said Ariel.

Ariel's parents came by her and placed their hands on her shoulders and leaned on her. Later they went home Ariel was in her room feeling upset about how Carlica and her friends were to her and her being nervous to perform in public more. Then Ariel's parents came in.

"Hey mom dad I want to go to bed now." said Ariel, sitting at her bed.

"Right now but it's too early." said Regina, sitting next to Ariel.

"Baby girl you're not going to go to bed now." said Kylestone, sitting next to her too.

"Then can I be left alone in my room for the rest of the day?" said Ariel.

"Baby are you trying to avoid us because we've been bothering you, usually you still want to hang out with us at this time of day?" said Regina.

"No no." said Ariel.

"Is there something wrong baby." said Kylestone.

Kylestone put his arm around Ariel and his other hand on the bottom of Ariel's waist and he felt something in Ariel's pocket.

"Baby what's in your pocket?" said Kylestone.

Ariel grabbed it out.

"It's a brochure to a <u>BLOSSOM SPA</u>." said Ariel.

"Looks very nice." said Regina.

"Yes it does, but where did you get this brochure from?" said Kylestone.

"Yes, I don't see anywhere where they were handing them out." said Regina.

"Neither did I." said Kylestone.

"I uh got- it from- the trash at the mall." said Ariel.

"Baby where did you really get it? It sounds like you're lying." said Kylestone.

"Okay it was given to me by someone but look it's just a brochure to a spa. Why do you need to know so much about it?" said Ariel getting mad.

"Baby why can't you just be honest with us?" said Regina.

"Is there something wrong with you that you want to be alone? Usually you like hanging out with your family longer?" said Kylestone.

"Look I just want to be left alone so go now." said Ariel, starting to get more mad.

"Little baby girl you're looking even more mad if something is bothering you you have to tell us." said Regina.

"It bugs me that you guys aren't leaving me alone." said Ariel, putting the brochure on the desk in her room.

"Baby we just want to know if you're okay and that you're not doing something bad you know we care about you." said Kylestone.

"It's something that I don't need you guys' help with." said Ariel, going farther up her room.

"Don't be getting away from us you don't need to be like that." said Regina, mad while she and Kylestone both got off of Ariel's bed coming up to Ariel.

Ariel said nothing.

"If you're going to be this way then you can stay in your room for the rest of the day as punishment." said Kylestone mad.

"And tomorrow she should too and there should be more talking about this to her tomorrow as well." said Regina to Kylestone.

"Your right Regina." said Kylestone.

Then he and Regina left and went downstairs to the living room. The two of them sat on the couches with their parents while Regina and Kylestone were looking mad.

"You two don't seem okay." said Pocahontas.

"Ariel is not being herself and we don't know why." said Regina.

"What has happened to her?" said Kylestone.

Ariel opened the door to her room very quietly so no one would hear her then she went downstairs and opened the door quietly and closed it quietly too and went outside to go to the spa.

"Maybe you guys need to give her time to calm down." said Tarzan.

"Would if she like this because she's upset she's not a singer because of her being nervous? She loves music and dancing it's a skill she adores so much and she does want to do it for something like performing." said Kylestone.

"She should understand that even without being a singer or dancer or both she can still be a fun loving girl." said Zinnia.

Zinnia got out a scrapbook of photos of Ariel when she was younger and opened it.

"Just look at how happy she is, aww." said Zinnia looking at a photo of Ariel when she was a little human/snake monster girl.

"Yeah, mother can I take that scrape book to Ariel? This could make her feel better." said Kylestone.

"If it has a chance then sure." said Zinnia.

"Thank you." said Kylestone.

Kylestone grabbed the scrapbook from Zinnia and went upstairs to Ariel's room and knocked on Ariel's bedroom door.

"Baby." said Kylestone.

Kylestone knocked but there was no reply.

"Baby girl listen please don't be feeling upset I have something to make you feel better." said Kylestone.

Ariel still didn't reply.

"Baby?" said Kylestone after knocking again.

Kylestone opened the door and saw Ariel not in her room so he went downstairs.

"Ariel's gone." said Kylestone.

"What!" the rest of Ariel's family said.

"I looked around the house and I couldn't find her." said Kylestone.

"What, oh no my baby girl." said Regina.

"Have you tried calling her?" said Tarzan.

"She left her phone." said Kylestone.

"Where would she have gone to?" said Pocahontas.

"Maybe she wanted to go to a friend's house." said Regina.

"We'll should look at those places." said Tarzan.

"I'll look to see if Ariel is at any of the parks." said Kylestone.

"Zinnia, why don't you stay here in case she comes back?" said Tarzan.

"Sure, oh I hope she's okay." said Zinnia.

So they all head out to find Ariel. Ariel arrived at the BLOSSOM SPA and opened the doors that were unlocked and went inside.

"Hello, is anyone here?" said Ariel.

Ariel saw no one but she loved how the spa looked inside.

"Wow, this place is beautiful." said Ariel.

Matilda, Nagaila, and Tuckles appeared behind Ariel.

"Hello you." said Matilda.

"What you, Carlica said you weren't coming." said Ariel to Matilda.

"I'm guessing she didn't say we were coming either." said Tuckles.

"Where are Carlica and Mesha, Manora, and Mingmi?" said Ariel.

"Finally I get to catch you again." said Matilda to Ariel.

"No." said Ariel.

Matilda grabbed Ariel by the arm and pulled her up to her.

"Hey let go of my arm you can keep me hostage." said Ariel.

"Actually that's why we're here." said Nagaila.

Ariel tried to yack free but she saw a big daisy shampoo bottle and grabbed it and banged it on Matilda's hands.

"Ow!" said Matilda.

"Ah man I hate daisies." said Tuckles, feeling discussed.

Ariel quickly slithered after she threw down the shampoo.

"Get her." said Nagaila.

Tuckles accidently stepped on the shampoo that Ariel used that was also opened and splatted shampoo on the floor which Tuckles also stepped into.

"Ew I'm standing in daisy shampoo. Why am I standing in daisy shampoo?" said Tuckles discussed more.

Carlica went in front of Ariel.

"Carlica your friends are trying to kidnap me." said Ariel.

"That's why we wanted you here." said Carlica.

"What!" said Ariel all scared.

Ariel went past Carlica to get to the door but a giant brown reddish hand with skinny six fingers grabbed her around her arms and waist and it scared Ariel even more she started shivering a little and did not know who's hand was grabbing her. Who's hand was grabbing her turned her to see who was grabbing her and it was a human/ monster who's bigger than a human, has big eyes, a big mouth, a round square head, thin crescent shaped ear at the top round points of her head, nostrils no nose, her upper arms are longer than her forearms, and she walks on twenty- six arms and hands instead of feet and legs that are the same as the two other arms and hands she has she uses as regular arms and hands. Ariel notices the dress she was wearing which is the same dress Carlica wears.

"Carlica?" said Ariel.

"Yep freaked out by my walloi form huh." said Carlica.

"W-w-wall-oi?" said Ariel.

"Yeah they don't sell this kind of human to monster formula at stores or anywhere the formula was made by my grandfather and he had it be kept in the family and it still is now." said Carlica.

"Let me go Carlica I need to get back to my family." said Ariel, trying to get herself free.

Carlica put another one of her hands around Ariel's mouth.

"Mmuhmum." said Ariel, with her mouth covered by Ariel's hand.

"Ariel you can't be let go Matilda, Nadeline, and Tuckles are going to take you with them to that cool building own by Sasha Coldstone while Hailey, Nagaila, some of our other friends, and I are going to hang at the big house own by Sasha Coldstone that isn't covered in vines for a while." said Carlica.

"Carlica knows how to make keys for the locks without using the key own by who has them it's how we get in." said Mesha, who appeared.

Then Manora and Mingmi appeared.

"Yeah this place is actually not supposed to be open now." said Manora.

"Mmuhum!" said Ariel, surprised still with her mouth covered by Carlica's hand.

Carlica leveled her hand around Ariel's arms and waist more down Ariel so Matilda could tie Ariel with rope. Ariel made a teardrop from her eye while Matilda tied her up wishing she stayed with her family. Carlica's friend Neevya did a scream they heard and came over to them.

"Hey guys I did it. I finally beat my record of screaming the quietest when I'd pinched myself." said Neevya.

"Ah okay good for you Neevya." said Manora, who don't care.

"I am so glad Neevya is going with Carlica after they take Ariel." whispered Mingmi to Mesha.

After Ariel became fully tied up Nagaila came in front of Ariel and Carlica moved her hand off Ariel's mouth so Nagaila could put white tape over Ariel's mouth.

"Mmmumhuumm." said Ariel, now with tape over her mouth.

Carlica placed Ariel laying down on one of Carlica's hands while another one for her hands was placed under Ariel's head to hold up the upper part of Ariel.

"Aww." said Carlica liking how Ariel is placed.

Ariel tried to get free while Carlica handed Ariel to Matilda and Matilda held Ariel the same way but by using her arms and hands.

"Finally I got you now, aw cute you are." said Matilda to Ariel.

Ariel did not like it that she made a mad face at Matilda and then turned her head away from her.

"Like I care about that." said Matilda to Ariel.

"Let's go now." said Nadeline.

So Matilda, Nadeline, and Tuckles left while Matilda carried Ariel in her arms into one of their cars but before Matilda entered in there with Ariel, she had Ariel's head moved laying on Matilda's other arm then they drove off after they got in. Kylestone was looking for Ariel at the park.

"Where could she be, what a minute." said Kylestone, thinking he might know where Ariel is.

Ariel was brought by Matilda, Nadeline, and Tuckles inside <u>HANGING STARS SPOT</u> and Matilda brought Ariel into one of the rooms on the second floor where a big makeup mirror is and Matilda placed Ariel on the pink swivel stool chair attached to the floor for the makeup mirror.

"There we go." said Matilda, after placing Ariel on the pink swivel stool chair attached to the floor for the makeup mirror.

"Hmmhummhumm." said Ariel.

Matilda removed the tape from Ariel's mouth.

"OW, what are you all going to do to me?" said Ariel to Matilda.

"Well you don't need to wear clothes to go out in public when you're that human/monster you are, so I'm going to remove your clothes and that dark red leather jacket of yours too." said Matilda to Ariel.

"What." said Ariel.

Matilda untied Ariel. Matilda removed Ariel off the seat Ariel tried to slithered away while Matilda was grabbing onto her, and while Matilda took Ariel's clothes off and her dark red leather jacket, then she tied her up again with the dark brown rope and placed her back on the seat.

"Now let's try putting makeup on you." said Matilda, getting out a blush powered with a face brush stick from her pocket.

"No I don't like makeup." said Ariel.

"Well at least it will be done by me. I'm a fashion genius." said Matilda.

Tuckles came up to them wearing a golden color vest.

"Hey check out what they have in the costume room." said Tuckles.

"Tuckles hold it there's something wrong with your outfit." said Matilda.

"What?" said Tuckles.

209

"That vest." said Matilda, pointing at it and staring at it.

"Oh really I didn't think of it not going with my outfit." said Tuckles.

"I thought it looked nice." said Ariel.

"What do you know." said Matilda to Ariel.

Tuckles took it off.

"I was going through a big pile I grabbed from the costume closet which is right here." said Tuckles.

Tuckles opened the door that's next to Matilda and it was costume closet.

"Huh, I wonder if there's anything good in here." said Matilda.

Matilda reached into the closet by putting her hand in and put out the first thing she grabbed without knowing what it was.

"A boa, eww I hate these things." said Matilda, quickly trying to get it off her hands by flicking it.

The boa tickled Ariel's nose.

"Aachoo." sneezed Ariel.

Then Matilda quickly picked it up by a pitch and threw it in the closet and closed it.

"I'm going to go play more dressing up." said Tuckles.

But before Tuckles left she stopped and she and Matilda looked over at Ariel crying.

"What the heck is up with you?" Tuckles said to Ariel.

"I don't want to be here with any of you." said Ariel.

"Don't be crying it will mess up the makeup unless you want to make things worse for you." said Matilda.

"No no no I'll stop." said Ariel.

"Tuckles do you have your small box of tissues with you?" said Matilda.

"Yeah why are one of you about to sneeze?" said Tuckles, getting her small box of tissue out for her pocket.

Matilda grabbed a couple and used them to wipe the tears off of Ariel's face.

"Oh for tear wiping. Now why didn't I guess that?" said Tuckles.

"Yeah why don't you." said Matilda.

Matilda finished and then gave the tissues to Tuckles.

"Throw those tissues out somewhere and don't let anyone find them." said Matilda to Tuckles.

"Got it." said Tuckles.

Tuckles left. Matilda got out more white tape and placed it on Ariel's mouth then she started putting the blush powder on but she made Ariel sneeze from making a lot go in the air near Ariel's nose. Kylestone arrived at the big house that Sasha bought for the same reason for the <u>HANGING STAR SPOT</u> that isn't covered with vines but Carlica and some of her friends were already inside.

"Fabulous place this is." said Carlica, still in her walloi monster form.

"Oh yes it's not as big as the building but it's still wonderful." said Neevya.

Carlica went up the stairs where her friends were. Kylestone arrived at the door.

"Sasha says this place does lock until 11:00 p.m." said Kylestone, opening the door.

Carlica and her friends heard the door open they turned off the lights and tried to look who was there entering through the doorway without being spotted and saw it was Kylestone.

"Huh that's, isn't he?" whispered Neevya.

"Yes distract him so I can catch him. We need him caught too." whispered Carlica to Hailey.

Hailey got closer to the edge of the balcony of the stairs.

"Oh hey it's you Kylestone don't you recognize me?" said Hailey, still keeping herself hidden standing on the inside balcony next to the stairs.

While Hailey was talking Carlica was sneaking behind Kylestone.

"What, who are you?" said Kylestone.

"You know- a- her- she's a-friend-of yours." said Neevya keeping herself hidden too while standing on the inside balcony next to the stairs.

Carlica bought out one for her hands and grabbed Kylestone around his arms and waist.

"Huh." said Kylestone, realizing that something grabbed him.

Kylestone looked and saw Carlica in her walloi form.

"Aahh!" said Kylestone, scared.

"Hello Kylestone what a surprise." said Carlica.

"Who are you?" said Kylestone.

"Don't you recognize me?" said Carlica.

Kylestone noticed who she was the same way Ariel did.

"Carlica." said Kylestone.

"Yes now you know good for you but I say late." said Carlica.

"Good jod catching him Carlica." said Neevya, now having herself shown to Kylestone along with Hailey and Carlica's other friends.

"You know you need to work on your acting skills." said Carlica to Neevya.

"It's true." said Neevya.

"You know Carlica only told me to do the talking." said Hailey to Neevya.

"I know but I wanted to get in." said Neevya.

"Carlica you can't do this to me." said Kylestone.

Carlica wrapped another one of her hands around Kylestone's mouth.

"Mmhumm." said Kylestone, with his mouth covered.

"You need to speak more clearly? I have no idea what mmhumm means." said Carlica.

"Hhummmhuum." said Kylestone.

"Now that we caught you, ladies, get the ropes tie him up." said Carlica.

"Humm." said Kylestone, being leveled down so Nagaila can tie him.

Carlica moved her hand lower around Kylestone's arms and waist so Nagaila could tie him up.

"Oh by the way this formula that turns me into having the ability to transform in a walloi which is my monster form name was made by my grandfather had it kept in the family so no one outside my family owns it I've been talking fast about it because I didn't like having to repeat explaining stuff again after a while since I already told Ariel." said Carlica.

"Hummmhum." said Kylestone, while being tied up.

"Yeah you hear what she said." said Hailey to Kylestone.

After Nagaila fully knotted the rope around Kylestone Carlica removed her hand from his mouth then Nagaila put white tape over his mouth.

"Are we going to be taking him where Ariel is now?" said Varoge.

"We should Varoge in case someone comes here who isn't someone we're out to kidnap since he got to have told someone he has gone here, wait a minute." said Carlica.

Carlica stuck her hand into Kylestone's pockets and got out his phone.

"To be sure no one will track you down." said Carlica.

"Hold on Carlica may I?" said Varoge.

"Well okay." said Carlica, handing Kylestone's phone to Varoge.

Varoge grabbed the phone from Carlica and broke it in two and put the pieces in her pocket.

"Okay now let's go." said Carlica.

"Oh wait Carlica could I be the one to-?" said Nagaila.

"Alright." said Carlica, handing Kylestone to Nagaila.

Nagaila grabbing Kylestone but did not hold him how Matilda did with Ariel instead she held him with her arms around him up to where the rope around him stops and has him facing the same way she is.

"Okay now let's go." said Carlica.

So they left. Where Ariel still is with Matilda.

"And there." said Matilda, finishing putting makeup on Ariel.

When Matilda was done she turned Ariel to the mirror and Ariel did not like having makeup on her and she threw a fit about wanting it off.

"Relax I was never going to keep it on you I just wanted to try putting it on you and actually I prefer right after I'm done you have it off, so." said Matilda.

Matilda grabbed Ariel off the seat and carried her to where there is a sink and placed her sitting on the counter next to it.

Kylestone was brought to **HANGING STARS SPOT** too with Carlica and her friends including Mesha, Manora, and Mingmi.

"Hhuumm." said Kylestone.

"Sorry I really want to know what he's saying." said Varoge.

Varoge removed the tape from Kylestone's mouth.

"OW, you guys have been hanging out here?" said Kylestone.

"Yeah this is a great place." said Varoge.

"Okay you know what he said." said Carlica.

Carlica placed another piece of white tape over Kylestone's mouth.

"Mmmuhhmmm." said Kylestone.

Then they continued walking. In the room where Ariel is with Matilda removing the makeup off Ariel's face with a wet washcloth Matilda rubbed a wet washcloth on Ariel's left cheek and finished removing the makeup.

"There, it's all off now just got to dry your face." said Matilda.

Matilda grabbed a dry cloth and rubbed it on Ariel's face to dry her face off.

"Okay then." said Matilda, after she finished.

Then she grabbed Ariel off the counter and carried Ariel back on the seat Ariel was on earlier then Matilda removed the tape off Ariel's mouth again.

"Ow!" said Ariel.

Then Matilda turned Ariel around and started to untie her.

"Are you letting me go?" said Ariel.

"No." said Matilda, untying Ariel.

"What are you going to do to me now?" said Ariel, feeling nervous.

"Well there's someone who you'll be with here who I got a text about earlier." said Matilda, still untying Ariel.

After Matilda untied Ariel, Ariel tried to get away but Matilda held on to her before she could even leave the seat. Then Matilda held onto Ariel the same way Nagaila is holding Kylestone. Ariel and Matilda were facing the door. Ariel tried to get out of Matilda's arms but just then there was a knock.

"The door's not locked you know." said Matilda.

"Oh right." said Neevya behind the door.

"Out of the way Neevya have Nagaila go first." said Carlica, behind the door.

Carlica opened the door and Nagaila came in first with Kylestone still in her arms. Kylestone and Ariel both saw each other.

"Huh, dad!" said Ariel, trying to get to him but Matilda still had her arms around Ariel.

Nagaila stopped walking then she dropped Kylestone on the floor on his left side.

"Let me go, I need to know if he's okay." said Ariel, trying to get out of Matilda's arms.

Matilda did let go of Ariel and she quickly slithered to her dad. He was okay and Ariel and removed the tape from his mouth and untied him and then he got up but they were still both sitting on the floor.

"Oh my little baby what were you thinking about slithering away?" said Kylestone, while he and Ariel hugged each other.

"I'm sorry." said Ariel.

"Where are your clothes and your leather jacket?" said Kylestone.

"They were removed just like yours are going to be." said Tuckles.

"You're going to-" said Kylestone.

They grabbed Kylestone.

"No let him go." said Ariel.

But Ariel got grabbed by Matilda and they removed his tank top and scarf then they grabbed his upper arm bracelet. Kylestone grabbed onto his upper arm bracelet and tried to pull back away from them.

"Let go of that, that was given to my father for his sixteenth birthday that he gave to me." said Kylestone, trying to pull it back.

But it was still taken from him by making him lose his grip. Then they let go of Ariel and Kylestone and Ariel and Kylestone sat on the floor with their arms around each other.

"Please let us go." said Ariel.

"You guys are not allowed to leave." said Carlica.

"So you guys have your vehicles parked in areas in the woods that's not far from here." said Kylestone.

"Uh-huh." said Neevya.

"Young lady I am very mad at you for slithering away and because of you disobeying me and your mother you have us both captured." said Kylestone.

"I'm sorry dad I didn't want this to happen. I wanted to go to the spa because I was invited-." said Ariel.

"Invited by who?" said Kylestone.

"That would be me but it was to capture her," said Carlica.

"You were hanging out with her." said Kylestone to Ariel.

"Well not exactly." said Ariel.

"I'm confused." said Kylestone.

"You know what I don't need to hear this because I know what happened so have them be put in one of the bedrooms and fork the door so they don't get out since none of the bedroom doors have locks." said Carlica.

"Um, couldn't you just grab them you are able to do that." said Nagaila.

"Oh right." said Carlica.

So Carlica grabbed Ariel and Kylestone with each one of her hands around their arms and waist.

"No you can't." said Kylestone.

"We can, I'm saying this in my human form." said Veza.

Veza changed into her yovola form.

"We can, and I'm saying it in this form." said Veza.

Then Veza changed back into a human. Then Carlica carried Ariel and Kylestone to a bathroom and dropped them in there on the bed then Nadeline forked the door so they couldn't get out. Kylestone tried to open it but he couldn't then he went back to the bed with Ariel.

"Huh." said Kylestone, upset with his head down and eyes closed.

Ariel felt scared about how her dad is going to be to her. Then he opened his eyes and turned his head at Ariel with a mad face at her then lifted his head up.

"Continue on telling me what happened, right now." said Kylestone.

Ariel felt scared and nervous to speak.

"You heard me!" said Kylestone.

Where Regina is she has been calling Kylestone.

"Kylestone if you're not in trouble please answer me I'm worried about you." said Regina, calling through her phone.

Just then Pocahontas and Tarzan came up to Regina in their family car.

"Any luck mom and dad?" said Regina to her parents, through the car window opened.

"No we couldn't find Ariel or Kylestone." said Tarzan.

"Did he answer?" said Pocahontas.

"No he would have called me back by now I think something bad happened to him, oh where is my husband

and baby." said Regina, putting her head down on where the window is in.

Pocahontas and Tarzan got out of the car to comfort Regina.

"We're worried about them too." said Pocahontas, with her hand on Regina's back.

"It's true but it's getting really late and we need to get home. Do you want me to tell Zinnia about Kylestone?" said Tarzan, with his hand on Regina's back too.

"Thanks dad but I'll tell her." said Regina, lifting her head up.

So they all got into the car and headed home. Zinnia was in the living room sitting on the couch making jewelry in a worried and tired way then Regina came to Zinnia nervous to tell her about Kylestone first she sat on the couch with Zinnia.

"Regina wants wrong did you guys find Ariel?" said Zinnia.

"Did she or Kylestone come back?" said Regina.

"I wish they did but no." said Zinnia.

"So they're both missing." said Regina.

"Did you just say both, meaning my baby is missing too?" said Zinnia.

"I'm afraid so." said Regina.

"Oh no no not my baby boy too." said Zinnia, getting up from the couch after putting her jewelry down.

Zinnia covered her face with her hands.

"No no." said Zinnia.

"We'll go to bed and try finding them in the morning and spread the word out." said Regina, with her hands on Zinnia's arm.

Then Zinnia and Regina hugged each other.

"Oh Zinnia I hope they're okay." said Regina.

"Me too." said Zinnia.

At the room where Ariel and Kylestone are being kept in.

"And that's what happened." said Ariel.

"Are you serious!" said Kylestone, mad.

Just then they heard banging on the door of the room they're being kept in.

"Simmer down with the yell. I wouldn't mind it if I wasn't trying to go to sleep." said Hailey, behind the door.

"You should not be near those girls for that reason, they're bad." said Kylestone to Ariel.

"I'm sorry." said Ariel.

"And because of you doing that now we are both in this situation." said Kylestone.

Ariel felt sad.

"You know most kids don't have this stuff happen to their fathers, unbelievable Ariel!" said Kylestone, grabbing the light switch next to the bed they are in.

"Hey what did I say." said Hailey, behind the door of the bedroom Kylestone and Ariel are being kept in.

"Sorry." Kylestone said to Hailey.

Then he turned off the light and went to sleep. Ariel and Kylestone both were in the same bed Ariel didn't go to sleep she just laid down in the bed with the blanket over her and started having tears falling from her eyes.

At Ariel and her family's house, Regina laid in her and Kylestone's bed on Kylestone's side with her dress and necklace still on her and not with the blanket over her because of how upset she was feeling and had her arms around her pillow under her chin.

"Everyone look I'm juggling rubber spiders." said a man outside.

Regina, Tarzan, Pocahontas, and Zinnia opened the curtains and saw the man and a few more people with him doing things like juggling, playing the accordion, holding out relighting sparkers, all while on rollerskates.

"Don't those guys have any idea how late it is?" said Tarzan.

"Too bad they don't know where Ariel and Kylestone are your dad and I asked them earlier and the one with the accordion fainted with upsetness when he heard what we told them but they did say they keep an eye out for them." said Pocahontas to Regina.

"Whoa." said Regina.

At the room where Kylestone and Ariel are, Ariel got out of the bed and put her pillow down on the floor next to the bed and grabbed a blanket to place over her and fell asleep. Later in the middle of the night Kylestone woke up realizing where he is and feeling sad about it and turned to where he thought Ariel was but saw her gone and he got worried so he got out of bed and looked by the bed on Ariel's side and saw her sleeping on the floor and he didn't want that for her so he lifted part of the blanket on the bed on Ariel's side and picked her up and placed her there and then put the blanket over then he went to bed and put his arm over Ariel. Later it became the next morning Nagaila, Matilda, and Tuckles were awake.

"Okay girls you know what to do." said Matilda.

In the room where Ariel is with Kylestone Ariel woke up and realized she was not on the floor then Kylestone woke up once Ariel lifted his arm that's over her.

"What, but I was on the floor." said Ariel.

"I know, and I brought you here because I would rather have you sleep in a comfy bed." said Kylestone.

"Sm." said Ariel starting to cry again.

"Baby." said Kylestone.

"I don't want to talk right now." said Ariel.

Kylestone looked at the lamp and saw a note on it that said: Don't be a singer like disgrace Ivern. Kylestone got mad about that note he ripped it off and crumpled it and threw it on the floor. Nadeline came up to their door while holding plates. Ariel and Kylestone both sat on the bed hugging each other worried about what was going to happen when they heard Nadeline coming in. Nadeline left the plates of scrambled eggs and waffles on the floor by the door.

"What you guys are eating for breakfast." said Nadeline to Ariel and Kylestone.

Then Nadeline fork locked the door. Kylestone got off the bed and grabbed the plates and handed one to Ariel then they started eating but sadly. Their family and friends were all looking for Ariel and Kylestone outside.

"Okay guys I did a radio announcement to try telling everyone to keep an eye out for Ariel and Kylestone."

said Darent's dad, who came up to them with Darent and Darent's mom.

"And I sent the word out to the entire police force and some of them had a panic attack about the son and granddaughter of a dead singer they adore so much have gone missing." said Belyndica's dad, who came over with Belyndica's mom and Belyndica with a mankin.

"And I told this gal to keep an eye out for them." said Belyndica, setting her mankin standing up.

"Thanks you guys." said Regina.

"Thank you." said Pocahontas.

"Thank you." said Tarzan.

Zinnia leaned herself against the wall of a dinner all sad.

"Thanks." said Zinnia.

Regina and Pocahontas and Tarzan went to Zinnia to comfort her.

"We're still here with you." said Tarzan, with his hand on Zinnia's back and the other one on her arm.

Belyndica, Dilia, Pennya, Ocieana, and Mabel all hugged the dinner wall.

"Why are you gals hugging the diner?" said Natasha.

"Aren't they also hugging the diner wall too because they love it?" said Ocieana, pointing at Zinnia, Regina, Pocahontas, and Tarzan.

"Guys that's not why." said Chrysalis.

"Oh." said Belyndica, Dilia, Pennya, Ocieana, and Mabel.

"Maybe the temperate jungle tribe knows anything about what happened to them?" said Chrysalis.

"Temperate jungle tribe?" said Regina.

"Yeah they're Noodle's neighbors they're people and people/monsters who live in the temperate jungle by Noodles house and her barns." said Chrysalis.

"They also have beautiful flowers there Sue always tries to grab them." said Jerrica, with Sue in her arms.

"Sue's a flower grabber." said Aaron.

"And a cute one." said Chrysalis.

"And we can show them our outfits." said Lumia, dressed as a tree.

So are Swifta, Agnesa, Dayla, Mirabel, Cherryette, Bessa, Cleo, Falla, and Constance.

"Oho, nice costumes." said Dava.

"Thanks." Chrysalis' friends dressed as trees said.

"You girls are going there dressed as trees?" said Jaser.

"Yeah those guys love trees so much that that's why they live in the temperate jungle by Noodle's house and her barns." said Constance.

"Yeah we thought they would like to see us dressed as trees." said Cherryette.

"Uh, okay." said Jaser finding it a little weird.

"Great idea guys." said Chrysalis.

"There's a path by my house and my barns that leads to them in the temperate jungle." said Noodle to Regina, Tarzan, Pocahontas, and Zinnia.

"Come on." said Chrysalis.

At the room where Ariel and Kylestone are being kept in Ariel and Kylestone finished eating and placed their plates down then they heard the door trying to be open.

"Oops forgot to unlock this door." said Matilda behind the door.

Ariel knew it was her so she quickly tightly hugged her dad.

"Ow, baby that's really tight." said Kylestone.

Matilda opened the door and came in with Nagaila and Tuckles and they had Carlica in her walloi form at the door entrance blocking it.

"Are you guys done? We came to get your plates." said Nagaila.

"Cute as a button you are." said Matilda to Ariel.

Matilda tried to pinch Ariel's cheeks again but Ariel and Kylestone pushed her hand away.

"Don't try to do that to my daughter." said Kylestone to Matilda.

"Leave me alone and my dad." said Ariel.

"Still like that how you were at the mall." said Matilda.

"Baby did you meet her earlier when you were at the mall?" said Kylestone.

"Well I um, yes." said Ariel.

"What happened there?" said Kylestone.

"Oho a show, don't know why I made popcorn but I'm glad I did." said Carlica, grabbing and eating her bowl of popcorn.

"Well I tried to catch her at the mall but she kept getting away." said Matilda.

"What! Is that true you don't mention about seeing, what her name is at the mall when you were with Carlica." said Kylestone.

"Huh, yes." said Ariel.

"But the way my name is Matilda." said Matilda.

"I'm Nagaila by the way." said Nagaila.

"And my name's Buckles, oops I mean Tuckles." said Tuckles.

"Anyway we're going to giving you guys baths soon but in spread bathrooms." said Nagaila.

"What." said Ariel and Kylestone.

"Dawa." said Matilda looking at Ariel.

Ariel didn't like how Matilda was staring at her then Matilda grabbed Ariel out of Kylestone's arms Nagaila had Kylestone in her arms when he got up to grab Ariel back and Matilda had Ariel with her arm around Ariel against her and started to pinched Ariel's cheek.

"Ow you're hurting me." said Ariel.

"Don't hurt my baby." said Kylestone.

But then Nagaila covered his mouth with her hand.

"Mmmhmm." Kylestone said, with his mouth covered.

"Can it." said Nagaila to Kylestone.

"Aacoua." coughed Carlica, which they all started at. "Went down the wrong pipe."

Matilda got an idea she put her hand that was pinching Ariel's cheek over Ariel's mouth and grabbed Ariel's mouth moving it back and forth.

"Mmmmhumm." said Ariel while Matilda did that.

"Aw you feel so soft." said Matilda.

Kylestone thought what Matilda was doing was weird.

"Mmummhum." said Kylestone with his mouth covered.

Chrysalis and her friends arrived at the temperate jungle tribe.

"Now remember even though they live in a temperate jungle they still live how we do with things like electronics so you can talk to them how we do to each other." said Chrysalis.

"Whowy awesome costumes!" said a man, who is a temperate jungle tribe member to Chrysalis' friends dressed as trees.

"Thank you." said Chrysalis' friends, dressed as trees.

"Your guys' costumes sure are a hit." said Chrysalis.

"Oh hey there's my dad and mom." said Trudy, pointing at them.

"Hey everyone and Trudy." said Trudy's dad, while his wife waved at them.

The rest of them waved back and Trudy went over and hugged her parents.

"Mom dad did you find anything on where Ariel and Kylestone could have gone?" said Trudy.

"Sadly no." said Trudy's mom.

"Hey guys." said Nia.

"Hey Nia." they all said.

"Yep that's me." said Nia.

"Ah man Nia is it true that you or anyone else in this temperate jungle doesn't have a clue where Kylestone and Ariel are?" said Chrysalis.

"Yeah it's true." said Nia.

"Well Kylestone is not at the big stay at the house that my great-grandma bought that isn't covered in vines that's the place he said he was going to before he went missing." said Chrysalis.

"It's true my parents and Zinnia and I checked there." said Regina.

"That's a mystery nice trees outfit you guys." said Nia to Chrysalis' friends dressed as trees.

"Thanks Nia." said Chrysalis' friends dressed as trees but feeling a little sad about Kylestone and Ariel.

"Oh man." said some of the people in the temperate jungle tribe, feeling sad too.

"Yeah those guys have been very upset lately about the son and granddaughter of Ivern missing they're really big fans of Ivern." Nia said to Regina, Tarzan, Pocahontas, and Zinnia.

"Sometimes they do get excited when you say Ivern's name oh and another thing they get crazy scared when you mention an owl." whispered Chrysalis to Regina, Tarzan, Pocahontas, and Zinnia.

"An owl?" whispered Regina.

"Yep." whispered Chrysalis.

"Hey Chrysalis you were whispering to Regina, Tarzan, Pocahontas, and Zinnia not to mention an owl right?" said Cherryette.

"AN OWL, WHERE!?" said some of the temperate jungle tribe members, scared.

"Oops sorry about that!" said Cherryette.

"Come down you guys there's no- what you guys are scared of!" said Chrysalis.

So the temperate jungle tribe members that are scared of owls stopped panicking.

"Wow they are that scared of- those things?" said Regina.

"Yep." said Chrysalis.

"Wow they love trees so much that they don't care that they're living in an area where you're more likely to see- that what Chrysalis said, than where we live." said Tarzan.

"They do know that right?" said Pocahontas.

"Yep we told them that." said Chrysalis.

Chrysalis got out her phone and set it to the instrument choice playing to singing app and got out her music lover bracelet and started singing then while her bracelet shone yellow light with pink and blue polka dots on it making everyone feel better. Then she stopped and put her phone and bracelet away.

"Do you guys feel better?" said Chrysalis.

"Yeah." said Everyone.

"Hey, who here brought this FAKE owl?" said Agnesa pointing at a "fake" owl on a tree branch low enough for her to touch it.

"Ah Agnesa that's a real owl." said Chrysalis pointing at it too.

The owl turned its head to Agnesa and made a hoot sound.

"Oh." said Agnesa.

But Agnesa and Chrysalis and their friends and family weren't scared but some of the temperate jungle tribe members were and started panicking.

"AH, AH, AH." the temperate jungle tribe, who are scared of owls yelled.

"Calm down it's just an owl!" said Chrysalis.

"They're acting like owls eat them." said Tarzan.

"Don't worry I help take care of this stuff for them." said Chrysalis.

Chrysalis got out her phone and set it to the instrument choice playing to singing app and got out her music lover bracelet and started singing then while her bracelet shone purple light with white messy shaped flickering lights and Chrysalis did that close to the owl to shoo it away with the bright lights from her bright light music lover bracelet and it worked and the owl flow away then Chrysalis stopped sing and put her phone and bracelet away again.

"Oh, oh, ah man, thank goodness, thanks Chrysalis Loom." said the temperate jungle tribe people, who are scared of owls.

"Another use for those bracelets." said Calvis.

In one of the bathrooms of <u>HANGING STARS SPOT</u> where Ariel and Kylestone are being held at Matilda, Tuckles, and Nagaila were setting up Ariel and Kylestone's baths Nagaila placed a yellow cylinder plastic pitcher on the round table next to the bathtub.

"Okay Tuckles did you grab the shampoo?" said Matilda.

"Yep it's right here." said Tuckles, holding out the shampoo bottle.

"Honey mustard shampoo Tuckles really you got that disgusting shampoo." said Matilda.

"Well I like it." said Tuckles.

"Tuckles we're not using that." said Nagaila.

Nagaila notice something else.

"And you didn't get the towel either." said Nagaila.

"Okay fine I'll get a different shampoo bottle and the towels." Tuckles said, getting up.

In the room where Ariel and Kylestone are being kept in.

"I wonder how they're planning on cleaning us separately." said Ariel.

Kylestone didn't say anything, he had his head down feeling sad Ariel felt really bad then she started to cry. Once Kylestone heard her he got out of position and wrapped his arms around Ariel and rubbed her on the back with his hand.

"Sh sh sh." said Kylestone to Ariel.

"I'm really sorry dad sm, even if I did do what I was planning to do I still shouldn't have done it sm." said Ariel while crying.

"Baby I don't understand why you didn't tell what you were doing or what has been happening to you. Do you think that your mother and I aren't there for you?" said Kylestone.

"No it's just well, I didn't want to interfere with you or mom or anyone." said Ariel.

"Baby your mother and I want you to be okay, if we have to help you with some we would want to than not." said Kylestone.

"Dad." said Ariel with her arm around her dad.

"What is it baby?" said Kylestone.

"There's something else I didn't tell you about when Carlica and her friends came to our table when we're eating at the <u>GLAMOR PAL MALL </u>they left me a note to meet them in a store at the mall so lied about leaving behind my phone to go there and that's where the stuff I told you about started to happen." said Ariel.

"What." said Kylestone, with his hand on his hip.

"I really am sorry dad sm." said Ariel crying.

Kylestone moved his hand that was on his hip and wrapped it around Ariel again then he kissed Ariel on the forehead.

"At least you told me the truth." said Kylestone.

Another tear dropped from Ariel's eye then Kylestone kissed her close to it on her cheek and wiped it away.

"I promise not to lie any more." said Ariel.

"That's my baby girl." said Kylestone.

"I really wish there was something for me to do for you." said Ariel.

"Well actually there is something." said Kylestone.

"What?" said Ariel.

"It's something we used to do together, here lay yourself in my arm." said Kylestone.

Ariel had herself placed laying in her dad's arm and he had her against his chest.

"I don't remember doing this?" said Ariel.

"Of course not." said Kylestone.

Then he started rocking her.

"Because you were a little baby when this happened." said Kylestone.

"You're rocking me." said Ariel.

"Yes do you like-." said Kylestone.

Kylestone was about to finish talking but he knew Ariel did like it because she snuggled against his chest and curled up in him more and she smiled with her eyes closed.

"Aw." said Kylestone.

Kylestone was about to kiss her on the cheek again but Ariel opened her eyes knowing what he was trying to do and she moved her head and had him kiss her on the lips on purpose she did. Kylestone felt surprised but gave in on it then they stopped kissing once he moved his head up. At their house in Regina and Kylestone's room, Regina was looking at photos of her and Kylestone in the hospital after Ariel was born and she's turned into the monster form she is now.

In Regina's flashback of that time Regina was in the hospital bed holding baby Ariel wrapped up in a blanket with Kylestone sitting next to on the bed Regina was in fourteen years ago.

"Aw, look how healthy she is." said Regina fourteen years ago.

"She's so cute." said Kylestone fourteen years ago, with his hand behind baby Ariel.

Then he removed his hand off baby Ariel then baby Ariel started wiggling.

"Mmma mm." said baby Ariel.

Then baby Ariel stopped moving and making sounds during that Kylestone fourteen years ago and Regina fourteen years ago were concerned that baby Ariel was going to cry but she didn't.

"Aw, you're our one and only little baby. What should we call her?" said Regina fourteen years ago.

Kylestone fourteen years ago and Regina fourteen years tried to come up with a name for baby Ariel.

"I think she should go by a name that begins with the letter A." said Regina fourteen years ago.

"How about, Ariel?" said Kylestone fourteen years ago.

"Ariel, that's pretty for her." said Regina fourteen years ago.

"You're a loving baby Ariel." said Kylestone fourteen years ago.

"Come snuggle with mommy Ariel." said Regina fourteen years ago.

Regina fourteen years ago had her snuggling with baby Ariel and then Regina's flashback stopped.

"Oh where are they?" said Regina.

In one of their living rooms Zinnia was looking at a picture of her and thirty-one years ago with Kylestone when he was a baby then she had a flashback of the time when she was sitting on the couch while holding baby Kylestone wrapped up in a blanket on her lap.

"What an adorable good boy you are Kylestone." said Zinnia thirty-one years ago.

"It's true he barely even cries at night." said Ivern when he was alive thirty-one years ago sitting on another couch after putting down his magazine to show his face.

Zinnia thirty-one years ago kissed baby Kylestone on the head while Ivern when he was alive thirty-one years ago came sitting next to them but then Zinnia thirty-one years ago smelled baby Kylestone's blanket and noticed it smelled odd so she unfolded him out of it.

"Honey can you watch our baby while I quickly go get him another blanket and put this one in the wash?" said Zinnia thirty-one years ago.

"Of course." said Ivern when he was alive thirty-one years ago.

Zinnia thirty-one years ago gave baby Kylestone to Ivern thirty-one years ago when he was alive then she quickly got off the couch and slithered to go do what she said. Ivern thirty-one years ago when he was alive laid his head on baby Kylestone but then he started to cry.

"What's wrong?" said Ivern thirty-one years ago when he was alive.

He looked at baby Kylestone and saw that he was crueling himself up shivering like he was cold.

"Oh you're cold." said Ivern thirty-one years ago when he was alive.

He tried to think of something.

"Here." said Ivern thirty-one years ago when he was alive.

He put baby Kylestone into his shirt he's wearing through his neck hole and held him while baby Kylestone was in there with his head out, and then baby Kylestone stopped crying then they both snuggled together. Then Zinnia thirty-one years ago quickly slithered back with another blanket.

"Okay I'm back." said Zinnia thirty-one years ago, slithering back with another blanket.

Then she realized what the two of them were doing.

"Aw that is so adorable." said Zinnia thirty-one years ago.

Then she sat on the couch too next to them.

"You want to also?" said Ivern thirty-one years ago when he was alive to Zinnia thirty-one years ago.

"Well yes but you-." said Zinnia thirty-one years ago.

"It's okay that I just did it I really want you to do it too." said Ivern thirty-one years ago when he was alive.

"Okay thanks honey." said Zinnia thirty-one years ago.

She put down the blanket on the couch and Ivern thirty-one years ago when he was alive took baby Kylestone out of his shirt and gave baby Kylestone to her and she did the same thing with baby Kylestone putting him in her mid-length sleeves boat neck sweater and she held him in there with his head out and then baby Kylestone and Zinnia thirty-one years ago snuggled each other.

"Aw that is cute." said Ivern thirty-one years ago when he was alive.

Zinnia stopped her flashback.

Pocahontas came into the room where Regina is in.

"Regina Chrysalis is here." said Pocahontas.

"Okay mom." said Regina.

Chrysalis came into the room too.

"Hey Regina my family and friends and I were wondering if you guys wanted to come to the CREEPY CREEP CENTRAL that Dakota's dad owns don't worry it's not scary honest." said Chrysalis.

"CREEPY CREEP CENTRAL why is it called that?" said Regina.

"It used to be a house for wealthy people to live in for two hundred years. Now it's a place where they sell costumes and Halloween stuff but since Halloween is a once a year thing they mostly sell clothes there for any time of the year we thought it would cheer you guys up because of them, you know, and we're also going to pay for anything you guys want there too." said Chrysalis.

"Why don't we go Regina?" said Pocahontas.

"Okay I'll tell dad and Zinnia." said Regina.

Zinnia was still in the same room when Regina came in.

"Zinnia you want to come to this <u>CREEPY CREEP CENTRAL</u> with us that Chrysalis and her friends and family want to bring us to. They said they want to pay for anything we want there because they want to cheer us up and also Dakota's dad owns that place." said Regina.

"Sure I know my son and granddaughter wouldn't want us to keeping ourselves in the house." said Zinnia, looking at the photo she was looking at earlier.

Regina came up to her and leaned against Zinnia and looked at the photo too.

"Aw, Zinnia you alway find me as a daughter to you. Do you want me to spend more time near you to make it feel like you still have a kid with you?" said Regina.

"Oh yes I would love that." said Zinnia, putting the picture frame with the photo in it down.

"I really don't like seeing a sweet mother-in-law like you upset." said Regina.

"I don't want you upset either Regina." said Zinnia, with her hand on Regina.

"We should go now to not keep them waiting." said Regina.

"Uh-huh." said Zinnia.

So they left the room to go to the others but everyone else all walked into the room too before Regina and Zinnia left.

"Hi Zinnia, are you coming too?" said Chrysalis.

"Yeah I am." said Zinnia.

"Great." said Chrysalis.

"Good to know." said Cherryette (not wearing her tree costume) yelling through the window by them in the room.

"Whoa." they all said, when they saw Cherryette.

"Are you on a ladder because that window is high?" said Tarzan.

"Yeah I wanted to know if you guys were coming." said Cherryette.

"You could have just answered the door." said Zinnia.

"Hey I got to use this ladder for something plus I want to climb it." said Cherryette.

In the room where Ariel and Kylestone are where they are still doing the rocking and snuggling thing together Kylestone started kissing Ariel on the cheek a few times and it made Ariel laugh quietly.

"My little baby girl." said Kylestone.

Just then they heard the door opening and they stopped what they were doing hugged on each other tightly and came in with Falyby and Eny and had Carlica block the door entrance in her walloi from again.

"Okay so here's how it's going to go. Falyby is taking Ariel while I take Kylestone." said Eny who is a human/

monster who looks like a human who is four feet taller than her original height and has green skin with diagonal black lines and thinner purple ones and black at the edge of her fingers and underneath her hands and very thin fingernails and very thin nail plate and her ears looks like her hands. Eny grab Kylestone's chin up to her.

"So you're the one I'm incharge of." said Eny.

"Ow." said Kylestone.

"Don't do that to him." Ariel said, while trying to pull Eny's hand off him.

Eny did let go but made Ariel and Kylestone fall.

"I was just trying to do a face to face talk meaning I'm serious about what I am saying." said Eny.

"You don't need to squeeze my face." said Kylestone, rubbing his chin.

"Yeah somethings I do that by mistake." said Eny.

"Eny are you sure you know how to use a rope?" said Falyby.

"Ha ha don't worry about it, honest." said Eny.

"Honestly I don't know what I'm going to expect but anyway come with me Ariel." said Falyby.

Eny grabbed Kylestone's arm and pulled him out of Ariel's arms then Falyby grab Ariel before Ariel got off the bed to try and escape.

"Hey guys you interested in having a cup of cranberry juice?" said Tuckles, who came into the room holding a tray of glass cups of cranberry juice by having Carlica let her go through.

"Tuckles we're doing something right now plus Eny and I don't like cranberry juice." said Falyby.

"It looks like blood to me, so freaky." said Eny, feeling weird out.

"Oh yeah right I also better go put this tray down somewhere my arms are getting tired." said Tuckles.

Then Tuckles left the room. Chrysalis, Regina, Tarzan, Pocahontas, Zinnia, and their friends arrived at the **CREEPY CREEP CENTRAL** and Chrysalis' friends who were wearing tree outfits were not wearing them.

"Wow so this place used to be a house for wealthy ones." said Zinnia.

"Yep." said Chrysalis.

"Fun place this is with the mask." said Venelope holding a flower mask.

"Wow very pretty one that is." said Regina.

"You guys have got to feel this place's wall." said Ocieana.

"Ocieana you've been hugging that wall for five minutes are you tired of standing there?" said Natasha.

"I can't help it it's so smooth." said Ocieana.

"This is a smooth wall Ocieana but I think you're going too far with it." said Princeson, while he felt the wall with his hand.

"Okay you guys are right." said Ocieana.

So Ocieana got off the wall. Just then Justina showed up.

"Hey guys sorry I'm late, my mom took a wrong turn." said Justina.

"That's okay Justina." said Chrysalis.

Justina breathed too close to Pennya, Mabel, Cassandra, Kathleenie, and Marge because she was panting from running.

"Okay Justina two things one it's not a big deal that you're late and two your breath smells bad." said Pennya.

"Yeah you need to brush your teeth, your breath smells like elck." said Kathleenie.

"Sorry I was up really late last night bat watching and I got too caught up in it." said Justina.

"Well since we're here why don't you buy yourself a creepy breath mint?" said Marge.

"Creepy breath mint?" said Tarzan.

"Yeah they sell them here, there right here." said Chrysalis, grabbing a clear holder of some to show it to them.

"Whoa." said Tarzan.

"Yeah they have mints shaped like spiders, centipedes, witches, vampires, ticks, mice, and piranhas, you guys interested?" said Chrysalis to Regina, Tarzan, Pocahontas, and Zinnia.

"Ah no thanks." said Tarzan, looking a bit weird out.

"If you want they also make ones in white to make it less odd looking." said Chrysalis, holding the clear holder of white ones.

"Still no thanks." said Tarzan.

Regina, Pocahontas, and Zinnia didn't look like they wanted them either.

"Okay." said Chrysalis.

Then Chrysalis placed them down. Just then Tinka came running over to them.

"Hey guys have any of you seen Dannya?" said Tinka.

"Oh hey there she is." said Chrysalis, pointing at her.

Dannya was pushing a tray cart with bubbly orange juice in a big clear bowl over a small fire.

"Why am I smelling orange juice?" said Heviner.

"I believe that's what's boiling in Dannya's bowl." said Chrysalis.

They all went over to Dannya.

"Dannya what are you doing?" said Darent.

"I was thinking that if those kidnappers, clearly Ariel and Kylestone were taken by kidnappers." said Dannya.

"Yeah we all think that." said Chrysalis.

"Maybe if their kidnappers are here and they smell and find this orange juice I mean who doesn't love orange juice they might come here to take it and we will catch them when they come for it." said Dannya.

"Ah man if I was a thief I would take that orange juice." said Butterscotch, looking at Dannya's bubbling orange juice.

"You see it would work for Butterscotch if she was a thief." said Dannya.

"Just let Dannya do it." said Chrysalis to everyone.

They all agree with Chrysalis.

"Hey Regina, Tarzan, Zinnia, Pocahontas do you guys want to sleepover at my house because of what happened to Ariel and Kylestone?" said Shenatha.

Regina, Tarzan, Zinnia and Pocahontas looked at each other and smiled and nodded.

"Okay Shenatha sure and thanks." said Regina.

"Thank you." said Tarzan, Zinnia, and Pocahontas to Shenatha.

In the room where Ariel and Kylestone were kept together until Falyby took Ariel, Eny was still in the room with Kylestone with him laying on bed on his stomach while she was trying to be sure she tied him with the rope right.

"Falyby thinks I can tie with rope right well. I am checking to be sure I did it right." said Eny, checking the knot.

"Clearly I'm going to be stuck here for a while." said Kylestone, while being bothered.

"Well at least you're somewhere comfortable you can't argue with that." said Eny.

"You're not planning on having me take a cold bath are you?" said Kylestone.

"Oh yeah I forgot about how long the water temperature will stay warm. I might have to unplug the drain and refill it." said Eny.

"I have a feeling I would be waiting for it to refill." said Kylestone.

Eny rubbed Kylestone's shoulder.

"Oho you have your mom's skin." said Eny.

"How do you know what my mother's skin feels like?" said Kylestone.

"Actually I don't I just wanted to say that." said Eny, back to checking how tight the rope is around Kylestone.

Just then Nadeline came into the room.

"Hey mine if we talk for a while?" said Nadeline to Eny.

"Not now Nadeline I'm still checking this rope and I need to stay focus." said Eny.

"You've been at it for a while." said Nadeline.

"That's what I've been telling her." Kylestone said to Nadeline.

"Well I wanted to tell you that we're going to be going back to the big house for those singers who this building was meant for later in the day since it's got be okay now for us to go back at that time because clearly they already investigated it to see if there's anything on him, who you have tied up, missing." said Nadeline.

"Look please let my daughter and I go." said Kylestone.

Then Nadeline covered his mouth with her hand.

"Stick with no being our answer." said Nadeline.

Then Nadeline felt a spitball at her.

"Hey, Eny!" said Nadeline.

"It wasn't me it was– um can you move your hand from him?" said Eny.

Nadeline did move her hand from Kylestone then Eny pushed the straw into his mouth.

"It was him." said Eny, while Kylestone spat the straw out.

"Give it up, his arms are tied up." said Nadeline.

"Okay fine." said Eny.

"You're always doing weird things Eny like before you heard him Kylestone speak you though he was a girl." said Nadeline.

245

"You thought I was a girl?" said Kylestone to Eny.

"Well you were wearing that bracelet." said Eny.

"It was a men's upper arm bracelet." said Kylestone.

"You better watch yourself Eny." said Nadeline, while she left the room.

"Huh, are you trying to check if the rope around me is tight enough or are you just wanting to play with the rope?" said Kylestone.

"Actually both." said Eny.

"You and I clearly aren't going to get along." said Kylestone.

In the bathroom where Ariel is with Falyby. Falyby was filling up the bathtub that's rectangle shaped and clear while Ariel was lying on her back on the floor tied up wiggling.

"Auh." said Ariel trying to get free.

"Hey I said keep quiet it's bad enough Matilda forgot to fill this tub with water now I have to do it and wait." said Falyby.

Ariel felt scared then someone grabbed the edge of her tail and pulled her up.

"Someone's got-." said Ariel.

Falyby grabbed Ariel and had her look at her face and placed tape on Ariel's mouth.

"I told you to keep it quiet or I will make you myself." said Falyby.

"Mum mhum." said Ariel trying to tell her something.

But Falyby just put her down laying on the floor again and whoever was grabbing Ariel grabbed her again by the tail and pulled her and Ariel saw it was Matilda doing that.

"Come to me." said Matilda.

"Mmummmmmummm." said Ariel flipping out about not wanting to go with Matilda.

But Falyby walked up standing right behind Matilda.

"Matilda get out." said Falyby.

"Oh hi Falyby yeah you're right I'm going to go." said Matilda looking at her.

So Matilda left the bathroom and Falyby grabbed Ariel again and placed her back where she was. Ariel turned and looked at the side of the bathtub watching the water rise and pretended she was underwater. At the <u>CREEPY CREEP CENTRAL</u>.

"Hey everyone look at this costume we're wearing." said Javada, wearing a costume that her little sisters are wearing too and are all attached to each other.

"Whoa." said Kert.

"That's unusual." said Slecks.

"It looks fun actually." said Chrysalis.

"What are you girls dressed as?" said Tarzan.

"You girls look like messy color black, gold, and purple octopuses that are bejeweled with heads shaped like scuba diving helmets from the 1920s and with some of your tentacles attached to each other." said Pocahontas.

"Yeah whoever made that costume was making up their own monster." said Raymen to Javada, Zila, Lalo, and Darma.

"I still like it." said Lalo.

"Me too, yeah, oh-huh." said Javada, Zila, and Darma.

"Looks like we know what they're wearing for Halloween." said Chrysalis.

Calvis and Rowshella came over to them.

"Hi." said Kert's little sisters to Calvis and Rowshella.

"Whoa." said Calvis shocked.

"Wow I've never seen a costume like that before." said Rowshella.

"Kert are your little sisters wearing that costume?" said Calvis.

"Yep by the why it's nice you and Rowshella are a couple now." said Kert to Calvis.

"Same thing with you and Slecks now being a couple." said Calvis to Kert.

"Hey guys look what we found in the basement here." said Constance, walking over with a terrarium of worms.

"Whoa they sell those things here?" said Tarzan.

"Yeah sometimes they sell unusual stuff like that here." said Chrysalis.

"Hey guys check out these costumes Navia and I are wearing." said Princeson dressed as a jungle prince.

"Like them." said Navia dressed as a jungle princess.

"Who you guys look great looking." said Chrysalis.

All of Chrysalis' friends agreed.

"Nice look you guys." said Patty.

"So Navia you're going around wearing a skunk on your head?" said Arianie.

"Excuse me." said Navia.

"You don't find that a complement?" said Arianie, feeling worried she said something mean.

"No Arianie she doesn't." said Amelia.

"Oh sorry." said Arianie to Navia.

"It's okay Arianie." said Navia.

"Okay everybody if you are scared of worms don't go into the room with the brown door closed because there was an accidental drop with one of the worm terrariums." said a man through the P. A. system.

Justina still walked there anyway.

"Justina, you're seriously going to go in that room?" said Darent.

"So what they're just worms." said Justina.

"Of course Justina wouldn't mind she doesn't even care if she's touching a spider web with or without a spider." said Chrysalis.

"Wow I'm not brave enough to touch that." said Zinnia.

"No wonder her mom and dad asks her to take care of the spiders that unexpectedly come in." said Gaddy.

"Glad the worms aren't in this room." said Heviner.

"Hey look a worm." said Zila.

Zila picked it up and grabbed it.

"Got it." said Zila holding the worm.

"Um okay Zila just keep that back from me." said Heviner, not wanting the worm near him.

"Okay who is it anyway?" said Zila.

"Oh there's that worm I forgot to mention that I was looking for it." said Constance.

Zila handed Constance the worm and she put it back in the terrarium.

"Thanks Zila." said Constance.

Kylestone was placed in a bathroom in the bathtub that looks just like the one in the bathroom that Ariel is in. First she placed him in and untied him but kept her hand grabbed to him to prevent him from slithering away and poured water on him with her hand and then put soap on a ball cloth loofah and rubbed it on him.

"Lucky for you the water temperature was good when we got here so it don't need to be refilled and I was able to properly tie rope wait until I tell Falyby." said Eny.

Just then Matilda came into the bathroom and walked by the tub Kylestone is in and stood on the side of it that Eny isn't sitting on her knees at. Kylestone looked at Matilda with his head facing her but his back still in a way for her to see.

"Well I got curious about what's happening in here. I already got kicked out of the bathroom that Ariel was in." said Matilda.

Then Kylestone turned himself completely at Matilda.

"Hey what are you doing? I haven't finished cleaning the front of you." said Eny to Kylestone.

"In a minute." said Kylestone.

"Don't tell me to wait." said Eny.

Kylestone was about to speak but Eny grabbed Kylestone's other arm too and faced him the other way.

"Just hold on a minute." said Kylestone.

"You stay how I want you to." said Eny.

"Huh, okay listen I'm talking to you Matilda." said Kylestone, trying to look at Matilda with his head turned as much as he can.

"Even though you're not facing at me and it looks like you're talking to the wall, ha ha." said Matilda.

"Don't make this rude and what I'm trying to tell you is to leave my baby girl alone if you don't care about how upset or bothered she's feeling. So unless you're going to treat her right leave her alone." said Kylestone.

Matilda pinched Kylestone on the cheek and not how she did with Ariel.

"Ow, what was that for?" said Kylestone rubbing his cheek that was pinched on his arm and shoulder.

"That's a pinch that's to hurt someone not how it was when I did it to Ariel." said Matilda.

"Yeah but how you did it to Ariel was still painful even though not as much as you did it to me and she didn't like it and you didn't care." said Kylestone.

"Well I'm leaving." said Matilda.

Kylestone watched Matilda leave hoping Ariel will be okay. In the bathroom where Ariel is Falyby placed Ariel in the bathtub and removed the tape from Ariel's mouth and untied her and grabbed on to Ariel's arm so she doesn't slither away too then Falyby poured water on Ariel with her hand and put soap on the ball cloth loofah and rubbed Ariel with it.

"Are you all sad because you miss your mommy?" said Falyby, teasing Ariel.

"I miss my entire family and friends." said Ariel.

"Like I care." said Falyby.

"I knew you say that." said Ariel.

Just then they heard a knock on the bathroom and Falyby went over dragging Ariel by the arm until Ariel hit at the edge of the bathtub.

"Ow." said Ariel.

Falyby opened the door and saw Matilda.

"Huh." said Ariel scared.

"You think it's fine that I come in and watch Ariel while you take a break, right?" said Matilda.

"No no no." said Ariel.

"Well fine but if she's missing I'm going to be going to you." said Falyby.

Ariel tried to hide herself behind the bathtub wall.

"You know I can see you the bathtub you're in is clear." said Matilda.

Matilda grabbed Ariel's other arm that Falyby isn't holding on to and they dragged her up the tub then Falyby let go of Ariel and left the room leaving Ariel feeling scared of being stuck with Matilda. Matilda pulled on Ariel's upper arm to her.

"Ow, what are you going to do to me?" said Ariel.

"You have been mean to me enough and I'm getting back." said Matilda.

"What no no please don't." said Ariel, trying to get Matilda to let go of her arm.

But Matilda grabbed Ariel's other upper arm too.

"Let me go, I wasn't being mean to you, you were being mean to me." said Ariel, trying to yank herself out of Matilda's hands.

"You need to learn your lesson." said Matilda.

Matilda slid her hands up to Ariel's wrists and placed then both in her one hand and tied a rope around Ariel's wrists together and Matilda held onto the stick out laces to not have Ariel interfere with what she is trying to do and she dragged Ariel with her while she walked first Matilda went up to the circle small table where the shampoos are kept on and she swapped them out with look alike bottle and putted them in a bag she had with her. Ariel knew Matilda was not replacing them with something good. Matilda dragged Ariel over while walking to the ball cloth loofah hanging on a O-ring clip attached to the bathtub and replaced that with a look alike and put the good one in her bag. Ariel felt hopeless then she looked by her and saw a very long thread from Falyby's dress that most of it in the water but a part of it out that Matilda didn't notice. Matilda wasn't looking because she was grabbing out the good shampoos to looking at them while Matilda did that Ariel tied the thread into a lasso and throw it at the small circle table and grabbed one of the bad shampoos and pulled it over to her and placed it between her pit and did the same thing to the good one in Matilda's bag but she had the good one be placed in the water and she placed the thread around the bad one just by twirl it around and gently threw it in Matilda's bag and pulled on the thread to come back to her and she keep on doing the same thing until she swapped them all including the loofahs.

"Now before I go." said Matilda.

Matilda dragged Ariel over where the "bad" loofah was hanging on the O-ring clip attached to the bathtub and tied

Ariel to the O-ring clip ring in a way she couldn't open the O-ring to remove her from it.

"And to be sure you don't tell Falyby." said Matilda.

Matilda got out a piece of light brown tape and put make up glue on it and placed it on Ariel's mouth.

"Mmumm." said Ariel.

"Now I'm going to go use these good items I have that you won't be enjoying, but you need to understand I am doing this for your own good." said Matilda, while she placed her hand on Ariel's cheek.

Ariel moved her cheek from Matilda's hand mad.

"Mmmmmhummmm." said Ariel trying to pull herself free.

"But don't worry that make up glue will only stay on you for a few minutes, oh and I will be back to do more." said Matilda walking away.

After Matilda left Ariel kept trying to get herself free then Falyby came back.

"Well let's get back to what we were doing." said Falyby.

Falyby looked at the small circle table and noticed the shampoos weren't there.

"So you have the stuff underwater huh." said Falyby to Ariel.

Ariel nodded yes.

"I know Matilda tried to do something and I will not act like I have been fooled by her plus I'm bothered by her so did you do something to prevent that from happening?" said Falyby.

Ariel nodded yes again.

"I'm guessing you used this thread here of mine." said Falyby, grabbing it out.

Again Ariel nodded yes.

"I knew it would come in handy if I left it here plus I didn't want to throw it away at a time I don't have to, now where we're we." said Falyby, collecting the stuff out of the water.

Falyby put shampoo on the loofah again and rubbed it on Ariel. Tuckles was walking by a bathroom door that Matilda is in when she heard Matilda scream.

"You accidentally put the water on too hot, don't worry you're not the only one!" said Tuckles.

"Aaaahhh!" screamed Matilda.

At the **CREEPY CREEP CENTRAL** Chrysalis and Regina went down to the basement.

"My this is a nice looking basement." said Regina.

Regina saw a fake couch that's made of very hard plastic and sat on it.

"Is this a model of a couch that was down here when this was a house?" said Regina.

"Actually that is the actual couch that belonged to the last people who lived here for a home." said Chrysalis.

"Really even this couch isn't made from wood, cloth, or leather?" said Regina.

"Yeah I was surprised when I was told that too and a lot of others." said Chrysalis.

"Hey Chrysalis we can hear your voice." said Dayla, inside the vent between Chrysalis and the couch Regina is sitting on.

"Dayla, are you in the vent?" said Chrysalis, talking to the vent.

"Yeah." said Dayla.

"I'm going to open the vent hatch." said Tinka.

So did that and Chrysalis and Regina saw Tinka and Dayla in the vent and also Bessa, Butterscotch, Cherryette, and Gaddy.

"Whoa you girls are in the vent too." said Chrysalis.

"If the store owner is okay with it and the vent is safe to go in through then yeah we're good with it." said Bessa.

"I'm only in here to watch Butterscotch and Tinka." said Gaddy.

"I like it in here." said Dayla.

Dayla grabbed out a clear thermos of tomato soup.

"And I like drinking tomato soup in here too." said Dayla.

"Well if you guys are okay and having fun." said Chrysalis.

Dayla opened her thermos and drank a little of her tomato soup. Just then Mesha, Mingmi, and Manora.

"Chrysalis are you talking to the vent?" said Mesha.

"Oho I'm glad I'm not the only one." said Manora.

"Actually I'm talking to my friends." said Chrysalis.

"The vent hallway is your friend you mean?" said Mingmi going over to see.

"No." said Chrysalis.

Mingmi looked through and saw Bessa, Butterscotch, Cherryette, Gabby,Tinka, and Dayla in there.

"Hi." said Bessa, Butterscotch, Cherryette, Gabby, Tinka, and Dayla.

"Aaahh." said Mingmi frighten when she saw them.

Chrysalis' other friends came over and saw them in the vent and Mingmi screaming.

"Whoa you guys really did go into the vents." Jaya.

"Huh you girls are weirdos." said Mesha to Bessa, Butterscotch, Cherryette, Gabby,Tinka, and Dayla.

"Yeah we know you mean girls say that a lot. Why do you guys keep saying what we already know?" said Bessa.

"Yeah you girls are being weird about that." said Butterscotch to Mesha, Manora, and Mingmi.

"And just so you know we can also be other things besides being weird, like." said Dayla.

Bessa, Butterscotch, Cherryette, Gabby, and Tinka nodded yes.

"I can sound tough listen to my growl, gggrrrhhhrrr." said Dayla with her fist up.

The strangers who saw and heard Dayla do that all applauded her.

"Who cares about growling compared to singing which I'm more amazing at than you guys." said Mesha.

"Really you don't know for sure." said Bessa.

"What is it me against you?" said Mesha.

"Me I wasn't setting up a sing off also I want to enjoy being in the vent if I don't have to." sad Bessa.

"Well are any of the rest of you willing to sing against me?" said Mesha.

"If you guys don't mind I will." said Regina getting up off the hard plastic couch after she put her bright light music lover bracelet on.

"Okay Regina." said Chrysalis.

Mesha went first and she sang after she set up her phone to play the instruments she wanted to her music and her bright light music lover bracelet placed on her wrist and while she sang her bracelet made dark purple light with pink spots and some of them had white rings around them and others were enjoying it then Mesha put her bracelet and phone away. Then it was Regina's turn after she set her phone to play her instruments she wanted to her singing and she sang while her bracelet made a mix up of yellow and red light with orange spots and white eight point stars in the orange light and everyone loved it even more then Regina finished and put her stuff away too.

"Unbelievable." said Mesha.

"Well you girls looked like you were shocked at how good Regina performed." said Chrysalis to Mesha, Manora, Mingmi.

"Yeah you girls looked almost as surprised as some of the temperate jungle tribe members when they get scared of an owl." said Axa.

"An owl where?" said four people, coming up scared to of them were the ones who carried Vargoe on a stretcher.

"I said almost as surprised as some of the temperate jungle tribe members when they get scared of an owl, not that there's an owl here." said Axa.

"Relax there's no owl." Chrysalis said to the four people.

The four people calmed down.

"They're scared of them too." said Tarzan.

"Why are you four scared of them so much?" said Manora.

"Why would we not be." said one of them, who is a man.

"Are you four friends of Mesha, Manora, and Mingmi?" said Chrysalis to the four people.

"Yes we are and sorry that we're late to cheer on you while you were singing against- uh Regina." said one of them, who is a lady.

"You guys should be, you guys missed the whole thing." said Mesha.

"But we did see some of it." said the other one of them, who is a man.

"Hey everyone here is a display of the pies for sale at the <u>SWEET AS CANDY BAKERY</u> with Ivern's face on them." said a man, holding a big pie tray with multiple pies on it with Ivern's picture and a lady holding the other side.

"Oh wow!" said the people they walked by.

"Seriously unbelievable that they thought you sang and performed better than me." said Mesha to Regina.

Mesha got so mad she kicked a big tall rolling stool with Halloween masks on it and it rolled to the lady holding the pie tray's left side and made her fall and she and the man on the other side fell too and made the pies fly in the air.

"Look out." the man and women, who were holding the tray and others by them said.

Chrysalis and her friends ran and Tinka closed the hatch but Mesha, Manora, Mingmi and their four other friends did not move and once they saw the pies and so Mesha, Manora, Mingmi and their four other friends got hit by them and got pie on them too.

"Are you serious?" said Manora.

Tinka opened the hatch and Chrysalis and her friends came back over.

"Whoa that was surprising." said Chrysalis, looking at Mesha, Manora, Mingmi, their four other friends covered in pies.

"Better than being near an owl." said another one of Mesha, Manora, and Mingmi's four friends, who is a woman.

"You're way too odd." said Manora to her, Manora, Mingmi's four friends.

Then Mesha, Manora, Mingmi, and their four friends left.

"That sure we ruff for them." said Pocahontas.

In the bathroom where Kylestone is being kept Eny poured water on him again and grabbed him out of the bathtub and she placed a lay out blanket on the floor and placed him on top and rubbed him dry with a towel, then folded the blanket around him, and picked him up with her hand around him and took him out of the bathroom. In the bathroom where Ariel is she still had her wrists tied and her mouth covered by light brown tape stuck with make up glue. Falyby also poured water on Ariel with her hand and untied Ariel's wrist and placed a lay out blanket on the floor and put Ariel on it while Falyby rubbed a towel on Ariel while Ariel tried to pull off the tape but she couldn't and it kept hurting her mouth when she tried. Then Falyby folded the blanket around Ariel and grabbed her with her hand and carried Ariel out and into a room where her dad was already in and placed her in there and closed and locked the door. Kylestone quickly got off the bed he was sitting on and hugged Ariel out of the blanket she was in.

"Oh, my little baby." said Kylestone.

"Mmmuhmmmmu." said Ariel, still trying to pull the tape off.

"Oh here we'll pull it together." said Kylestone, with his hand grabbed to the tape edge too.

They both pulled it together and it came off.

"OW!" said Ariel.

Ariel lips hurt some much she cried, but Kylestone kissed Ariel on the lips to make her feel better.

"Huh." said Ariel, feeling her lips feeling better.

Then they both hugged each other. Chrysalis and her friends were all leaving the <u>CREEPY CREEP CENTRAL</u> and were walking outside on the sidewalk.

"That place was fun." said Zinnia.

"Hey Chrysalis, speak to me." said Gaddy.

"Um hey Gaddy did you enjoy seeing worms?" said Chrysalis.

"The worms were fun and hey why don't you talk to the puppet?" said Gaddy.

Gaddy held up her puppet on a stick with another stick under its mouth in front of Chrysalis' face.

"Well Gaddy's puppet did you like the worms?" said Chrysalis.

"The worms were wiggly terrific." said the puppet.

"Ha ha did you think they were slimy enough?" said Chrysalis to the puppet.

"Oh yes they were but man I wish I was that slim, take it from me, I'm crazy." said the puppet.

Everyone laughed.

"Good find Gaddy." said Tarzan.

"Yep." said Gaddy.

Belyndica's dad drove over in his police car.

"Hey dad any luck finding Ariel or Kylestone?" said Belyndica.

"Sorry I'm afraid not." said Belyndica's dad.

"On." said them all.

"On." said a group of photographers.

"On." said a group of strangers.

Just then they saw the flower shaped bus drive by with people riding on the top of it with telescopes and binoculars.

"People are riding on the top." said Kert.

Yeah they added seats and seatbelts to that bus' top once they heard that Ivern's son and granddaughter were missing to look out for them better." said Chrysalis.

"Oh so that's why the bus skipped its stops today." said Swifta.

"Well I'm going to go get myself a smoothie." said Chrysalis.

So Chrysalis left to go get one.

"See you guys later." said Chrysalis.

"Okay." they all said.

At the room Ariel and Kylestone are being kept in, the two of them were hugging each while Ariel sat on her dad's lap while he sat on the bed.

"And that's what happened in there during my bath." said Ariel, while tears dropped from her eyes.

"Really." said Kylestone.

Kylestone kissed Ariel on the head.

"I'm worried what Matilda will do to me. She said she's not done with me." said Ariel.

"I'll try to protect you baby." said Kylestone.

Then he kissed her again on the forehead and a couple times on her cheek but Ariel still felt sad and started to cry more and her dad noticed.

"Oh baby I promise I won't let her do anything to you." said Kylestone.

"It's not just that I really am sorry that I brought you into this kidnapping mess." said Ariel.

"Baby I told you I still love you and want to care for you and I'm not mad at you so can you please stop crying about feeling guilty?" said Kylestone.

"I know you do but still I can't help but feel this way but I'll try." said Ariel.

"Good baby girl." said Kylestone.

Just then they heard the door opening and they saw Matilda coming in.

"Don't think about escaping the door Falyby is guarding it outside of it, I don't know have my plan to teach you a lesson failed but like I said I'm not done with you." said Matilda to Ariel.

Ariel hugged her dad tightly and her dad blocked Ariel with his arm covering her.

"Stay away from my baby." said Kylestone to Matilda.

"You think I'm going to listen to you." said Matilda to Kylestone.

Matilda grabbed Kylestone's arm and tried to pull him away but Ariel grabbed her dad's other arm to prevent that from happening.

"Ah ow." said Kylestone.

"Let go of my dad. I won't let you do anything to him." said Ariel.

Matilda did let go of Kylestone to push and knock down Ariel while she was yanking on her dad and made Ariel hit the floor on her left side.

"Ow." said Ariel.

Kylestone quickly went to her and picked her up in her arms while he still sat on the floor with her laying in his arms.

"My baby are you alright?" said Kylestone.

"I'm fine." said Ariel.

Kylestone turned her more facing him.

"My baby, my little baby girl." said Kylestone, while lifting her up to him.

"I want to say something that I really feel like saying now after heard what happen, I knew you would be like this by the way I'm talking to you Kylestone being just like your pathetic father how awful is to be like him at least he's not around bothering us because he's dead so now we have a pathetic rack like you around." said Falyby.

Kylestone started to feel like crying.

"Don't say that." said Kylestone.

"Why should anyone listen to you? You belong to be kept with us to be held captive." said Falyby.

"Dad." said Ariel, worried that her dad was about to cry.

"Is that why you wish he was here so you're not the only one pathetic at least?" said Falyby.

Kylestone got up off the floor with Ariel and had her stand up and grabbed her by the wrist and brought her with him up to the wall and placed her against his chest with his arms around her so she's kept with him while he placed his head against the wall crying.

"Well I believe I'm done here." said Matilda.

So Falyby and Matilda left the room and locked it again while Kylestone kept crying with his feelings hurt.

"Didn't cry dad." said Ariel, looking up at him.

But Kylestone kept crying so Ariel snuggled with him with her arms around him and kissed him on the heart a few times all while smiling then Kylestone started to cry less and looked at what Ariel was doing to him. Even though Ariel stopped hearing him crying she still kept kissing him on the heart and snuggled with him had her arms around him and smiled and it made him feel better.

"Sm huh, sm." said Kylestone, while crying less.

Then he had both his arms around Ariel, and he stopped laying his head against the wall.

"Oh, my little baby girl." said Kylestone, still having tears coming from his eyes but smiling.

Then he sat on the bed with Ariel on his lap with his arms around and her still doing the same thing to him. Then he started kissing her on the head again a couple times.

"See you're a good girl I'm glad you made me feel better thank you." said Kylestone.

"You know I care about you no matter what." said Ariel.

"I know and I care about you no matter what too." said Kylestone.

Then Kylestone went back to kissing Ariel. Chrysalis arrived where to get a smoothie but there was a lady in front of her. Chrysalis couldn't see her face because of the big black hat she's wearing but she knew the lady has black hair and the lady was wearing a black trench coat.

"Okay ma'am here's your order." said a guy behind the counter.

"Uh, I don't order an Ivern cup." said the lady.

"Oh well we're giving these out to everyone oh man I'm a big fan-." said the man behind the counter.

"Okay, got it." said the lady, with her hand out wanting him to stop.

"And keep an eye out for his son and grandda-.' said the man behind the counter, before beginning interrupted by the lady again.

"Okay yes we know his son and granddaughter are gone everyone has been mentioning that." said the lady.

Chrysalis felt strange about the lady in front of her.

"I'm shocked to meet someone who doesn't want a our cups with Ivern on it." said the man behind the counter.

"I just want a cup without Ivern on it because I want to be sure that everyone else gets a cup with him on it." said the lady.

"Well they are going like crazy, but not as much as the Ivern cakes at the bakery, but we don't have any other cups so everyone who comes here will get one." said the man behind the counter.

"Oh really great." said the lady.

"And also keep an eye out for the rotten horrible lady who dared kill the singer Iver-." said the man behind the counter, before getting interrupted by the lady the third time.

"No need to say it! It's too sad to hear and I know" said the lady.

"Yeah I shouldn't continue I'm about to cry just thinking about it." said the man behind the counter.

The lady left and Chrysalis watched her walk away.

Regina was at the store going grocery shopping while pushing a cart feeling a little sad then she ran into Taffada and Raymen while Trixie was being held in Taffada's arms.

"Hi Regina are you feeling okay?" said Raymen.

"Still feeling sad but okay." said Regina.

"You know you did a great job singing and how lovely you made your bracelet light up, and how you moved while enjoying your singing." said Taffada.

Regina saw a paper of Trixie on a diaper box in Raymen and Taffada's cart.

"Thanks I appreciate it and I see Trixie is on the diaper box." said Regina.

"Yep and adorable she is." said Raymen.

"When they take her picture they aren't using their cameras on flash?" said Regina.

"Oh no that's not good for a baby we know that." said Raymen.

"Oh good just checking." said Regina.

"Trixie is on a few other boxes in the baby aisle." said Taffada.

"Oh how nice." said Regina.

Regina entered the aisle where Trixie's picture was shown on boxes.

"Aw she looks so cute." said Regina looking at them.

Then Regina started to have a flashback of when Ariel was a baby. In Regina's flashback she and Kylestone were doing the dishes together while baby Ariel was wrapped up in a blanket napping lying on a pillow far enough from the sink while on her right side.

"Aw." said Regina fourteen years ago while looking at baby Ariel.

Regina fourteen years ago dried her hands and pet baby Ariel on baby Ariel's left side.

"Great job making her." said Kylestone fourteen years ago to Regina fourteen years ago.

Then Kylestone fourteen years ago rubbed his head on top of Regina fourteen years ago and Regina fourteen years ago rubbed against him while laughing silently with her mouth closed. Just then baby Ariel started crying.

"Oh shot I got to feed her now." said Regina fourteen years ago.

"You do that I'll continue on." said Kylestone fourteen years ago.

"Thanks honey." said Regina fourteen years ago.

Regina fourteen years ago grabbed baby Ariel, and started to feed her.

"My she looks like she was hungry." said Regina fourteen years ago.

Regina stopped her flashback.

"Wherever the two of you are my husband and baby I hope you both are alright." said Regina.

Chrysalis was at Dilia's house where Dilia makes her formulas which is what Dilia is doing.

"Still no luck finding them." said Chrysalis.

"I don't have any luck finding them either but while I was searching for them I did find some things to use for my formulas." said Dilia.

"At least you found that stuffs." said Chrysalis.

Chrysalis looked over by Dilia and saw some paper towels, bowls of soup, and ice cream in a mini freezer.

"You have all that stuff next to you because you miss Ariel and Kylestone so much?" said Chrysalis.

"Well yes but most of that stuff is there because I want them just because I want them, Chet and Fern got the stuff for me and yes they know about what I told you about most of the stuff I'm not using them just to get stuff." said Dilia.

"That's good." said Chrysalis.

"I told them to only give me paper towels not only because I can use them for tissues but also to clean up my messes, speaking of messes." said Dilia, while pouring things into a beaker that's inside a cylinder glass container with its lid off.

"What formula is that?" said Chrysalis.

"Watch what happens." said Dilia.

Dilia put in a drop of water into the beaker and quickly shut the lid and the formula exploded pink stuff but not straight up it exploded out wideout like flower pebbles bursting out and from the top too.

"Wow." said Chrysalis.

"Don't worry about that stuff getting on you it's harmless." said Dilia.

"So it does that when you put water in it?" said Chrysalis.

"Actually with any liquids, oh and I made others over there." said Dilia, pointing at the table with other beakers of that same formula by the door on the table.

Just then Darent and Venelope can enter the room. Darent was holding a bottle of berry juice with no lid.

"Hey guys what's going on?" said Darent, while accidently dropping some of his berry juice into one of the beakers.

"Guys get away from that beaker and hide." said Chrysalis, going under cover.

"Stay away from it." said Dilia, doing the same thing Chrysalis is.

But it was too late for Darent and Venelope the beaker exploded green stuff on them. Chrysalis and Dilia were clean and saw Darent and Venelope were not.

"Ah man." said Darent.

"I actually don't mind my dress having this green on it. This stuff stays permanent on clothes right?" said Venelope.

"Actually no it explodes from liquids such as water but it can come off from water." said Dilia.

Just then Justina came into the room and saw what happened.

"Whoa." said Justina shocked.

In the room where Ariel and Kylestone, are kept in hugging each other on the bed they suddenly heard the door being open and they hugged each other more tightly and in came Nadeline, Eny, Neevya, Hailey, Manora, Mesha, Mingmi, and Carlica still in her walloi form.

"What are you here for now?" said Kylestone.

"Well the one who's incharge of us wants to show herself to the two of you guys now and who wanted us to kidnap you guys." Nadeline to Ariel and Kylestone.

"You guys have heard of her before and of course you guys have." said Eny.

"What do you mean?" said Ariel.

"Well because of something she did twenty years ago." said Nadeline.

Ariel and Kylestone had faces like they think they know what Nadeline is talking about.

"About your father who's her grandfather." said Nadeline to Kylestone.

"Huh." said Ariel and Kylestone shocked.

"Her she's here." said Kylestone.

"Where is she?" said Ariel mad.

"She is here and she's a friend of ours." said Falyby, who came into the room.

"I'm guessing she not you Falyby." said Ariel.

"Right on that." said Falyby.

"Who is she?" said Kylestone.

"Me." said a lady with a big black hat covering her face and wearing a long black trench coat standing leaning on the doorway edge that Carlica is not blocking.

She then slowly lifted the hat up her face until they clearly saw her entire front head and she did have black hair but she was no one who they've seen before.

"You." said Kylestone, mad with his teeth together.

"You guys probably never knew my name I'm AmeraAmara." said the lady.

"Am- Amera-Am- Amara?" said Ariel.

"Try practicing it." said AmeraAmara to Ariel.

AmeraAmara walked up to Ariel and Kylestone, and they went up the bed until they hit the end of it.

"My Kylestone I remember when you were a little boy, my have you grown." said AmeraAmara.

"You left us that note on the lamp in the room we were in didn't you and you gave Falyby that note to pass around to other singers too?" said Ariel to AmeraAmara.

"Yes you're right on both of those." said AmeraAmara.

"That was my father who you killed." said Kylestone.

"Zip it I wanted to be a singer my whole life but I wasn't expected because everyone thought my voice didn't sound good enough from hearing your father Ivern's singing, they thought my voice wasn't good they alway said Ivern's voice

272

is too good and after hearing him my voice sounds like they should forget about. Hearing me sing every judge and everyone kept saying that to me I couldn't stand it." said AmeraAmara.

In AmeraAmara's flashback. Ivern was slithering then AmeraAmara in her big black hat and long black trench coat came in front of him.

"Excuse me." said Ivern when he was alive twenty years ago.

But AmeraAmara twenty years ago wouldn't let him pass her even when he turned back.

"Are you wanting an autograph?" said Ivern when he was alive twenty years ago.

"No." said AmeraAmara twenty years ago.

"Is something wrong?" said Ivern when he was alive twenty years ago.

"Oh yes making someone like me not living your life of a singer." said AmeraAmara twenty years ago.

"I don't understand." said Ivern when he was alive twenty years ago.

"I wanted to be a singer!" said AmeraAmera twenty years ago.

Ivern when he was alive twenty years ago tried to get away from her but she grabbed him by the arm and then both arms and had him down in a way he was not standing.

"What are you doing?" said Ivern when he was alive twenty years ago.

"Because of you everyone thought that my voice should be forgotten compared to your's!" said AmeraAmara twenty years ago.

Then AmeraAmara from twenty years ago threw him on the street (no being shown) but unexpectedly a car ran over him (no being shown). Once after that happen AmeraAmara twenty years ago became shocked that she killed him and she quickly ran off. That was it with AmeraAmara's flashback that she told Ariel and Kylestone while thinking about it.

"And that was how it went." said AmeraAmara.

"Wow I was told that story more than once before and I still feel shocked hearing it." said Neevya.

Ariel and Kylestone were both breathing deeply with tears from their eyes.

"That was my father he didn't do anything you to wrong." said Kylestone.

"If you don't kill him and just be happy for him you would be living a life on the run." said Ariel.

"Say what you want I'm mad at him, of course you freaks say that the ones who share his DNA." said AmeraAmara.

"I'm guessing you're the one who destroyed the snake blood bottles at the store." said Ariel.

"Of course, I hate snakes because they remind me of him." said AmeraAmara.

"Um, can we take them to the big house that's not covered by vines, but is next to it now?" said Carlica.

"Well yes Carlica we'll take them now, tie them up and place them in the bag." said AmeraAmara.

So AmeraAmara left the room while everyone else in the room tied Ariel and Kylestone up with the dark brown ropes and placed white tape on their mouths and placed them in the bag and tied it up and Nadeline carried them out. Regina arrived at the temperate jungle where the temperate jungle tribe members are.

"Regina are you okay? You look like a tear is about to fall from you?" said Chrysalis.

Chrysalis saw Regina wipe a tear from her eye that just started to fall.

"I was looking at images of Trixie on diaper boxes when I was grocery shopping and then I started to think when Ariel was a baby." said Regina.

"Ah man." said Chrysalis.

"I came here to slither around to calm me." said Regina.

"Hey guys." said Lumia who came to them.

Just then they saw Bessa walking weirdly without her glasses.

"Bessa where are your glasses?" said Chrysalis.

"I accidentally dropped them, oh hey Chrysalis I just found Kylestone (really Bessa was looking at Regina) you were at the temperate jungle tribe area the whole time what the heck." said Bessa.

"Where I don't see Kylestone?" said Lumia.

"Lumia, Bessa has really bad eyesight without her glasses and she's mistaking Regina for Kylestone." said Chrysalis.

"I am?" said Bessa looking at Regina.

"Yes you are." said Regina.

"Oh I recognize that voice, sorry Regina." said Bessa.

"Oh hey, here are your glasses." said Chrysalis picking them up.

Then Chrysalis handed Bessa her glasses and Bessa placed them on her face.

"Yep you guys are right." said Bessa now seeing clearly at Regina.

"Good thing they were found." said Chrysalis.

Kylestone and Ariel got put into a room and were taken out of the bag by Carlica only having her arms in the room and Carlica untied Ariel and removed the tape from her mouth and closed the door and locked it right after then Ariel untied her dad and removed the tape from his mouth. Ariel tried to open the door hoping for a mistake with locking it but it was locked good. Then Ariel looked behind her and saw her dad laying on the bed sideways but not sleeping but he was crying and Ariel quickly went to him and comforted him on the bed once Kylestone felt Ariel he turned the other side and they wrapped their arms around each other. Where AmeraAmara is in the big house not wearing her black trench coat or big black hat.

"I can't believe it after that boy's father's death and what I told him he still hasn't learned his lesson and he's having his daughter agree with him." AmeraAmara said to Tuckles.

"Oh issues." said Tuckles.

"That Kylestone and his father go together like combs and hair dryers." said AmeraAmara.

"That makes, no sense." said Tuckles.

"Oh I'll show you want makes sentence when you don't agree with me." said AmeraAmara.

AmeraAmara punched her fist to the furniture table next to her and it broke in half and it broke the table's legs too.

"Oh yes I get that, but you better have that be fixed or replaced because that table is not ours." said Tuckles.

"What's happening here?" said Matilda coming over with Nagaila.

In the room where Kylestone and Ariel are being kept Matilda, Tuckles, and Nagaila came in while Falyby blocked the doorway.

"Ah." said Ariel scared.

"You're coming with us Kylestone." said Matilda, grabbing Kylestone's arm.

"No." said Ariel.

But Ariel got grabbed by Nagaila having Nagaila's arm around her and Nagaila did cover Ariel's mouth with her other hand while Matilda and Tuckles tied Kylestone up.

"Let us go." said Kylestone.

Tuckles tied a thick cloth around Kylestone's mouth.

"Mmuhmmm." said Kylestone.

Then they carried Kylestone out of the room while Ariel watched, worried that AmeraAmara might do something to her dad. Nagaila let go of Ariel and tossed her on the bed then Nagaila ran out and Falyby closed and locked the door. Kylestone got placed in a room where he was tied to a chair while trying to break free.

"Mmmuhhmmmm." said Kylestone trying to break free.

Just then AmeraAmara came into the room up to with a glass of water in her hand Kylestone.

"You thirsty? Well you're not getting any" said AmeraAmara, waving the glass of water up and down close to Kylestone's face.

AmeraAmara drank the water and placed the cup down.

"Disappointing right." said AmeraAmara.

Kylestone turned his head away from AmeraAmara.

"Now doesn't that sound familiar?" said AmeraAmara.

Kylestone moved his head back to her and AmeraAmara moved down the thick cloth from his mouth.

"Let me and my baby girl go." said Kylestone.

"I was afraid you would be like this." said AmeraAmara.

"I can't believe what you did to my father sm, I miss him dearly." said Kylestone, starting to cry.

"Enough with crying and focus on me." said AmeraAmara.

Kylestone tried to stop.

"Are you trying to stop?" said AmeraAmara.

"Sm yeah." said Kylestone.

"That's a good boy, now listen if you want to get over this with your father then forget him." said AmeraAmara.

"I won't." said Kylestone.

"Won't?" said AmeraAmara, confused.

"It's better than not." said Kylestone.

"You're unbelievable and your father was a jerk." said AmeraAmara.

"No he was not." said Kylestone.

Just then Neevya opened the door by them and stuck out with half of her body past the door and both AmeraAmara and Kylestone stared at her.

"Hey guys I couldn't help but hear your conversation so during it I'm welcoming myself to back up AmeraAmara." said Neevya.

"No thanks Neevya I want to handle this myself plus you don't seem helpful for that." said AmeraAmara.

"I have a possibility to figure it out remember when I finally got the TV to work?" said Neevya.

"All you had to do was push the on button on the remote." said AmeraAmara.

"Well I got it to work." said Neevya.

"Get going." said AmeraAmara.

"Okay fine." said Neevya.

Neevya closed the door then a second later she opened it again.

"But just so you know my opening still stands for later." said Neevya.

Then Neevya closed the door and left.

"Odd indeed." said AmeraAmara.

In the room where Ariel is being kept Ariel was on the bed clinging on the blanket while sitting up crying a little feeling worried just then Ariel started hearing the door open and she got off the bed feeling scared and went under the bed and into the room came Matilda, Nagaila, and Tuckles.

"Uh did we walk into the right room because I don't see Ariel, unless my vision is fating oh my gosh is it?" said Tuckles.

"It is not." said Nagaila.

Nagaila started whispering something to Tuckles.

"Oh okay." said Tuckles.

Ariel was wondering what was happening.

"Hey you look behind you." said Tuckles, showing her face to Ariel under the bed.

"Ah." said Ariel when she saw her.

Then Ariel got pulled out of the bed by her tail.

"Ah." said Ariel.

Nagaila was the one who grabbed Ariel by the tail and lifted her up by grabbing onto Ariel's tail.

"Let go." said Ariel trying to get Nagaila to let go of her tail.

"You don't think we wouldn't think of you hiding under the bed, well except for Tuckles? Plus we were able to see you when we entered." said Matilda.

"Foolish girl." said Nagaila to Ariel.

While Ariel was trying to get Nagaila to let go of her tail, Nagaila made Ariel hit her head on the floor by lowering her down and then back up.

"Ow." said Ariel, while rubbing her head.

Nagaila laughed quietly with her mouth closed.

"What's AmeraAmara going to do to my dad? She is with him isn't she?" said Ariel.

"Yes but she's not going to hurt him, maybe." said Matilda.

"What." said Ariel.

But then Ariel got her mouth closed by Nagaila's hand snapping Ariel's mouth together. Ariel tried pulling Nagaila's hand off.

"Oh by the way Matilda you better remember to do better when you try to teach someone a lesson after what happened to you trying to teach Ariel a lesson in the bathroom." said Nagaila.

Ariel stopped what she was doing.

"Mmu mmuhm mmumh mhmm?" said Ariel.

"Ah what does what she said mean can someone translate?" said Tuckles.

"I believe she said you guys know about that." said Matilda.

Ariel nodded her head yes.

"Yes we do and so much of it to get you to learn your lesson." said Nagaila to Ariel.

"Mmhm mh mmumm mmum mmm mum mmu mmuhm." said Ariel madly.

"Uh can someone translate that too?" said Tuckles.

"She said; learn my lesson you're the ones who should." said Nagaila.

"Oh fussy." said Matilda.

Ariel went back to trying to get Nagaila to let go of her mouth.

"Well let's go now." said Matilda.

So they walked out while Nagaila carried Ariel in the position she's holding on to Ariel. In the temperate jungle tribe area Regina was slithering around with Chrysalis.

"Hey Chrysalis and Regina, Nia's parents made great soup you guys interested?" said Noodle with a bowl and spoon standing outside Nia's house with Nia next to her.

"But you guys are going to have to wait for my parents to finish their next batch." said Nia.

"Okay." said Chrysalis.

"Sure." said Regina.

Noodle put a spoon full in her mouth but then quickly spit it out.

"Ah this taste like bart." said Noodle.

Nia looked at Noodle's bowl.

"Oh that's actually dirt water you were tasting." said Nia.

"What why would you have this?" said Noodle.

"I accidentally dropped my ring in the mud and I was trying to clean it and I must have forgotten to put that bowl away." said Nia.

"Oho." said Chrysalis.

"Hey guys." said Cherryette hanging on a tree branch with Lumia and Shiloh and Kiri.

"Hi." said Lumia.

"Hey guys you four are hanging on a tree branch like that." said Chrysalis.

"Hi aren't you girls' arms tired?" said Regina.

"Well you see Lumia, Kiri, Shiloh and I were hanging on the tree admiring the view but we didn't want to let go so we put make up glue on our hands to the tree branch to stay on longer but we used the wrong glue." said Cherryette.

"So now we're waiting for Zita to get back with the glue remover." said Shiloh.

"Hey guys I'm back, so far I came here quickly." said Zita with the glue remover.

"You want to know something else, I feel like I'm ripping off my arms." said Lumia.

"Here I will help." said Chrysalis.

"Me too." said Regina.

So Chrysalis, Regina, and Zita helped Lumia, Cherryette, Kiri, and Shiloh get removed from the tree branch.

"Oh man thanks guys." said Kiri.

"Thanks." said Lumia, Cherryette, and Shiloh.

Chrysalis' other friends came over to them. Just Carlica (in her human form), Veza, Vargoe, Neevya, Mesha, Manora, and Mingmi came over to them.

"You girls were seriously hanging on the tree for that long?" said Mesha.

"Well actually it was an accident." said Shiloh.

"I'm surprised you guys would touch a tree. Trees are filthy." said Neevya.

"Trees are very helpful actually." said Chrysalis.

"Yeah." said all of Chrysalis' friends.

"Is everything going okay here?" said Sasha, who came over with Ard.

"We were having a talk about trees." said Fredricka.

"You guys alway live your lives as celebrities working or not." said Carlica.

"By the way Carlica what do you do with your friends?" said Chrysalis.

"Oh that well, we hang out at nice places I stay in." said Carlica.

"Do you hang out with your friends a lot?" said Fredricka.

"Oh yes a lot." said Carlica.

"Do you have any other friends besides Vargoe, Veza, Neevya Manora, Mingmi, and Mesha?" said Chrysalis.

"Well I do but don't be expecting me to bring them to you, seriously don't." said Carlica.

"Well if they are nice we would like to meet them." said Sasha.

"Don't care." said Carlica.

"Watch how you talk to that teenager." said a lady, walking by them to Carlica.

"I'm not a teenager I'm a senior citizen." said Sasha to the lady by them.

"Oh really my bad but still." said the lady by them before walking away.

"We told that same lady five times that us who are senior citizens aren't teenagers, this morning." said Ard.

"You should keep an eye on how you talk Carlica, you're like a crazy mad psycho." said Dakota.

"Not as crazy mad psycho as the lady who killed Ivern." said a man who walked by them.

Then he continued walking and looked like he was about to cry.

"Yeah that guy is still weeping about Kylestone and Ariel missing." said Nia.

"So what those two are missing who cares?" said Carlica.

"We care." said Pocahontas.

All of them but Vargoe, Mesha, Manora, Mingmi, Veza, Neevya, and Carlica agreed with Pocahontas.

"Really if you guys didn't care about them you all wouldn't be sad about them gone now would you." said Carlica.

"It's good to care about others." said Chrysalis.

"And that same thing with Ivern who cares that he's dead?" said Carlica.

The people walking behind Carlica all gasped with disappointment about what Carlica said.

"How dare you." said a man to Carlica.

"Unbelievable." said a woman, who's with the man to Carlica.

The people who were behind Carlica all continued walking.

"We all care about Ivern too." said Pocahontas.

Everyone but Vargoe, Mesha, Manora, Mingmi, Veza, Neevya, and Carlica agreed with Pocahontas.

"Okay look I don't want to talk or hear about Ivern ever because I dislike him-." said Carlica.

Again people behind Carlica gasped with disappointment about what Carlica said.

"Eck." said Carlica disgusted.

Carlica turned her head at them.

"Hey look there's an owl." said Carlica lying.

"AN OWL, WHERE?" said the scared people, who gasped behind Carlica.

"An owl where?" said Neevya scared.

"Everyone relax there's no owl Carlica lied!" said Chrysalis and her friends.

Everyone who was scared calmed down.

"Carlica what the heck you got me scared." said Neevya.

"I was too desperate to get them back, but anyway can we go now we don't need to keep talking to these guys." said Carlica.

Vargoe, Mesha, Manora, Mingmi, Veza, Neevya, and Carlica left.

"Rude they are." said Jared.

"I hope Ariel and Kylestone will be found by Chrysalis' birthday tomorrow." said Emily.

"Yeah we all do." said Chrysalis.

Zinnia started feeling so sad like she was dropping herself a little.

"Zinnia." said Pocahontas patting her.

"Zinnia do you want us to go home now?" said Regina.

"Yeah I think I need to." said Zinnia.

"By the way Shenatha we already finish packing so we're prepared for your sleepover." said Regina.

"Good news to know." said Shenatha.

"Oh but Regina we can wait until Nia's parents are done making you a bowl of soap." said Zinnia.

"Are you okay with waiting?" said Regina to Zinnia.

"I can handle it." said Zinnia.

"Okay thank you." Regina said to Zinnia.

At the room where Ariel is with her arms crossed against her chest while being tied up and her mouth covered by a thick cloth Ariel was being held by Matilda by laying in Matilda's arms around her on Ariel's stomach and Ariel was not liking it that she had a serious bothered face. Matilda just finished knotting the knot to the rope around Ariel.

"There we go, hey Tuckles." said Matilda.

"Yeah?" said Tuckles.

"Keep an eye on Ariel while she's laying here on the couch." said Matilda placing Ariel on the couch.

"Sure but you don't have to worry about me watching her." said Tuckles.

"I would have asked Nagaila but she's doing something." said Matilda.

"Well I can prove I'm good." said Tuckles.

"You better." said Matilda.

Matilda exits the room Tuckles sat by Ariel laying on the couch.

"You know I've seen Matilda holding you and Nagaila but I haven't." said Tuckles.

So Tuckles picked up Ariel in her arms and got off the couch with her and walked around with her.

"Tuckles, Nagaila and I are coming back now and if you're holding Ariel put her down now." said Matilda.

"Oh." said Tuckles.

Tuckles did place Ariel down but face first in the trash can next to her. Matilda and Nagaila came back into the room and saw where Tuckles put Ariel seeing Ariel's tail wiggling out of the trash can.

"Tuckles really, why would you put her there?" said Matilda.

"Well you said to put Ariel down now so I did as quickly as I can." said Tuckles.

"I didn't think you would do that." said Matilda.

Nagaila lifted the garbage lid of the garbage can and lifted Ariel out.

"Hand her to me." said Matilda.

So Nagaila gave Ariel to Matilda.

"Hey Matilda aren't you coming with us to go out?" said Tuckles.

"Sure I will just have to do something with Ariel here." said Matilda.

Once Ariel heard what Matilda said her eyes opened very wide with shocking fear then Ariel turned her head at them.

"Mm mmmm." said Ariel while shocking her head no.

Ariel really tried to shimmy and shake out of Matilda's arms. Nagaila and Tuckles left while Ariel watched them.

"Now then." said Matilda to Ariel.

Ariel kept trying to get out.

"Oh enough with the squirming you know you won't escape from it." said Matilda.

Ariel stopped because she knew Matilda was right. Matilda tied a rope to the rope around Ariel to a pole that's there in the room for a house design. At Chrysalis' house Chrysalis was in her room.

"I wonder if Texia's workers have ever secretly hung out at the big hang out and preparing for the performance house, wait a minute, maybe they could be there right now some of them know how to make keys or could have gotten a key copy." said Chrysalis.

So Chrysalis left to go to that big house. At Shenatha's house Regina, Pocahontas, Tarzan, and Zinnia were there to sleepover. Zinnia was in a room by herself then she decided to go to the big balcony that's at Shenatha's house. Once Zinnia got there she saw Regina already there sitting looking at the view from it.

"You decided to come out here too." said Zinnia.

"Yeah." said Regina.

Just then they saw from the balcony a big light shining like it was coming from a giant flashlight.

"What is that coming from?" said Regina.

"Huh?" said Zinnia.

"Let's see." said Regina.

So they left. Where light was coming from was from a giant flashlight that Geena had wrapped around her and she was knocking stuff over with it.

"Muw- ha-ha." laughed Geena.

Geena kept causing more trouble with her flashlight just then Chrysalis came over to her and then so did Zinnia and Regina.

"What the heck?" said Zinnia.

"Oh well looks like I got myself some heros to try and stop me well this is the time I prove how using a flashlight in the dark can be good for bad." said Geena.

"You better watch it you." said Chrysalis in front of Geena.

"Oh yeah." said Geena.

Geena tried to lower her giant flashlight on Chrysalis but Chrysalis knew she be doing that and stepped away and lifted the giant flashlight up with her hand before it could go down to her head.

"What." said Geena.

Chrysalis used both hands and was strong enough to make Geena get off the ground while Chrysalis pushed the flashlight down to the ground. Regina and Zinnia came over to them.

"Chrysalis can you help us lift the flashlight up words so we can talk to who's using this giant flashlight face to face?" said Regina.

"Sure." said Chrysalis, helping them.

"Oh hey I'm back up, oh wait now I'm upward in a wrong way." said Geena, now laying on her back on the flashlight.

Regina and Zinnia grabbed Geena's arms to prevent her from escaping while tying the straps she used to attach the flashlight to her around her wrist.

"Okay I'm calling the police now." said Chrysalis getting out her phone.

"What the heck with causing mischief with this giant flashlight of yours?" said Regina to Geena.

"Well I wanted to show my friends how bad it is to use a flashlight. We had an argument at the building we were in before going back to the big house to stay at." said Geena.

"Okay they're on their way, and what building and big house are you talking about?" said Chrysalis.

"Okay I shouldn't be talking more I just realize I said too much." said Geena.

"You tell us what building and big house you were talking about right now." said Regina.

"Yeah right snake lady." said Geena to Regina.

"Parten me." said Regina.

"You tell us- what's your name?" said Chrysalis to Geena.

"Geena." said Geena.

"You tell us Geena or else we'll make you talk." said Chrysalis.

"How are you going to do that?" said Geena.

Chrysalis tried to think then she looked by her and saw an owl on the tree close to them.

"Oh hey look an owl." said Chrysalis, pointing at it.

"Oho." said Regina and Zinnia, looking at it admiring it.

"An owl!" said Geena, scared.

Geena looked and saw the owl too.

"Oh my gosh it is an owl get me out of here!" said Geena.

"I'll get rid of the owl if you will tell us–." said Chrysalis.

"Tell you the building and big house I'm talking about? Okay I'm talking about a very lovely building with a cheetah pattern couch that's like forty-five minutes from here by driving for stars and a big house next to another big house with giant vines all it for stars too." said Geena.

"What!" said Chrysalis, Regina, and Zinnia.

Geena looked at the owl and it turned its head at her.

"Ah man the owl just looked at me!" said Geena.

"Okay I'll get rid of it now." said Chrysalis.

Chrysalis put on her bright light music lover bracelet when she got closer to the owl and sang making her bracelet shine golden and purple light and it scared the owl away. Then Chrysalis put the bracelet back in her pocket and walked back to Regina, Zinnia, and Geena.

"Regina you said that the last time Kylestone sent you a text was when he was going to the big house next to the one covered in vines he must have gotten captured there and the kidnappers took him to **HANGING STARS SPOT** in the meantime before coming back to that big house." said Chrysalis.

"You must be right Chrysalis." said Regina.

"So that pink shampoo drop I found on the ground at that building must have been left by them." said Chrysalis.

"Not only that." said Zinnia, retying Geena's wrist after untying Geena's wrist.

Zinnia held up the bracelet Geena was wearing that is actually Kylestone's.

"Hey that's Kylestone's bracelet." said Regina.

"Yeah." said Chrysalis.

"So you and your friends did capture him." Chrysalis said to Geena.

"Chrysalis we need your great-grandma's key to the big house get in." said Regina.

"Actually I have it with me. She let me take it when I told her I was going to the big house next to the vine covered house." said Chrysalis, holding the key up after taking it out of her pocket.

"Okay and we'll call the cops and text everyone about it on the way there let's go." said Regina.

So Chrysalis, Regina, and Zinnia went to go save Ariel and Kylestone leaving Geena where she is.

"I just hope the cops get here before that owl comes back." said Geena.

At the big house next to the house cover in vines in the room where Kylestone is being kept in AmeraAmara left but Kylestone was back having the thick cloth over his mouth and he started having tears fall from his eyes just then he heard whispering behind the door (which is Chrysalis saying to be sure that no one will lock the door again while during their rescue mission) Chrysalis kicked the door down and in the room they saw Kylestone.

"Oh my gosh." said Chrysalis, seeing him.

Regina and Zinnia saw him too and he saw all of them and was surprised.

"Mmmuhmmmuhm." said Kylestone, while trying to stretch himself free to get to them.

Regina and Zinnia quickly slither to him and untied him. Regina untied the thick cloth around his mouth and once she did that the two of them kissed each other while Zinnia was untying the ropes around him. Regina stopped their kiss and untied the ropes around his tail to the chair that was to prevent him from slithering away on the chair but Regina still held her right hand on Kylestone's face.

"I was so afraid I wouldn't see any of you again." said Kylestone.

"We felt the same about you and Ariel. Do you know where she is?." said Regina.

"She's here too." said Kylestone.

"She is." said Chrysalis.

"Yes but she's being kept in another room." said Kylestone.

Once Regina finished untying Kylestone she kissed him and Kylestone put his arms around Regina and Regina did the same thing to him once his mother finished untying him and then his mother Zinnia placed her arms on him while they slithered out of the room.

"I'm so happy to have my baby boy back." said Zinnia.

"I'm glad to be back with you mother." said Kylestone, while he rubbed his head against her.

"Do you know what room they have Ariel in?" said Chrysalis.

"The last time I saw her she was in that room next to this one." said Kylestone, looking at the door to the room.

"But there's nothing on that door to lock it, but she could still be in there tied up." said Chrysalis.

So they went over to the room's door and Chrysalis kicked it down but Ariel was not in there.

"Oh no they took our baby out of this room." said Regina.

"Looks like we got some searching to do." said Chrysalis.

In the room where Ariel is being kept in Matilda wasn't in it but Ariel was still were she is and was laying on the floor all sad just then she saw Chrysalis kick the door to the room she's in down and she saw Chrysalis and her parents and grandmother and they quickly came to her. Regina got to Ariel first and Regina placed her arms around Ariel and Ariel against her chest on her lap and then Regina started kissing Ariel on the forehead before removing the thick cloth from Ariel's mouth.

"Mom." said Ariel.

"Oh my little baby girl." said Regina, snuggling with her while untying her.

"Grandmother." said Ariel, while Zinnia kissed her on her forehead.

Kylestone and Zinnia were snuggling with each other while Ariel and Regina were snuggling with each other and they were all next to each other sitting on the ground. Just then Ariel grabbed Kylestone's wrist and kept it in her hands.

"You're not hurt dad are you?" said Ariel.

"Don't worry I'm fine." said Kylestone.

Regina kissed him on the cheek but then Kylestone started to cry.

"Honey?" said Regina.

"Baby what's wrong are you crying tears of joy?" said Zinnia.

"I'm really sorry dad that I made you meet her." said Ariel.

"Who?" said Chrysalis.

"Baby you've said sorry enough." said Kylestone.

Kylestone kissed Ariel on the head and Ariel started kissing the palm of Kylestone's hand.

"There's something you all should know." said Kylestone.

"What is it and baby girl where did you slither off to and then got captured? Who captured you guys? We figure out how you go capture Kylestone." said Regina.

Regina and Kylestone both kissed each other again.

"Oh and we got this back." said Zinnia, holding out Kylestone's bracelet.

"Oh hey my bracelet thanks mother." said Kylestone.

Kylestone put it back on him on his upper arm.

"By the way why are you guys not wearing your clothes or accessories? By the way this reminds me of when you were a baby my baby boy your dadda wanted to see you with nothing on to see the actual mutant snake form of the baby he made happen." said Zinnia.

"Okay okay mother! Please not now and they took our clothes and accessories to be rude to us." said Kylestone.

"But baby I wasn't saying anything inappropriate. It's okay for people in our mutant snake forms to go out in public not wearing clothes, which is what form you were in when that happened." said Zinnia.

Regina started kissing him on the cheek again.

"I know but you see-sm." Kylestone said, while starting to cry again.

Before Kylestone told what had happened Chrysalis saw AmeraAmara's big black hat and long black trench coat hanging on a hook.

"Hey that hat and coat that's the exact same hat and coat the lady who was in front of me was wearing at the smoothie place who didn't want an Ivern cup she's the one who wanted you guys capture isn't she and I sure you Kylestone were crying because your mom was talking about your dad and you felt sad hearing about him after meeting her because she's the lady who killed him." said Chrysalis to Kylestone.

"Yes." said Kylestone.

"What!" said Zinnia, shocked.

"Are you serious her." said Regina.

"Oh-huh her name's AmeraAmara." said Ariel.

"AmeraAmara uh." said Chrysalis.

Zinnia started getting up and sat against the window that's behind her feeling upset and shocked.

"I just can't believe this she killed my husband and she had my baby and granddaughter get captured." said Zinnia.

"But we're back now grandmother." said Ariel, laying next to her.

"Mother." said Kylestone, laying next to her too.

Kylestone kissed Zinnia on her cheek.

"Yeah you're both right." said Zinnia.

"How did she and the others get in here?" said Chrysalis.

"Carlica knows how to make keys without using the original." said Ariel.

"Wait Carlica is a part of this too?" said Chrysalis.

"Yes and she's a mutant, a walloi that is." said Ariel.

"A walloi never heard of that human/monster?" said Chrysalis.

"That's because her grandpa made the formula and it only has been kept in her family and has the ability to transform to human and walloi again without using the reverse formula." said Ariel.

"Whoa." said Chrysalis.

"Now baby girl tell me everything about how and what happened when you got captured and about your dad too." said Regina, while placing Ariel around her arms.

"And remember baby you promise you will tell the truth for now on." said Kylestone.

"I know okay mom." said Ariel.

Chrysalis' friends enter the big house too.

"Okay guys let's get searching." Mirabel.

"All of you guys be careful." said Mirabel's mom.

In the room where Chrysalis is with Ariel, Kylestone, Regina, and Zinnia.

"And I'm really sorry for what I caused." said Ariel.

"Baby, your dad's right you need to tell us what's going on with you even if it means we have to stop being happy at the time." said Regina.

"I'm sorry I really am sorry." said Ariel.

"Well at least it's fixed now." said Regina.

"So Falyby was working with AmeraAmara the whole time and is a friend of hers. A lot of freaky things I have found out today." said Chrysalis.

Just then they heard banging on the door of the room next to them and they exit the room and saw Chrysalis' friends with Chrysalis' other friends Fawn, Nillia, Arianie, Nia, Axa, Pennya, Mabel, and Cassandra knocking the door with a dragon over their heads banging on the door with it.

"What are you guys doing?" said Chrysalis.

"Oh hey Chrysalis." said Pennya.

"Oh my gosh Ariel and Kylestone." said Mabel.

"Ah man, sweet." said Chrysalis' friends.

"Awesome." said Cherryette.

Cherryette got out sparklers and sparkled them.

"Whoa." said Jistopher, next to Cherryette.

"Don't worry they're lights not hot fire." said Cherryette.

"That explains why you don't light them up with fire." said Jistopher.

"What are you guys doing with that dragon in front of the door?" said Zinnia.

"Well if any of those intruders were behind the door we figured we would give them a jump scare to catch them better." said Fawn.

"Okay." said Chrysalis.

"Hey who's over there." said Swifta, in another area where she couldn't see them or them seeing her.

Swifta was coming over with a chair over her shoulders.

"You better show yourself and stay still or else I'll make you stay still with this high chair, I mean chair." said Swifta.

"Don't worry Swifta, it's us." said Chrysalis.

"Oh." said Swifta, placing the chair down.

Swifta came over to them.

"Oh my gosh you guys have been found." said Swifta, seeing Ariel and Kylestone.

"Hey where's Zita?" said Bemma.

"Hey guys." said Zita, in the room they haven't opened the door yet.

Chrysalis opened the door and they saw Zita in a blanket chest.

"Zita what are you doing in there?" said Constance.

"I thought I should hide in here and come out to catch the intruders." said Zita.

"Okay Zita." said Chrysalis.

"Clever." said Cherrycake.

"Thank you Cherrycake." said Zita.

"Hey Zita we found Ariel and Kylestone." said Loua.

"Really." said Zita, coming out.

Zita got out of the room and saw Ariel and Kylestone.

"Great seeing you guys again." said Zita.

"We're glad to be back with you guys." said Kylestone.

"Oh-huh." said Ariel.

"And by the way why are guys not wearing your clothes?" said Belyndica.

"They were taken." said Ariel.

"Ariel Kylestone." said Pocahontas.

Pocahontas and Tarzan both slithered through Chrysalis' friend and saw Ariel and Kylestone and they hugged them.

"Thank goodness you guys are back." said Pocahontas.

"We missed you both." said Tarzan.

"We missed you both too." said Ariel.

"We did." said Kylestone.

"Are you both okay?" said Pocahontas.

"We're fine." said Kylestone.

"Hey guys it turns out that the ones who captured Ariel and Kylestone took them such as Falyby and Carlica who's secretly a mutant called a walloi and are being led by AmeraAmara who killed Ivern twenty years ago." said Chrysalis.

Everyone who didn't know about that became shocked.

"What do you just say?" said Rowshella.

"The lady who killed Ivern." said Fern.

"What's a walloi and Carlica's a mutant." said Dilia.

"Are you sure? And thank goodness we found you guys Ariel and Kylestone." said Marleen, coming over with Walter holding Ariel and Kylestone's clothes and accessories.

"Yeah and we found your guys' clothes and accessories." said Walter, holding them out.

"Thanks." said Ariel and Kylestone, going over to get them.

The two of them grabbed their clothes and accessories and started putting them on.

"Amer-a-Ama-, what's her name again?" said Javada.

"AmeraAmara." said Chrysalis.

Ariel and Kylestone finished putting their clothes on.

"Well we looked all over the place but we haven't found any of the intruders." said Navia's dad.

"They must have all left, what about HANGING STARS SPOT?" said Chrysalis.

"My cops are still searching around there but so far they have found no one." said Belyndica's dad.

They all started going to the front door just then Chrysalis looked by her at the window and saw Nadeline looking through a peek.

"Hey." said Chrysalis, pointing at her.

But Nadeline started running away once Chrysalis pointed her out.

"Oh man that was Nadeline someone who works for AmeraAmara." said Ariel.

"Ah man, it looks like she's going to tell AmeraAmara and her friends not to come back here." said Chrysalis.

"Well in case she doesn't we'll have cops keeping an eye on the place and HANGING STARS SPOT if they return." said Belyndica's dad.

"Do you guys want to spend the rest of night at your guys' house so Ariel and Kylestone can enjoy being back home with you guys because you can and we can do the sleepover with you guys and Ariel and Kylestone a different day?" said Shenatha's dad to Ariel's family that weren't kidnapped.

"Yeah you guys can." said Shenatha's mom.

"I do miss our house." said Ariel.

"Plus it will feel like we're back home and not captured." said Kylestone.

"Well I really want to enjoy you guys back at the house." said Pocahontas.

"Okay." said Tarzan.

"Okay we can do that." said Shenatha.

"Plus we can make our sleepover more fun for next time." said Shenatha's mom.

Nadeline did tell AmeraAmara and the others about what she found out.

"They know now and they found Ariel and Kylestone." said AmeraAmara.

"I'm afraid so." said Nadeline.

"Well at least we didn't get caught." said Tuckles.

"Well looks like we'll just have to recapture them and I want their entire family captured too." said AmeraAmara.

Chrysalis and her family and friends went back to their houses. At Kert, Javada, Zila, Lalo, and Darma's house Javada, Zila, Lalo, and Darma were hanging out in the living room.

"Can't believe the mean lady has been this close to us." said Lalo.

"We better stay alert." said Zila.

Just then they heard a loud pound and an angry howler.

302

"That doesn't sound like mommy or daddy or Kert." said Darma.

"You're right it must be the mean lady AmeraAmara or her mean friends." said Javada.

"Quick grab a pillow and let's get her." said Zila.

So Javada, Zila, Lalo, and Darma each grabbed a pillow and went to where they heard the sounds.

"We're going to get you." said Lalo, while they were coming over.

But before they hit with their pillows they saw their mom on the floor sideways.

"Whoa whoa." said Kert, Javada, Zila, Lalo, and Darma's mom, stopping them.

And she did stop them before they hit her.

"What's going on here?" said Kert, Javada, Zila, Lalo, and Darma's dad, who appeared.

"We thought mommy was the mean lady or her mean friends." said Javada.

"Yeah mommy why were you pounding and howlering?" said Zila.

"Because I slipped on your guys' toy dump truck that is what happens when you don't pick up your toys." said Kert, Javada, Zila, Lalo, and Darma's mom to Javada, Zila, Lalo, and Darma.

"Okay mommy." said Zila.

"We'll pick up." said Javada.

"We don't want something like another false alarm or getting hurt." said Darma.

At Ariel's house Ariel's dad Kylestone was looking out the big window of a living room of theirs alone just then his mother came over to him and hugged him and he hugged her too.

"It's so good to have you both back." said Zinnia.

"I know." said Kylestone.

"Look I understand how you feel after meeting that lady and she doesn't feel sorry for what she did." said Zinnia.

"I know you do and sm she told me sm the whole story of how she did it sm it felt like I was reliving the time." said Kylestone, starting to cry.

"Oh I get that it does feel heartbreaking I know you were close with him." said Zinnia.

"This really is a time for you to be comforting me." said Kylestone.

"I knew it would be but you're also comforting me too." said Zinnia.

"Yeah you both were so happy with each other." said Kylestone.

Ariel was in another room wrapped up in a blanket sitting on a form with her mom Regina's arms around her.

"Mm, oh how we missed you both." said Regina.

But Ariel was feeling too sad and Regina recognized it.

"Baby are you feeling scared after what happened to you?" said Regina.

"Yes but I'm also upset about what trouble I caused dad." said Ariel.

"Baby your dad said he's not mad at you about it anymore and wants you to start being happy." said Regina.

"I know he keeps telling me that but I just can't get over it." said Ariel.

"Don't think that and snuggle with your mom okay." said Regina.

"Okay." said Ariel.

"And remember what you dad said he said you were later being a good girl to him such as helping him feel better when his feelings got hurt, remember that." said Regina.

"Yeah." said Ariel.

"Oh and since your dad started rocking you again can I do that to you?" said Regina.

"Okay mom." said Ariel.

Ariel had herself placed between her mom's arm and her mom's chest and then Regina started rocking her and Ariel smiled during it and during when Regina began kissing Ariel on the cheek and top of her head too.

"And you know baby others teasing you doesn't mean you have a problem." said Regina.

Ariel rubbed her head against her mom.

"You know anyone who's mean to you will be in trouble with someone like me like how dare those mean human/monster girls like that one who put you in the garbage can or try to give you a bad bath or that one who banged your head against the floor." said Regina.

"Thanks mom." said Ariel.

"My little baby girl." said Regina.

Regina went back to kissing Ariel on her cheek and forehead. Pocahontas and Tarzan came into the room where Kylestone and Zinnia were hugging each other.

"Kylestone are you okay?" said Pocahontas.

"I just need to relax myself." said Kylestone.

"Well you look like you're doing a good job at it." said Tarzan.

"Is there something else you need?" said Pocahontas to Kylestone.

"No thanks, I'm good." said Kylestone.

"Okay but I do want you and Ariel to take this medicine. I want to be sure you guys have your strength after what you guys have been through." said Tarzan pouring the medicine into a spoon.

Tarzan placed the spoon into Kylestone's mouth and Kylestone though it had a strange taste that he clinged on to his mother very tightly.

"That tastes very odd." said Kylestone.

"Well at least you took it better than I have." said Tarzan.

"It's true." said Pocahontas.

The four of them laughed then Regina entered to them.

"Honey, can you come with me to our baby?" said Regina to Kylestone.

"Is something wrong with her?" said Kylestone.

"She's okay but she told me she wants you." said Regina.

"Okay I'll go." said Kylestone, getting out of his mother's arms.

Kylestone went to Ariel with Regina, Tarzan, Pocahontas, and Zinnia. Ariel was still on the form but before Kylestone sat next to her his mother stopped him.

"Hold on baby." said Zinnia to Kylestone.

Zinnia grabbed a blanket and placed it on him.

"Thanks mother." said Kylestone.

Kylestone sat next to Ariel on the form and Regina sat on the other side of Ariel.

"Baby girl what do you need me for?" said Kylestone.

Ariel hugged her dad Kylestone and he hugged her.

"I want you with me." said Ariel.

"Okay." said Kylestone.

Tarzan slithered by them and poured the medicine into the spoon he's holding.

"Ariel, I want you to take this." said Tarzan.

Ariel opened her mouth and her grandpa placed the spoon in her mouth and Ariel swallowed it and she thought it tasted weird too and cling tightly on her dad.

"Ha she's taking the same why you did." said Tarzan.

Kylestone rubbed Ariel's back while Regina moved her face close to Kylestone.

"You two have really bonded." said Regina.

"Yeah, I'm so happy to be back with you." said Kylestone to Regina.

"So am I with you." said Regina.

"You make my life better." said Kylestone to Regina.

"And you're someone I want in my life." said Regina to Kylestone.

Regina and Kylestone both kissed each other.

"You're squeezing me." said Ariel, who was getting crushed by her parents squeezing against each other.

"Oh, oh sorry baby." said both Regina and Kylestone, giving Ariel some space.

"By the way baby and you Kylestone, we went to a temperate jungle tribe area in the temperate jungle next to Noodle's house and her barnes." said Regina.

"Really wow." said Kylestone.

"What are they like?" said Ariel.

"Well they live like us but in a temperate jungle." said Regina.

"Oh and by the way no one say owl there." said Pocahontas.

"Owl why?" said Ariel.

"Well some of the temperate jungle tribe members are terrified of owls some much just hearing the word scares them." said Tarzan.

"Seriously?" said Kylestone.

"Yep we were all surprised by it." said Tarzan.

"Do you guys want to go there?" said Regina.

"Sure." said Kylestone.

"Okay mom." said Ariel.

"Then it's planned." said Regina.

Regina kissed Ariel on the head a few times.

"Can we go right now?" said Ariel.

"No baby it's too late." said Kylestone.

"Please." said Ariel.

"No baby we want you to go to bed now." said Regina.

"Huh, okay." said Ariel.

So they all went to bed. At Chrysalis' house Chrysalis and her sisters were in the living room watching TV.

"Hey Chrysalis guess what the places where we bought your party supplies stuff all gave us refunds." said Walter, who came over.

"Refunds it's not because you returned the stuff for my party right?" said Chrysalis.

"No it's because you helped save Ariel and Kylestone who are the granddaughter and son of Ivern who they are big fans of." said Walter.

Chrysalis and her sisters' mom came over to them.

"Wow, those guys didn't scream if you said his name right?" said Marleen.

"No no they said they controlled that years ago." said Walter.

"I hope the other Ivern fans who scream when you say his name will do that." said Tiana.

"Anyway Chrysalis do you want to also have an Ivern cake for your birthday party too they're allowing us to have one on the house for everyone for your party?" said Walter.

"Sure, and I'm glad that we found Ariel and Kylestone in time to come to my birthday party." said Chrysalis.

Just then they heard one of Ivern's songs being played outside and they saw bright lights and parade floats through the window.

"Wow a parade." said Chrysalis looking at it through the window with her family.

"They're doing a parade this late." said Natasha.

"Yeah I ran into a person whose a part of this and he said they're doing a parade to celebrate that Ivern's son and granddaughter are found and returned now and that they now know the lady who killed Ivern twenty years ago and they really wanted to do it now even though they are going to do it again tomorrow." said Jimonthey.

"Whoa." said Chrysalis.

At Ariel's house, Ariel had her clothes on and her leather jacket on while she was writing a note in her room then she left her room and went into her parents room where they were sleeping by quietly opening the door. Ariel put the note on their lamp next to their bed and she kissed them both on the cheek before she left their room and quietly closed the door. The note that Ariel left said I WENT TO THE TEMPERATE JUNGLE TRIBE LOVE ARIEL. Ariel arrived at the temperate jungle tribe area and she liked it. In Ariel's parents' room Kylestone woke up and removed Regina's arms off him which woke her up.

"I'm just going to go get a drink of water." said Kylestone to Regina.

Kylestone looked at the lamp and saw the note Ariel left. Once he saw it he ripped it off the lamp with shockness.

"What, Ariel." said Kylestone.

"What is it?" said Regina.

Kylestone showed her the note.

"What, that girl we better go get her." said Regina.

So both Regina and Kylestone left their bedroom to go get Ariel. Ariel was looking at the trees and the houses.

"Wow this is cool." said Ariel.

Ariel looked up at the trees and saw an owl.

"Oh hey an-." said Ariel, before covering her mouth remembering what her grandma said.

Meanwhile Regina and Kylestone were slithering to go get Ariel and on their way there they slithered by the parade.

"Oh hey it's Ivern's son and his son's wife." said a man, on one of the floats.

Some of the ones going past them on the parade floats took pictures of Regina and Kylestone but on bright flash.

"Oh, ow, ow." said both Regina and Kylestone.

"Oops sorry we had them on flash." said one of them, who's a man.

Ariel was now in the tall grassy field near a lake touching the water with her hand just then her parents appeared.

"What are you doing out here?" said Regina behind Ariel.

"I wanted to see this place." said Ariel.

"Baby we don't want you out here without anyone you could have got captured again." said Kylestone.

"I wanted to prove that I'll be okay going to places on my own." said Ariel.

"Baby please listen to me and your dad and try to stay focus on keeping yourself safe." said Regina.

"Okay." said Ariel, getting up.

Kylestone and Regina both hugged her.

"But you know that Chrysalis' birthday is tomorrow." said Kylestone.

"Oh no I forgot about that please don't make me miss it. I've never been invited to a friend's birthday party." said Ariel.

Kylestone and Regina looked at each other and whispered.

"Alright you can still go to Chrysalis' party but you're still being punished." said Kylestone.

"Okay and I promise I won't sneak out again." said Ariel.

"Good to know." said Kylestone.

"What you're doing for punishment is vacuuming at the CREEPY CREEP CENTRAL." said Regina.

"Where's that?" said Ariel.

"That place is supposed to be closed tomorrow but Dakota's dad owns that place and said I can bring you guys in there to see it especially after what happened to you guys." said Regina.

"Although you baby are going to be checking it out in a different way with a vacuum." said Kylestone.

"I understand." said Ariel, disappointed.

"Come on, let's go home now." said Regina.

Ariel and her parents went home while her parents placed their arms across her shoulders. It became the next morning and now Chrysalis' 15th birthday. Chrysalis was coming down the stairs to the dinning room where her family set up a big breakfast that Chrysalis sat down for.

"Happy birthday Chrysalis." said her family.

"Thanks everyone." said Chrysalis.

"Finally we're having your party today." said Blinda.

"By the way Chrysalis the bakery who gave us the free Ivern cake just delivered it to us." said Nessia.

"Really can I see it?" said Chrysalis.

"Sure it's right there." said Nessia, pointing at it on the counter.

After Chrysalis set up her plate with breakfast foods she went over to see the cake and opened the box and saw it inside with her sisters looking over her shoulders.

"Wow that looks great." said Chrysalis.

"Yeah not only it has Ivern on it but it's also good art." said Gege.

"Still can't believe that I stood so close to his killer and those other things I found out about her yesterday." said Chrysalis.

"Yeah like wasting snake blood." said Gege.

"Man she really is bothered by Ivern that she hates snakes because they remind her of him." said Whittneya.

"Yeah and we better keep a look out for her too and her friends." said Chrysalis.

"Don't have to tell me twice." said Patty.

At Ariel's house Ariel and her dad and mom went over to the table to eat.

"Surprise Ariel and Kylestone we made your guys' favorite breakfast foods to welcome you back home." said Pocahontas.

"Oh wow." said Ariel.

"Thanks you guys." said Kylestone.

"Thank you." said Ariel.

Ariel and her family all sat at the table and started eating.

"When am I going to have to start vacuuming the **CREEPY CREEP CENTRAL**?" said Ariel.

"Why is Ariel vacuuming there?" said Tarzan.

"Well dad mine and Kylestone's own baby snook out of the house last night to go to the temperate jungle where that tribe lives by herself." said Regina.

"Ariel, that's not good." said Zinnia.

"I left a note." said Ariel.

"Yeah well at least you left a note." said Regina.

"But baby still that was bad." said Kylestone.

"I'm sorry I just thought you would worry about me going to places by myself after what happened and I wanted to prove you didn't need to worry and I really wanted to go to the temperate jungle and see the temperate jungle tribe area." said Ariel.

"We get it Ariel but still." said Pocahontas.

"I'm sorry." said Ariel.

"Eat up we're going there after breakfast." Regina said to Ariel.

So they all continued eating their breakfast. Later Chrysalis was walking with her friends to where another parade to celebrate Ariel and Kylestone being found and back home was happening at.

"Wow they went even bigger." said Chrysalis.

"Do you find this fun to have happened on your birthday Chrysalis?" said Dayla.

"Yeah I do." said Chrysalis.

"Too bad that Ariel is going to be vacuuming at the **CREEPY CREEP CENTRAL** but she is still going to be at your birthday party Chrysalis." said Dakota.

"Why is that happening to her?" said Chrysalis.

"Oh someone better tell her to vacuum the vents. I want them to be kept clean to continue crawling through them." said Cherryette.

"My mom said it's because she's being punished for sneaking out of the house to go to the temperate jungle where the tribe lives." said Dakota.

314

"Really." said Chrysalis.

"Yep it's true." said Dakota's mom.

"We're supposed to be seeing them to unlock the store for them not just for Ariel to vacuum there but also so her family can look around there with Kylestone." said Dakota's dad.

"I'm surprised she went out of the house at night by herself. I would be pretty scared to do that after being captured." said Arianie.

"Wow a parade." said Ariel, who came over with her family.

"Hi Ariel at least you're seeing some of it." said Chrysalis.

"Oh you know what I am doing later." said Ariel to Chrysalis.

"Yeah." said Chrysalis' friends.

"Oh and happy birthday Chrysalis." said Ariel.

"Happy birthday." said Ariel's family to Chrysalis.

"Thanks." said Chrysalis.

The parade finished going past them.

"Okay now that that's over come with me to the place." said Dakota's dad.

Ariel and her family went with Dakota's dad to the **CREEPY CREEP CENTRAL**. Dakota's dad unlocked the doors and let them in.

"This place is so big." said Ariel.

"Well then remember not to sneak out." said Regina.

Dakota's dad came back with the vacuum.

"Here's the vacuum." said Dakota's dad handing it to Ariel.

Ariel grabbed it and started it up and began vacuuming while her family looked around the place with Kylestone.

"Hey look at this." said Tarzan holding a plastic cage.

"Whoa what's it supposed to be for?" said Pocahontas.

"It's a part of a costume for a prisoner." said Tarzan.

"Oh." said Kylestone.

Ariel kept vacuuming and felt like she was hurting herself from bending too much.

"Ow." said Ariel.

"Baby didn't be thinking of tricking us that you've been vacuuming also there are security cameras here." said Regina.

"I wasn't going to mom, ow." said Ariel.

Regina grabbed a long scarf and threw it around Kylestone and pulled him up to her and they kissed each other. Chrysalis and her friends were all hanging out together outside.

"Hey guys look." said Chrysalis, pointing at a blimp in the sky.

The blimp said on it AMERAAMARA IS THE NAME OF IVERN'S KILLER and then it showed a drawing of her and it showed them again back and forth.

"Oh hey it's telling everyone who Ivern's killer is." said Chrysalis.

"And they're showing the drawing of her that Ariel and Kylestone told the forensic artist." said Belyndica.

"This bugs me." said Dayla mad.

"That AmeraAmara killed Ivern twenty years ago and is still on the run." said Stacya.

"That and the blimp is yellow, why is it not purple that will really catch attention, man I feel mad about it so mad I- I- going to do this with this wooden stool." said Dayla.

Dayla grabbed the wooden stool and tossed it but not in a dangerous way.

"Don't worry that stool's mine so it's no one else's I'm messing around with." said Dayla.

"Wait, why would you bring that stool with you?" said Trudy.

"Oh it's just in case I wanted to sit if the parade was going to go too long and I wanted to sit down." said Dayla.

"Well okay." said Trudy.

"Actually for today they should have it pink since it's Chrysalis' birthday and pink is your favorite color Chrysalis." said Dayla.

"Yeah plus you helped save Ariel and Kylestone." said Cherrycake.

"Yeah, oh well." said Chrysalis.

At the **CREEPY CREEP CENTRAL** Ariel was still vacuuming while she was doing that her parents came up to her.

"Okay baby we're going to go now." said Regina.

"And you're doing a good job vacuuming." said Kylestone.

"Thanks." said Ariel.

"And here's the keys to the place once we've left lock the doors okay." said Regina to Ariel.

"Okay mom." said Ariel.

"And call us when you're done too." said Kylestone.

"Okay dad." said Ariel.

Regina and Kylestone kissed Ariel and they left, leaving Ariel alone in the <u>CREEPY CREEP CENTRAL</u> while she kept vacuuming. Chrysalis and her family and friends were all hanging out in a smaller store that's not far from the <u>CREEPY CREEP CENTRAL</u>.

"Are you interested in anything Chrysalis?" said Marleen.

"I haven't found anything yet." Chrysalis said.

"Hey guys." said Tarzan with Zinnia and Pocahontas, waving.

"Hi." Chrysalis and her family and friends said.

"Where's Regina and Kylestone?" said Chrysalis.

"Oh they wanted to be in a room alone for a bit." said Pocahontas.

"You do mean they're here right?" said Chrysalis.

"Yeah." said Pocahontas.

"Let's try and find them." said Nillia to Arianie.

"Yeah." said Arianie.

"No you two if Regina and Kylestone want to be alone we have to let them." said Ratia to Arianie and Nillia.

"Ratia is right girls." said Nillia and Arianie's mom.

"Okay." said Nillia and Arianie.

"I wonder what they are doing." said Shenatha.

"Oh hey hematite and lepidolite rocks." said Tarzan going to them.

"Yeah they sell a lot of rocks here." said Fredricka's dad.

"These would be good for my medicines." said Tarzan.

"Oh well then good thing that someone like you who makes medicines found them." said Kert, Javada, Zila, Lalo, and Darma's mom.

Just then Kert, Javada, Zila, Lalo, and Darma's mom slipped and grabbed onto the door knob next to her but she made the door open wide and everyone saw behind the door was Regina and Kylestone kissed each other on the lips but they stopped and looked by them and saw that everyone saw them.

"Oh so that's what you guys were doing." said Chrysalis.

"Duh, pick up your toys." said Kert, Javada, Zila, Lalo, and Darma's mom to Javada, Zila, Lalo, and Darma.

Kert, Javada, Zila, Lalo, and Darma's mom held out the toy dump truck she slipped on.

"Girls really, that's the same toy dump truck your mom slipped last night." said Kert, Javada, Zila, Lalo, and Darma's dad.

"Sorry we're always forgetting to pick that one up." said Zila.

"Sorry about disturbing your guys' alone time." said Kert, Javada, Zila, Lalo, and Darma's mom to Regina and Kylestone, while getting up.

"Don't worry about it." said Regina.

Regina and Kylestone were leaving the room kissing while touching each others shoulders

"I think you're going to need one of those rock medicines that Tarzan is planning to make medicines that can help with stress." said Colleen to Kert, Javada, Zila, Lalo, and Darma's mom.

"It's true." said Tarzan.

"I think I might." said Kert, Javada, Zila, Lalo, and Darma's mom.

"We're sorry mommy it was an accident." said Javada.

"If we remember we would have picked it up." said Lalo.

"Yeah don't be planning on hitting or swallowing a rock." said Darma.

"Yeah that's dangerous." said Javada.

Everyone else laughed.

"What?" said Zila.

"What are you all laughing at?" said Lalo.

"That's not how you use rocks for medicine you have them in a safe way." said Chrysalis.

"Oh." said Javada, Zila, Lalo, and Darma.

At the <u>CREEPY CREEP CENTRAL</u> Ariel was still vacuuming but upstairs but she didn't know that the backdoors to the place were being unlocked because they were being unlocked quietly while Ariel was upstairs. The ones who were coming in by using a key copy were Matilda, Nagaila, and Tuckles.

"It sounds like someone's here. I can hear vacuuming from upstairs." said Matilda.

"Well we better keep quiet to steal from here there's a lot of stuff for us to use to protect us from being on the run worse now and to capture that mutant human to snake monster family AmeraAmara wants." said Nagaila.

Matilda, Nagaila, and Tuckles started to collect things and put them in bags.

"Do any of you guys wonder who is here upstairs vacuuming?" said Tuckles.

"Well kind of." said Matilda.

"Maybe I can take a peek." said Tuckles.

"Well okay but you better be careful." said Nagaila to Tuckles.

"Don't worry about it I'm really staying focused on not getting caught especially now." said Tuckles.

Tuckles quietly went up stairs quietly and took a peak at who was vacuuming and saw it was Ariel which shocked her so she quietly walked down to Matilda and Nagaila.

"Hey girls guess who else is here, Ariel." said Tuckles.

"Ariel." said Nagaila.

"Yeah she's upstairs vacuuming." said Tuckles.

"Luckily for us we have an opportunity to catch one of them." said Matilda.

While Ariel was vacuuming the second floor she didn't notice Matilda, Nagaila, and Tuckles were quietly sneaking behind her. While Ariel was vacuuming she stopped because she felt stiff from bending a lot.

"Want me to take over for you?" said Tuckles, behind Ariel.

"No I can't I'm being punished." said Ariel.

Just then Ariel gasped because she recognized that voice she heard but before she turned around Matilda grabbed her upper arms.

"Ah." said Ariel trying to pull herself out of Matilda's hands.

But Matilda pulled Ariel up to her and placed her arm across Ariel and her hand over Ariel's mouth.

"Wait until AmeraAmara finds out about this." said Tuckles.

At the smaller store not far from the <u>CREEPY CREEP CENTRAL</u> where Chrysalis and her family and friends are.

"Hey Texia, did you talk to your construction workers about you finding out who left that pink shampoo drop that Chrysalis found at <u>HANGING STARS SPOT</u>?" said Jindy, Tira, Irenie, and Candace's mom.

"I did a speech to them about it but still told them not to do what those bad guys did there." said Texia.

"Okay then." said Stacya, Lotusa, Bentha, Jannia, and Tarika's dad.

"This is a nice scarf." said Emily holding Batie in her arms.

Just then Emily noticed a rip in it.

"Ah man but it has a rip." said Emily.

"Don't worry about that Emily just sew it or ask someone like Dakota here. Her sewing motto is that she can sew it together right." said Cherrycake.

"Actually it's I can maybe sew it together right." said Dakota.

"Don't worry about it I can sew it when I get home." said Emily.

"Don't be expecting that popular tailor guy who lives in Germany to sew anything that guy's in jail for fighting against a tortoise." said Chet.

"Wait, he got thrown in jail for fighting a tortoise?" said Spencer.

"Yeah it was at a zoo and he really did not like tortoises." said Chet.

"Wow he sounds like he hates tortoises as much as AmeraAmara hates snakes." said Jaya.

"Well he doesn't hate tortoises as bad as AmeraAmara hates snakes, there hasn't been any saying of him destroying tortoise stuff." said Chet.

At the <u>CREEPY CREEP CENTRAL</u> Ariel was tied up with her mouth covered hanging on a nail in the top remain of a wall where a picture frame was while Matilda and Tuckles were collecting things to steal and Nagaila was tying rope around and across the bottom hole of the plastic cage with rope. Ariel kept trying to get herself free but she couldn't. Matilda came up to her and pushed Ariel making her swing while hanging on the nail.

"Mmhmm." said Ariel.

Matilda stopped Ariel from swinging and grabbed her chin and started messing around with it.

"Cute you are no wonder your daddy calls you baby." said Matilda.

Matilda placed her hands against Ariel's head on Ariel's cheeks and brought Ariel head against her head.

"I'm looking forward to you being back with me." said Matilda to Ariel.

Ariel was not. Then Matilda stopped touching Ariel's head and continued collecting things to steal. At the store where Chrysalis and her family and friends are at.

"Oh that's a pretty on." said Nillia, looking at Nia's phone with Nia and Arianie.

"What are you guys looking at?" said Chrysalis.

"We got curious about rocks." said Arianie.

"Look at this pretty on." said Nia.

Chrysalis looked at the rock picture on Nia's phone too.

"That is pretty but that rock is deadly." said Chrysalis.

"Because it's really hard if it hits your head." said Arianie.

"No just by being near it." said Chrysalis.

"Whoa no wonder we never seen it before at a store." said Nillia.

Chrysalis looked out the store window and saw a lady wearing a purple long trench coat and a big purple hat Chrysalis could see she had black hair and she looked like AmeraAmara when she was in front of Chrysalis at the smoothie shop. Chrysalis was thinking it was her and in case it wasn't Chrysalis thought of a plan.

"Hey guys I think that might be AmeraAmara out there in the purple trench coat and big purple hat and I have an idea to know for sure in an okay way if it's not her." said Chrysalis.

"I think Chrysalis is right." said Kylestone, looking at the lady in the purple trench coat and big purple hat through the window too.

The lady in the purple trench coat and big purple hat was still out there and saw Chrysalis and her family and friends come out of the store close to her and they were all spread around her. While Chrysalis set up her phone to play the instruments she wanted to her singing.

"Hey everyone guess what I'm going to sing one of Ivern's songs!" said Chrysalis.

Everyone cheered with excitement but the lady in the big purple hat and long purple trench coat froze with shocked. Chrysalis started to sing one of Ivern's songs and she saw everyone go wild but she kept an eye on the lady wearing a long purple trench coat and big purple hat and saw the she didn't seem like she liked it like everyone else that she was acting like she was bothered by it and she kept trying to get away from the song but Chrysalis' friends and family stood in her way to not have that happen then Chrysalis stopped sing.

"Auh." said the lady in the long purple trench coat and big purple hat on her knees bothered and mad.

"Everyone that lady is AmeraAmara who killed Ivern who's wearing the big purple hat and long purple trench coat." said Chrysalis.

"HUH!" said everyone, who didn't know that.

They went after the lady in the big purple hat and long purple trench coat and some people grabbed her and made her hat fall off revealing her head to them that she is AmeraAmara.

"Yes that's her." said Kylestone.

"HUH!" said everyone, looking at AmeraAmara.

"So that's what you look like with the hat off." said Chrysalis, looking at AmeraAmara.

"Yes and now you know." said AmeraAmara, mad.

"How dare you be so rotten." said Cherryette's mom to AmeraAmara.

"You're a meanie lady." said Zila to AmeraAmara.

"You don't mess with friends of ours or their relatives." said Marleen to AmeraAmara.

Meanwhile at the <u>CREEPY CREEP CENTRAL</u> Ariel felt sad but then she remember that she had the key to the place in her pocket so she reached her hand in there and grabbed the keys and cut herself free while Matilda, Nagaila, and Tuckles weren't looking once Ariel became free and got her mouth uncovered she slithered off. Just then Tuckles looked at where Ariel was and saw her gone.

"Ah girls we have a problem." said Tuckles.

Matilda and Nagaila looked where Tuckles was looking at too and saw Ariel gone.

"What." said Nagaila.

"Quick let's chase her." said Matilda.

So they did. Ariel slithered out of the place while Tuckles, Matilda, and Nagaila followed her. Meanwhile where Chrysalis and her family and friends are dealing with AmeraAmara, Zinnia went up to her.

"I can't believe you. You don't feel sorry at all for what you did?" said Zinnia to AmeraAmara.

"Uh what is it with you guys admiring Ivern?" said AmeraAmara.

"It's not supposed to be always about you AmeraAmara." said Chrysalis.

"I knew you would be saying that you're so not going to be a friend of mine." AmeraAmara said to Chrysalis.

"You're under arrest AmeraAmara." said Belyndica's dad, holding out his badge.

"Well then I better leave now. Carlica, guys!" said AmeraAmara.

Chrysalis looked and saw another lady in disguise up the crowd and thought she looked like Carlica and it was after she took her disguise off they saw Carlica reveal herself but once Carlica had her face shown she transformed into her walloi form and scared everyone but Chrysalis and her friends and family.

"AH!" said those, who aren't Chrysalis or her friends or family seeing Carlica's walloi form.

"Ah!" said a man, looking at Carlica's walloi form.

"WHAT THE HECK!" said a lady, looking at Carlica's walloi form.

"AH!" said a man, looking at Carlica's walloi form.

Two of the women who were grabbing on to AmeraAmara attacked the other ones grabbing on to AmeraAmara to help her escape because the two women were friends of hers. So AmeraAmara escaped running away not just with Carlica in her walloi form and the two women but along with Manora, Mesha, Mingmi, Nadeline (in her human form) and turn back to her monster form while running, Veza, Falyby (in her human form) and turn back into her monster form while running, Vargoe, Neevya, and Hailey they were wearing disguises too that came of while they were running but Chrysalis and her family and friends all now know what those women look like without their disguises on and were running after them.

"Deal with Ivern's granddaughter being missing!" said AmeraAmara.

"So that's what those other women look like and they're going after Ariel." said Chrysalis.

"It looks like they know where she is because they're running the way to where Ariel is." said Lamoria.

Regina looked at her phone while slithering after them and saw a message from Ariel that Matilda, Nagaila, and Tuckles were coming after her and that she left the CREEPY CREEP CENTRAL.

"Well they don't have my baby captured but getting chased by those other bad women who work side AmeraAmara." said Regina.

"Uh oh that means that Ariel's going to run into them while coming back to us." said Chrysalis.

Ariel was slithering quickly to get away from Matilda, Nagaila, and Tuckles but Ariel slithered in front of AmeraAmara and the other of her friends with her.

"Hey!" said AmeraAmara, looking at Ariel.

"Ah!" said Ariel.

Ariel slithered into the mall next to her to get away from them but they came into the mall too to get her but Chrysalis and Ariel's family saw them go into the mall.

"They must be chasing Ariel into the mall. Guys, they're chasing Ariel into the mall!" said Chrysalis.

So they went into the mall too. Ariel went upstairs once she entered the mall and everyone in the mall screamed and ran off once they saw AmeraAmara, Carlica, and the other bad women enter.

"There she is going upstairs." said AmeraAmara, pointing at Ariel.

"They're coming in too." said Hailey, looking at Chrysalis and her friends and family coming.

"Matilda come with me because you're holding that plastic cage you guys go all over the mall." said AmeraAmara.

So AmeraAmara and Matilda went upstairs to catch Ariel while the others went all over the mall. Ariel went to hide in a store in the mall upstairs in the clothes rack that's circle shaped and she peeked out to look out. AmeraAmara and Matilda went into the store where Ariel was hiding. Ariel saw them enter and felt very scared but just then her dad Kylestone came into the store too and he didn't see AmeraAmara and Matilda inside but AmeraAmara and Matilda spotted him when he got closer to them.

"Ha." laughed AmeraAmara, when she spotted Kylestone.

Ariel saw ArmeraAmara attack her dad and that made Ariel mad but she got a plan she removed the clothes from the hangers that were behind her while AmeraAmara put Kylestone into the plastic cage Matilda was holding and they tied his hands wrist to the plastic bars and his mouth with a white thick cloth that they also tied rope around the cloth knot to one of the plastic bars behind him.

"Well at least we will be escaping with you so let's leave now and get the others another time." said AmeraAmara.

Once AmeraAmara started to turn her head Ariel whacked her with the hangers Ariel had held tightly together in her hands and knocked her down then she did the same thing to Matilda and she made Matilda drop the cage Kylestone is in making it slide away with him in it.

"Dad." said Ariel.

But AmeraAmara got back up.

"Good thing that I'm very hard headed." said AmeraAmara, very mad.

"That's not going to help you against me." said Chrysalis, behind her.

Chrysalis and AmeraAmara fought against each other Matilda got up too and bet Ariel to grabbing the cage with her dad in it.

"Hold on Kylestone." said Chrysalis, while fighting AmeraAmara.

"Chrysalis, I got this." said Ariel.

"Okay just tell me if you need help." said Chrysalis, while fighting AmeraAmara.

Matilda ran with Kylestone to the closest exit of the store to her but Ariel went by her and pushed another one of those circled shaped clothes racks at her and made Matilda fall over again and drop the plastic cage Kylestone was being kept in and then Ariel pushed the circle shaped clothes rack down on Matilda. Ariel quickly untied her dad's wrist from the cage and opened it while her dad untied his mouth clear and once he got out of the cage they hugged each other. While Chrysalis and AmeraAmara fought each other out of the store.

"Thank you so much for helping save me." said Kylestone to Ariel.

"I won't let anyone hurt or be mean to you dad." said Ariel.

Kylestone kissed Ariel on the head and they went to get out of the store they were in but before they exit Carlica in her walloi form went in front of them.

"Ah!" said Ariel and Kylestone.

"You get away from us." said Ariel, feeling tough.

Chrysalis saw they were in trouble so she kicked AmeraAmara hard enough that she kicked her into Carlica knocking Carlica down.

"You guys okay and great job Ariel saving your dad." said Chrysalis.

"Thank you Chrysalis." said Ariel.

"Thank you." said Kylestone to Chrysalis.

But AmeraAmara got up again.

"Good thing Carlica broke my fall, ow kind of, how are you more stronger than me?" said AmeraAmara to Chrysalis.

Chrysalis and AmeraAmara went back to fighting each other.

"Ow." said Carlica in pain.

Carlica changed back into her human form and Ariel grabbed her by the part of the dress over her shoulders.

"Oh ow, Ariel I'm already in pain. Do you really think you need to do more to me ow, AmeraAmara is right, how is Chrysalis this strong?" said Carlica.

"Only if I have to but I am keeping an eye on you to bring you to prison." said Ariel.

Regina came over to them.

"Oh my gosh guys are okay." said Regina, hugging them.

"Our baby saved me." said Kylestone.

"And Chrysalis saved us." said Ariel.

"Ow." said Matilda.

The three of them looked at Matilda.

"Is that Matilda?" said Regina, mad.

"Yes." said Ariel.

Regina went over to Matilda.

"Someone get this off of me." said Matilda.

Regina moved the circle shaped clothes rack off of Matilda.

"Oh thanks." said Matilda.

But Regina grabbed Matilda the same way Ariel is with Carlica.

"You how dare you with what you have done to my baby and husband you better not mess with them again or you will be in trouble." said Regina to Matilda.

"Oh really okay I think I'd rather have that clothes rack on me again." said Matilda, scared.

Downstairs in the mall where Falyby is Dilia came up to her.

"Hey Falyby!" said Dilia, with her exploding liquid pink formula.

Dilia put water into her formula and threw it forward at Falyby and got it on Falyby such as Falyby's eyes.

"Ah my eyes." said Falyby.

"Cool Dilia." said LeLe.

"Nice." said LiLi.

"Thanks." said Dilia.

"Come on let's be sure she's taken down." said LuLu.

332

So they went after Falyby. Chrysalis kept fighting with AmeraAmara but it was easier for Chrysalis to fight her then earlier. Chrysalis went under a round table and kicked it up with both her feet at AmeraAmara knocking AmeraAmara down again and this time she did not feel like getting up.

"OW!" said AmeraAmara.

The police came over to her and grabbed AmeraAmara and placed handcuffs on her and they had all of the other women who works for AmeraAmara all arrested and brought over and Chrysalis' friends and family came over to where Chrysalis is near AmeraAmara.

"Wow all of you guys who are friends with AmeraAmara have been arrested too." said Chrysalis.

"Your friends and family are very tough." said Falyby.

"AmeraAmara you're caught too by that Chrysalis gal." said Nadeline.

"That means she's even stronger than you." said Hailey to AmeraAmara.

"Whoa." said Neevya.

"Yeah yeah don't bring it up." said AmeraAmara.

"Remember this Ariel that the prison outfits we will be wearing aren't our style so that's not really our style we would be wearing." said Mesha.

"Whatever." said Ariel.

Ariel hugged her dad. Regina went up to Tuckles and Nagaila and grabbed them by the dress where their necks come out.

"You two better stay away from my baby girl and husband or else you will be worrying about me." said Regina.

"Yeah we got it." said Tuckles, scared.

"I'm scared of her too." said Veza.

Veza changed into her yovola form.

"And this is what I look like scared in this form too." said Veza.

Then Veza changed back.

"That really was a weird form to look like." whispered Pocahontas to Chrysalis.

"Yep." said Nagaila, scared of Regina.

"We were pretty scared when Regina did that to us too." said Mesha.

"None of you bad ladies should mess with other family and friends." said Kylestone to AmeraAmara and AmeraAmara's friends.

"Yeah." said all of the good guys.

"You guys better watch it." said Chrysalis to AmeraAmara and AmeraAmara's friends.

"Yeah yeah we get it Chrysalis just don't hit us." said Mesha scared.

"Or kick us." said Mingmi to Chrysalis, while Mingmi felt scared too.

"Yeah don't do that to us." said Manora to Chrysalis, while Manora felt scared too.

"Relax I'm not going to hit or kick you guys." said Chrysalis.

"How are you so good at fighting?" said Uny to Chrysalis, while Uny felt shocked.

"That girl Chrysalis is amazing." said Falyby to Chrysalis, while Falyby felt shocked.

"You can't think that I'm mad at you now from when you brought me into being captured." said Kylestone to Ariel.

Zinnia came up to Ariel and Kylestone and hugged Kylestone's head and Regina kissed Ariel on the forehead while hugging Ariel and Kylestone and Regina kissed Kylestone on the lips while Regina's parents were near them. Ariel felt very happy that she got out her bright light music lover bracelet and started her phone to be able to play the music instruments she picked to her song and started singing to her dad even though she was in public and her bracelet shined white light with blue wiggly lines and pink light too and everyone but the ones arrested loved it. Then Ariel stopped and put her bracelet and phone away and kissed her dad on the face and Kylestone hugged her even tighter and showered her with kisses on her face.

"That was a very sweet thing you did for me baby thank you." said Kylestone to Ariel.

"Ariel that was amazing." said Chrysalis.

"Ariel, are you interested in being a new singer for me?" said Sasha.

"Really, yes." said Ariel.

"What, great now Ivern's granddaughter is going to be a singer too." said AmeraAmara, sarcastically and mad.

"Thanks Chrysalis you're the big hero." said Ariel.

"Yeah Chrysalis you saved my baby and I." said Kylestone.

"And you were the one who got AmeraAmara caught and those other mean women." said Elsa to Chrysalis.

"And helped us bring Ariel and Kylestone back to us." said Pocahontas to Chrysalis.

"You're a hero Chrysalis!" said everyone.

"Thanks guys." said Chrysalis.

Ariel went up to Chrysalis, and hugged her.

"Thanks Ariel." said Chrysalis.

Chrysalis hugged Ariel too. Then everyone but AmeraAmara and the other women arrested cheered for Chrysalis. Then a bunch of reporters and cameramans came up to her and she was all over the news.

"I'm here with Chrysalis Loom the singer and big hero." said one of the reporters.

"So am I." said another reporter.

"And me." said another reporter.

"Chrysalis Loom all of those Ivern fans are going to be majorly cheering for you for saving his son and granddaughter." said another reporter.

"Well in that case everyone have ear blockers with you. I know there are some Ivern fans who scream when they hear his name." said Chrysalis.

"Good thing to tell Chrysalis Loom." said another reporter.

AmeraAmara and her friends were placed in the same prison where Geena is in.

"You rat us out Geena." said Tuckles.

"Hey if you were that close to an owl you would." said Geena.

"Oh man you're right." said Tuckles.

"AN OWL WHERE?" said some of the other prisoners, scared.

"Zip you all there's no owl!" said AmeraAmara, extremely angry and with her hand stuck to her forehand.

"Oh." said all of the prisoners, scared mistaking there being one.

"Ah what happened to you?" said Matilda to AmeraAmara.

"I ordered a plum to have but they accidentally gave me a small bag of purple makeup glue that I popped opened when I grabbed it angrily and got on my hand and I accidently touch my forehand with my hand with that got the glue on it because of how mad I was and now it's stuck for twenty-four hours." said AmeraAmara.

"You look kind of funny." said Nagaila, about to laugh.

The other prisoners were laughing a little too at AmeraAmara. Tuckles held a small tape recorder making laughing sounds close to AmeraAmara.

"What are you using that for?" said Mingmi to Tuckles.

"So I can keep making laughs when I'm tired." said Tuckles.

"Oh genius." said Neevya to Tuckles.

"Yeah, genius right AmeraAmara?" said Tuckles.

AmeraAmara's anger grow.

"IF YOU DON'T PUT THAT THING AWAY I'LL SHOVE IT DOWN YOUR ESOPHAGUS!" said AmeraAmara to Tuckles.

"Okay okay, you know what." said Tuckles, scared.

Tuckles threw the tape recorder down on the ground and smashed it with her feet.

"There it's destroyed." said Tuckles.

Just then AmeraAmara felt something on her arm that's the arm to her hand that's stuck on her forehead.

"What is that on my arm?" said AmeraAmara, mad.

"Ah an actual owl!" said Tuckles, in fear.

Geena and the other prisoners who are scared of owls all went crazy scared in fear that they were knocking AmeraAmara down and bumping into her and also knocking down and bumping AmeraAmara's friends who aren't scared of owls.

"THAT DARN GAL CHRYSALIS!" said AmeraAmara, angry.

At one of Sasha's studios where Chrysalis birthday party was happening at. Chrysalis and her friends and family were having a big happy time. They were dancing to music and hanging out with each other.

"Chrysalis, this party is amazing!" said Cherryette.

"This party is so big and beautiful." said LuLu.

"Thanks guys." said Chrysalis.

They brought out the big cake with Ivern's picture on it and everyone came over quickly to see it.

"Whoa." they all said.

"So cool, hey dad I say you should go before me when they serve this cake." said Calvis.

"Why's that?" said Calvis' dad.

"Because you're a cool dad." said Calvis.

"Thanks Calvis." said Calvis' dad.

"And a good friend." said Walter.

"Thanks and so is everyone here who are all friends of mine." said Calvis' dad.

"Yeah." they all said.

"Finally that lady got put behind bars." said Zinnia.

Kylestone kissed his mother's cheek and Ariel hugged him while Regina and Kylestone kissed each other on the lips.

"Aw." said Pocahontas and Tarzan next to them, liking seeing Zinnia, Ariel, Regina, and Kylestone happy with each other.

Chrysalis walked over to the stage in the room.

"Hey Chrysalis, can my parents and I join you?" said Ariel, with her parents.

"Yeah sure that will be fun." said Chrysalis.

So Chrysalis, Ariel, Regina, and Kylestone all sang a song together with everyone enjoying it making it a happy birthday for Chrysalis.